CITRUS COUNTY

JOHN BRANDON

McSWEENEY'S RECTANGULARS
SAN FRANCISCO

www.mcsweeneys.net

Cover illustration by Keith Shore

Cover lettering by Brian McMullen

Second printing

ISBN: 978-1-934781-53-1

For John William Schneider Sr. (1930–2008)

PART ONE

Toby took his tacos outside and crouched on a curb. He knocked some sour cream off onto the concrete, devoured the tacos without tasting them, crumpled the wrappers and tossed them over his shoulder. The wind had given out, and there was no way to tell it was wintertime. Toby thought he might still be hungry.

"You littered."

Toby turned. He didn't get up. A little boy had snuck up on him. The boy's mother was still in the car, griping at someone on a cell phone.

"It's true," Toby admitted. "You've caught me in an unlawful act."

"Littering is bad for nature."

"Nature will be okay," Toby said. "Nature always wins in the end."

"You can get a fine. Up to five hundred dollars."

Toby looked up into the boy's face. Something was wrong with one of the boy's eyebrows. "When the time comes, you're going to make one heck of a hall monitor."

The boy looked from Toby to the wrappers. They weren't going anywhere—not the slightest breeze.

"Some people got it, some don't. You saw me gladly minding my own business over here and something about that bothered you."

"Are you going to pick them up?"

"You ever hear of an ice age?"

"Yes," said the boy.

"It might take a long time, but we're headed for another one. When the ice age hits, a couple of taco wrappers won't make much difference."

The boy shrugged. His knuckles were raw, along with his elbows. His T-shirt had a dolphin on it.

Toby stood and brushed his hands together, cleaning them of the gravelly dirt. He touched the boy's shoulder.

"Your mom doesn't love you as much as she used to. She thinks there might be something wrong with you. Is she right? Is there something wrong with you?"

The boy's mouth opened a bit and his funny eyebrow scrunched. He turned back toward his mother.

"You've noticed, haven't you? You've been monitoring her and you've noticed a difference in how she treats you."

The boy stared toward his mother in the car, waiting to state her case into the phone. Her eyes were pressed shut with impatience.

"It's all the bad thoughts you have," Toby said. "On the outside you're a hall monitor, but on the inside you're one sick lad."

Toby stopped at a 7-Eleven for a soda. The clerk was a young guy who wore bifocals and was always ready to harp on something. The counter was his spot in the world. Toby paid him in change. He took every penny from the little bowl near the register, and the clerk decided not to protest. He looked down on Toby through his spectacles as he accepted the payment.

Out in front they had dispensers of free newspapers and magazines. The things were free, but still nobody wanted them. Toby was finally out of the clerk's sight. He set his soda down and removed all the papers, armload by armload, and dropped them in a trash can. The papers belonged in the trash. Toby was only speeding things along. He had to shove the last stack down with all his weight, smudging the newsprint all over his arm.

He walked under billboards for realtors, all smiles and outdated haircuts. He passed power pole after power pole, each smothered in tacked flyers—runaway dogs, stolen ATVs, missing bikes. None of these things would be heard from again. In Citrus County, you couldn't keep anything unless you had a good hiding spot for it.

Toby wouldn't have minded walking all night, clearing his mind of everything. He wished he could skip the next years of his life, skip to the point when he would be his real self, whatever that would be. All the pale fascinations of his classmates—music, drugs, cutting themselves, sex—meant nothing to Toby. Drugs were pathetic. Flirting, degrading. Toby was in the doldrums. He was killing time.

The gas station. Scant light scarring the sky. Toby planted his feet and took a full breath, the air tart with petroleum. He saw the pay phone over near the air and vacuum. He was as weak as ever. Anything could make him weak—the wrong smell, the wrong tint in the sky, thinking about all the dragging afternoons he'd endured in his lifetime and all the afternoons to come. He was addicted to petty hoodlumism. He rested what was left of his soda on the metal sill, picked up the phone, dropped in coins, and dialed a number at random. A man with a Northern accent answered and Toby asked him if he believed his life was worth a damn, if he honestly believed anyone liked him.

"Who is this?" the man said, eager, like he got prank calls all the time.

"Nobody you'd understand," Toby told him.

"Pay phone," the guy said, apparently reading his caller ID.

"At the Citgo," Toby said.

"The Citgo? Tell you what, smart guy. I'm coming up there and I'm going to bash your brains in with a softball bat. How does that sound for a prank?"

"That would kill me, or at least do me grievous harm. That's what my uncle used to say, that he was going to do me grievous harm."

"I wish he had. It might've helped."

"A softball bat?"

"I use it for softball. I guess it's the same as a baseball bat."

"You're just saying you'd do that," Toby said. "You really wouldn't. You wouldn't murder a fourteen-year-old kid."

"I don't know," the guy said. "I think I might this time."

"Trust me, you'd think better of it. You're not like me. An idea strikes me, I'm helpless against it."

"The Citgo on Route 50?"

"That's the one."

The guy hung up. Toby looked at the phone in his hand then let it dangle by its cord. He slurped his soda until it was only ice and left the cup on the ground and walked the woods' edge. He found a spot to enter the tangled trees, angling toward Uncle Neal's property. He was taking the long way, out by the hardwoods, so he could check on the bunker. He wasn't going in. He only went in when he wanted to stay down for a long time. He liked to walk by, to see that the bunker was undisturbed. He didn't know whose property it was on. He'd been through that part of the woods a hundred times before he'd found it, a hundred times walking right past the bunker as he tromped through that hard-duned no-man's-land jumbled kittycorner to Uncle Neal's property. The bunker, with its ancient boards pushed in and cracked by tree roots, with its stench of hands and tarnish, with its muddy, mushroomed hatch door which had opened with a moist whiff and then a deafening silence. The bunker was from some terrible time, maybe not so very long ago but a different terrible time than the one Toby was in, a terrible time that had come to an end, one way or another.

Toby had a folding chair down there that he'd dragged from another part of the woods, and matches and candles and water. When he went down, he did nothing. Toby believed the bunker had a specific purpose for him, and he wasn't going to make a move until he parsed out what that purpose was. He wasn't going to hoard dirty magazines or fireworks or pretend he was camping. He didn't do a thing but sit in the chair and smell the smells. Sometimes he smelled vinegar. Sometimes the scales of fish. And each time he left, each time he finally climbed out, he felt that the bunker was sad to see him go. He felt he was leaving the bunker lonesome. Maybe nothing terrible had happened in Toby's bunker. It was one room, tidy in its way, plain. It could've been used for simple food storage and nothing else, back before refrigerators, back when the Indians were running around. Maybe this was a place for old-timey rednecks to keep their alligator meat away from vultures.

Mr. Hibma had given one of the kiss-asses a stopwatch and deemed her the umpire. Some days Mr. Hibma lectured. Some he allowed his classes to play trivia games. These were the two ways he could stomach teaching: losing himself in a lecture or daydreaming while the kids were absorbed in guessing.

"Mr. Hibma," the kiss-ass called. "Steven keeps saying 'retarded.' He said 'Australia's retarded nephew' for New Zealand."

"It should be noted," said Mr. Hibma. "One could as easily say Australia is the big retarded *uncle* of New Zealand."

Mr. Hibma knew he could teach for all eternity and it still wouldn't feel natural. He was a geography teacher but he didn't teach the subject of geography. He lectured about whatever he felt like and left the memorizing of topographical terms and state capitals to the kids. They had books. They had exercise manuals. If they were smart and curious they'd end up knowing a lot, and if they were dumb they wouldn't.

"Semifinal round," the kiss-ass announced.

Mr. Hibma listened as a boy named Vince who was known for giving out bubble gum tried to differentiate Asian countries.

"There are a lot of people crammed together," Vince said. "Short people?" He drummed his fingers, searching. "Not the one with the hanging ducks."

The kiss-ass called time up. Today's game was something akin to *The $10,000 Pyramid*. It was new to the kids. They'd never heard of *The $10,000 Pyramid*.

Mr. Hibma said, "Let me help. This is a country full of off-white folks who smile funny, eat raw fish, and wear the hippest shoes."

All the kids stared blankly except Shelby Register, who said, "Japan."

"Correct. I wouldn't trade you kids for all the tea in… Shelby?"

"China," she said.

Mr. Hibma sometimes viewed himself as a character in a novel. At the age of twenty-nine, he'd already experienced three things that mostly only happened in books. (1) As an infant, he'd been stolen from the hospital by a nurse. The duration of the abduction had been six hours and he'd been unharmed, but still. (2) He had unexpectedly inherited money. It was only $190,000 and he'd blown it in two years traveling around Europe, but still. (3) He had chosen his permanent residence by throwing a dart at a map. There hadn't been a town where the dart had stuck, but there weren't many towns in Citrus County, Florida. Citrus County was a couple hours north of St. Petersburg, on what people called the Nature Coast, which Mr. Hibma had gathered was a title of default; there was nature because there were no beaches and no amusement parks and no hotels and no money. There were rednecks and manatees and sinkholes. There were insects, not gentle crickets but creatures with stingers and pincers and scorn in their hearts. There was the smell of vegetation, every plant blooming outrageously or rotting by the minute. There was a swampy lake and a complex of aging villas surrounding that lake, and one of these villas was now Mr. Hibma's home.

Teaching had been the only job available to him, and for a while it was amusing, another lark, but now he'd been doing it a year and a half. It was February. It was Thursday. It was fourth period. Mr. Hibma was sick of skinny, smelly, hormone-dazed kids staring at him and lying to him and asking him questions. He was sick of their clothes, their faces. And the teachers were worse. Mr. Hibma did his best to keep to himself—ate in his classroom, avoided heading clubs or committees, kept all his discipline in-house instead of dealing with the office, and kept away from "7th hour," which was what the younger teachers called meeting at a Mexican restaurant Friday afternoon and getting drunk.

The teacher in the next room, Mrs. Conner, was not young and had likely never been drunk. She was about fifty, a grammar Nazi with bronze-colored hair who wore sandals that were too small and caused her toes to spill out onto the floor. She was an English teacher who refused to assign any literature that was morally corrupt. Poe was morally corrupt. "The Lottery" by Shirley Jackson was morally corrupt. Probably the Russians. Certainly the French. Mrs. Conner often informed Mr. Hibma that his shirt was wrinkled. She asked him pointed questions about his lesson plans, about all the games the kids played in his class. She and her husband, a retired cop or fireman or something, owned a mini-storage place. Mrs. Conner's classroom was decorated with posters about life not being a destination but a journey, posters of kittens hanging from ropes, posters of a ship or a whale with one word displayed across the top, like PERSISTENCE. Mr. Hibma often fantasized about murdering this woman. This was her last year of teaching before she retired and lived snidely off her pension and her husband's pension and their mini-storage profits, rising at dawn to greet her open days, getting more heavily involved in her church. The idea of letting her smirk through the last day of her twenty-fifth year as a teacher, loping around in her undersized sandals feeling as if everything she'd ever done was right, of letting her go home and sit on her porch on that warm June evening with her tea, and then, just as she dozed off, sneaking up behind her and... The idea sustained Mr. Hibma. The little table with the tea on it clattering down the porch steps. The look of disbelief on Mrs. Conner's blanched face when Mr. Hibma, what, slit her throat? He couldn't see himself doing that. He couldn't see himself shooting her, either. That part wasn't worked out. Mostly Mr. Hibma saw the look on her face. If the husband were there Mr. Hibma would have to kill him too. He didn't know what the husband looked like, but he saw him with sandy hair and a polo shirt and white sneakers. Mr. Hibma would put both their bodies in one of their own storage units. Mr. Hibma wondered if killers were born or made. He wondered that a lot. Mr. Hibma was a sad case. It was sad, he knew, to feel so powerless that you sat around idly dreaming of killing an old woman. Fantasies were for children and prisoners. Mr. Hibma did not feel like an adult and he did not feel free.

Despite failing to name their semifinal nation, Vince and his partner had advanced. Their opponents had broken a rule by using hand gestures and had been disqualified. It was Vince's team against Shelby and Toby. Shelby was the smartest student Mr. Hibma had, and Toby, well, smart wasn't the word. Cunning. Maybe he was cunning.

Shelby knew a lot about stand-up comedians. She had memorized the acts of Bill Hicks, Dom Irrera, Richard Belzer—nobody new, just stand-ups from years ago. She knew where these guys had gotten their starts and what jokes they were known for. She knew a lot about a lot of different things—literature, illnesses. Also, Mr. Hibma had noticed, Shelby seemed to want to be a Jew. She used words like *meshugana* and *mensch* and had brought matzo ball soup for ethnic food week and the days she missed school with a cold or stomachache were always Jewish holidays. Shelby lived with her father and maybe a sister in a little ranch house a stone's throw from the school. Her mother had died a couple years ago.

And Toby, denizen of detention, breaking rules in a way that seemed meant to reach a quota. There was no joy in his misbehavior, no rage. He didn't have friends but didn't get picked on. Neither of his parents were around. He lived on a big piece of property with his uncle.

Vince and his partner identified Morocco in seven seconds. Shelby and Toby had to beat that. Shelby trained her eyes coolly on the card. When the kiss-ass gave the signal, she said, "Where Bjork is from."

"I've heard of Bjork," said Toby.

"You're not allowed to talk," said the kiss-ass.

"Then how am I supposed to answer?"

"It was named to make people think it wasn't an inviting place to settle," said Shelby.

"You're allowed to guess countries," the kiss-ass told Toby. "You're not allowed to make comments."

"Shitland?" Toby offered. "That doesn't sound inviting."

"Time," blurted the kiss-ass.

Mr. Hibma informed the class that he'd gone to a flea market that past weekend and found a man selling movie posters for a dime each. He'd purchased three hundred. From here on out, these would serve as prizes. He presented Vince with *Midnight Run* and handed Shelby *The Milagro Beanfield War*.

"Let me get this straight," Vince said. "First place is a poster and second place is a poster?"

Mr. Hibma picked up a few stubs of chalk and shook them in his hand. "If Vince and Toby were gentlemen, they'd let the ladies keep the prizes."

"I'm not a gentleman," Toby said. "I don't think I've ever even seen a gentleman."

The lunch bell rang, ending the discussion and prompting a swift and sweeping exodus from the room.

"By the way, Toby," Mr. Hibma said. "You've got detention tomorrow afternoon for cursing."

Toby looked toward the ceiling a moment and then gave a dispassionate nod. Detention was a part of his life he'd come to terms with.

The silence in the classroom during lunch hour was irresistible. It turned Mr. Hibma's limbs to lead. Because it peeved some of the other teachers,

Mr. Hibma had no maps or charts or timelines on his walls. Instead, he'd hung prints by Dufy and Bosch. Because it peeved some of the other teachers, he made a point not to use the computer in his classroom. He didn't keep grades or attendance or lesson plans on it, didn't look up sample assignments on the Internet, didn't let his kids use it for research. As far as Mr. Hibma knew, the computer had never been turned on. Because it peeved some of the other teachers, Mr. Hibma had a cooler and a microwave in his classroom. This kept him out of the lounge.

He opened the microwave and deposited a frozen burrito. While he watched the seconds tick, he could not stop thinking about the playbooks in the drawer of his desk, the binders of formations, whirlwinds of stick-people and arrows. Princeton. Nebraska. Half-court press. The administration wanted Mr. Hibma to coach eighth-grade girls' basketball. The old coach had retired and all his plays and drills had been dropped off to Mr. Hibma with a not so subtly worded note mentioning that he was the only teacher in the school who did not head an extracurricular activity. The note reminded him that he'd promised, last year, to run the debate team, and that this promise had proven hollow. Mr. Hibma sat at his desk and blew on his burrito. If basketball had begun when it was supposed to, back in the fall, he'd have been able to stay hidden, to keep his head down and shuffle past this coaching business, but a conga-line of hurricanes, the nastiest weather ever to invade Florida, had blown all sports to the spring, giving the administration time to browse their options, to parse out a slacker and surround him and move in for the kill. And none of the hurricanes had even hit Citrus County. They'd hit the counties to the north and south, the counties most of Citrus Middle's opponents hailed from. Why not just cancel girls' basketball altogether? That was Mr. Hibma's question. The other coaches had stopped by one by one to assure Mr. Hibma that coaching was simple. You made them run, got them places on time, named a starting lineup—that was pretty much it.

Friday afternoon, when his detention was up, Toby exited the school and hiked into the February woods. He passed a clear-cut area pocked with piles of fill sand, a golf course whose construction had been halted years ago. Farther, there was a warehouse that seemed forgotten, that seemed to have been built by somebody who was now dead or had moved away. Statues of all sorts—gnomes, saints, water fowl—leaned against the warehouse's outside walls as if pleading to be let inside.

Toby hiked on, switching from this trail to that, imagining how he'd lose someone if he were being chased. He noticed a new bird's nest and climbed a low branch so he could look inside. Five pert eggs. They looked like toys, like decorations. Toby wished the mother bird would appear and run him off, pecking Toby's eyes, but that wasn't going to happen. These eggs were on their own and they'd run up against bad luck. Toby removed them one by one and slung them against the tree trunk. They didn't shatter like he'd hoped, just left splotches and rolled to rest on the ground. A shiver of joy ran through Toby, then immediately he was disgusted with himself. No matter how many speeches he gave himself, he couldn't keep himself in line. He was no match for his lesser urges. He was as much a junkie as those people who left empty gas cans and used rags all over the woods. He had about the same amount of purpose.

Toby lived with his uncle Neal on a few dozen acres in a concrete-block house. The property was lousy with sinkholes, but Uncle Neal said in a race between a sinkhole swallowing the house and nuclear destruction, he'd take the nukes. Toby entered the house and was enveloped by the familiar smell of fish sticks. Uncle Neal sat on a stool, clipping his nails. His hair was lopsided and his eyes watery. He always looked like he'd been shaken awake by a stranger.

"You're like a dog," he said to Toby. "Rattle your food bowl, you appear."

Toby sat at the table and took out his math homework. He could've done it in Mr. Hibma's detention, but Toby always made a point, when he was being disciplined, to stare at the nearest clock or out the nearest window. Toby did nothing in the bunker and he did nothing in detention, but the bunker was *his* nothing and detention was Mr. Hibma's. Detention sapped him and the bunker built him up.

"I'm sick of eating," Uncle Neal said. "Breakfast, lunch, dinner. Breakfast, lunch, dinner." He put on an oven mitt and took out the fish sticks. He divided them onto two plates and slid one of the plates to Toby.

"I have to work tomorrow." Uncle Neal filled his mouth with steaming fish stick and swallowed after one chew, getting it over with. "It's an all-day thing—semi-trailer of old fruit. Two brothers owned the company and they got in a fight and halted all shipments. Back in, like, the '80s."

As far as Toby could tell, Uncle Neal's business was to clean things that nobody else would clean, from grimed old engines to abandoned slaughterhouses. Toby's uncle, it was safe to say, was a pariah. He lived in a world of regret, if not remorse—about what, Toby couldn't say. Toby's uncle always joked about killing himself, and Toby had begun to suspect he wasn't joking. He didn't have much incentive to stay alive. Uncle Neal, like everyone else, believed Toby was a run-of-the-mill punk, another angst-ridden adolescent. He had no clue what Toby was capable of.

Another week of school had passed, more quizzes and study halls and, in the case of Mr. Hibma's class, more games. Shelby wasn't the new kid anymore, and she was grateful for that. She'd settled in and was more or less slipping through the days. People had their own problems. Shelby had been fooled about Florida, but that was okay. She wasn't the first. She'd imagined a place that was warm and inviting and she'd gotten a place that was without seasons and sickeningly hot. She'd wanted palm trees and she'd gotten grizzly, low oaks. She'd wanted surfers instead of rednecks. She'd thought Florida would make her feel glamorous or something, and there was a region of Florida that might've done just that, but it wasn't this part. It was okay, though. It was something different. It wasn't the Midwest. It wasn't a place where you could look around and plainly see, for miles, that nothing worthwhile was going on. Shelby would travel to better places when she was older, when she could chart her own course. She'd go to India and France. Shelby could see the mornings of her future, the foreign pink sunrises.

The sunrise *this* morning, in Citrus County, had been the color of lima beans. It had been a color you might see under peeled-off paint. Shelby had stuffed one pocket of her army pants with bagels, and into the other pocket she'd slid a shallow, lidded bowl full of lox. Once she and her father and her little sister had boarded the boat and snapped the straps of their lifejackets, Shelby spread her brunch feast, complete with sliced tomato and capers and cream cheese. They'd rented a pontoon boat and planned to cruise the spring system of Citrus County until they saw a manatee. They'd been told they could swim with the manatees if they liked. Manatees had no natural defense other than size, and that very size got them stuck in canals at low tide and cut up by boat propellers. The man who rented the boats had explained all this from beneath the brim of a blue ball cap adorned with the words IDLE SPEED, ASSHOLE! The man said Citrus County never got hit directly by a hurricane and, in his personal opinion, that's why the manatees had chosen this spot.

Shelby's father, a man with limp hair that parted and re-parted as the wind blew, a former boxer who spoke with an accent that could've come from anywhere, was always trying to expose his daughters to new things—new foods, new terrain, new ideas. He felt he had to be twice the parent, Shelby figured. And he was. Shelby did not feel deprived.

Shelby's sister Kaley had brought along her book about Manny the Manatee. Immediately after breakfast, Kaley stowed the book under a seat, along with her precious watch that always read 3:12 and the rest of the orange juice. Kaley would soon turn four. She looked up at Shelby, displeased that Shelby had seen her stash spot. This was something Kaley did lately—hoarded. She wore, as always, socks but no shoes.

After Shelby had cleaned up the remains of the bagels and lox, her father puttering them out into the deep water, she took out her vocab words. She had the definitions memorized. This week the theme was bureaucracy. She wanted to go through the whole semester without missing one word of one definition.

"You'd like my word from yesterday," her father said. "On my calendar at work: *poshlust*. It means bad art. It's Russian, I think."

Shelby folded the paper in her hands and slipped it into her pocket. "Mr. Hibma told us about that. Posh*lost*. We had that for a word. It means more than bad art. Means bad art that most smart people don't know is bad."

"Like what?"

"Mr. Hibma doesn't give examples."

"What do you mean?"

"He doesn't feel he needs to prove his statements. He feels that examples are petty."

"Well, his poshlost sounds like elitism to me."

"Mr. Hibma wishes elitism would come back into style."

"I met that guy," Shelby's father said. "He's one of those cool pessimists."

"Dad," Kaley broke in. "Will the manatee bite me?"

"No, the manatee loves you."

"Is he sleeping?"

"He might be."

"Where are we going?" Shelby asked.

"Not a clue."

Shelby's father had steered them down a river which had rapidly tapered into a house-lined canal. They approached a cul-de-sac. Shelby's father put the boat in reverse to avoid hitting a dock, then began to execute a three-point turn. The boat was unwieldy. An old man came out into his backyard in order to stare at Shelby's father as his three-point turn became a five-point turn, a seven.

"Thanks for your concern," Shelby's father shouted.

The man wagged his head. "There's a sign," he squawked. "At the mouth of the canal."

Shelby's father righted the boat and they headed back out to the main confluence of springs, past moss-laden oaks and palm trees that grew out of the ground sideways. They rounded a bend. The sun was out, warming the aluminum frame of the pontoon boat and the damp turf that covered the deck. Kaley, socks soaked, padded over and leaned on Shelby's leg.

Shelby closed her eyes and let the breeze tumble over her. She knew her family was getting by in the way people like them got by. They were making it. They did things on the weekends. Their moods went with the weather. In Indiana there were proven methods for dealing with misfortune—certain types of foods and certain types of get-togethers and certain expressions. Here Shelby's family was on its own, and that had been the whole point of coming here. There were things to do and they had to go find them and do them.

Shelby breathed the mild stink of the weedy water and soon her mind wandered again to Toby, a boy in her geography class. He'd been her trivia partner this past week. Shelby felt tingly, thinking of him. Or maybe it was the sun. She understood that her attraction to Toby was clichéd. She was considered a good girl and he a bad boy. There was a reason why it was clichéd, a reason why girls like Shelby, through the years, had become infatuated with boys like Toby. Regular boys were boring. There wasn't a way the regular boys could make her feel that she couldn't feel on her own. And Toby had calves like little coconuts and long fingers and his hair and eyes were the flattest brown. He wasn't in a clique. It seemed there was something about him you couldn't know right away. Shelby wanted his hands on her. She wanted to smell his hair. She wanted him to give her goose bumps. There were a lot of things Shelby wanted to do and she was pretty sure she wanted to do them with Toby.

The movement of the boat jostled Shelby. The waterway was opening up, ripples turning to waves, saltwater fishing boats speeding this way and that. The pontoon boat rocked. A pelican flew low over their canopy, its wings bellowing against the air, its crusty pink eyes narrowed, and Kaley squeezed Shelby's leg.

"That's a channel marker," Shelby's father said. "We're going out to the Gulf."

He waited for a break in the traffic and pulled a struggling U-turn, the waves clapping against the bottom of the boat. The engine was doing everything it could.

Shelby heard familiar voices and turned to see a couple of popular girls from her school wearing bikinis, sprawled on the front of a gleaming white boat. The boat was anchored. They waved as Shelby passed. They were eating pineapple.

"I can't thank you enough for not being slutty," Shelby's father told her. "Not that I'm counting my chickens. There's time yet."

"You're welcome."

"You've got character. You don't try and impress people."

"I'll say 'you're welcome' again and we can leave it at that."

"Maybe I'm doing something right," he said.

Shelby's father drove the boat and patted Kaley's head, guiding them past birdbathed back yards, past mangrove stands full of cranes. They ended up back near where they'd rented the boat and started off in yet another direction, down a wild-looking river shaded by vines. Kaley retrieved her book from under the seat and studied it.

Shelby was still thinking about the girls on the boat. She *had* chosen not to be one of them. In October her family had moved to Citrus County from Indiana and Shelby had immediately, halfway through her first day of school, been granted membership in the popular gaggle of girls. She was subjected to an onslaught of sleepovers, pool parties, and laps around the outlet mall. This lasted a month, at which time these girls could no longer deny that Shelby was uninterested in makeup, basketball players, the marital intrigues of celebrities, who would take whom to the dance. She didn't like the same magazines they did, didn't care to diet. She sometimes read books for pleasure.

Mr. Hibma assigned a family history project. He told the kids to choose one side of their families, whichever was less boring, and track it back as far as they could. They would present the history orally and wouldn't hand anything in.

"Those librarians get paid the same as teachers do," Mr. Hibma said. "Tell them to quit fiddling with paper clips and show you the genealogy section. And if you have to use the Internet for this, don't let me know about it."

Mr. Hibma went to his podium and began lecturing about assassination. He stayed broadly in the area of geography by informing the kids *where* certain assassinations had taken place, how the act of assassination had impacted different regions of the world.

"Assassination," he said, "helps everyone know what side they're on. It cuts through the shenanigans of voting and impeaching."

Mr. Hibma let this statement sink in, then touched on general points about revolution. He wanted the kids to understand that in the United States capitalism had become so monstrous that even the idea of revolution could be marketed and sold. Protest against a corporation could be sold *by* that corporation. Artists and moralists could no longer make their own revolutions; they had to depend on the poor. The problem was that the poor weren't poor. The poor had frozen pizza and cable TV and cigarettes. Hell, the poor had real pizza and DVDs and weed.

Mr. Hibma could drone for twenty minutes without thinking about what he was saying. There was nothing to do but observe the kids. It was like watching monkeys at the zoo—the scratching, the gnawing, the use of simple tools. One of the kiss-ass girls stared at Vince, the gum kid.

Vince stared over at Shelby. Shelby stared at the back of Toby. Toby stared down at the pages of a book about, it seemed, track and field, reading about, it appeared, pole vault.

"Pole vault?" Mr. Hibma asked, interrupting himself.

Toby looked up.

"I didn't know they did pole vault in middle school."

"If you want to do it they have to let you. Those two huge girls that failed can throw the shot and the discus further than any of the guys, and I can't run fast without someone chasing me, so I chose pole vault."

"They can throw *farther*," Mr. Hibma said.

"It's not even close."

"No, I mean you said *further*, but that's for intangible distances. For measurable distances it's *farther*."

"Okay."

"Would you like to read that book later or would you like detention?"

"I have to read this now," Toby said.

"We could schedule your detentions in advance. We could get a calendar with humorous pictures of puppies and fill it in from now till the end of the year."

Toby didn't answer.

"Where was I?" said Mr. Hibma. "I was about to tell you that the most rebellious thing a youngster can do is sit outdoors and listen to the birds. Sitting indoors in detention is about the least."

Mr. Hibma, without warning, walked out of the classroom. He did this now and again to shake the kids up, to force them to deal with freedom. Sometimes he returned in thirty seconds and sometimes he stayed gone the rest of the period.

He strolled to the end of the hall, to the big windows. Live oaks. Mockingbirds. A hill, or at least what passed for a hill in Florida. Mr. Hibma watched the groundskeeper for a time, jealous. The guy sat on that grazing tractor, letting his thoughts find him, watching the uncut section of lawn agreeably dwindle. Spread a little mulch. Eat a sandwich.

Mr. Hibma went to the lounge. He chugged someone's soda. Because it made Mrs. Conner angry, he used the ladies' restroom. He pissed on the seat and buried the bottle of hand soap at the bottom of the trash. He looked into the mirror and said aloud, "I am twenty-nine years old. I am a middle school teacher. I live in Northwest Central Florida. I inherited money from an old Hungarian man I picked up groceries for. I had a couple lengthy talks with him and sometimes walked his dog." Mr. Hibma cleared his throat. He looked at himself resolutely. "Sir, you spent one third of an inheritance on whores."

He came out of the bathroom. The tick of the clock had an echo. In three minutes the bell would ring and the lounge would fill with teachers. They would brag about how they'd dealt with their problem students. They would brag about what they'd said to pushy parents, brag about their students' test scores. They would brag about their weekends, about their houses and spouses and whatever else was handy to brag about.

When Toby got home from school he found Uncle Neal in the kitchen, shoving jars and small appliances around on the countertop. He went ahead and asked his uncle what was wrong.

"Stupid nail clippers are lost. Somebody ate them or somebody stole them." Uncle Neal stared at Toby in a way that was meant to convey fraying tolerance. "And we're out of freaking ketchup," he said. "You used the last of it."

It had been a long time since Toby had been scared of his uncle. This was a guy who'd never given Toby a gift, even at Christmas, who used to ground him for speaking too many words in a day, who used to slap him in the back of the head if he had a nightmare and woke Uncle Neal up. It hadn't taken Toby long to grow numb to his uncle's harassment, and it hadn't taken long after that for his uncle to get bored with harassing Toby. He still gave Toby shit, but nothing like before. Somewhere in there Uncle Neal had stopped drinking and had taken up smoking things. The guy was pathetic and Toby had to live under his roof for the foreseeable future. Toby had found that the best way to keep his uncle out of his business was to come around once a day and let him bitch, even if all he had to bitch about were clippers and condiments. As long as Toby came around, Uncle Neal didn't go looking for him.

After detention the next day, Toby headed for the track-and-field tryouts. A bunch of other kids were going too. This was the kind of thing kids did. Toby walked past the faculty parking lot, the garbage bins. He rounded the trailers. There was Shelby Register, sitting on a bench at the little playground, reading a newspaper. The middle school had once been an elementary school, so it still had this kiddie playground and low water fountains you almost had to get on your knees to drink from.

Toby took a moment to watch Shelby. She wasn't as transparent as the other kids at Toby's school. He sort of hated her because everything was easy for her, but somehow she felt like an ally. She had misery in her and she didn't give it away. She kept it and believed in it. She was like Toby; she was fine with whatever people thought she might be, fine with being underestimated. She was pretty without looking like all the other pretty girls. She wasn't ashamed of being smart.

A toddler with red hair was on the swing, kicking her feet and tucking them. Toby walked up beside Shelby and for a moment she didn't notice him. He wasn't sure why he was stopping, wasn't sure what he wanted to happen. Shelby had crisp tan shorts on instead of her old army pants. Her legs were ghastly white. She had wisps of hair falling over her ears. Shelby thought she was better than everyone else, and maybe she was right. She wasn't better than Toby, though, because Toby wasn't playing the same game.

She lowered her paper. "You can sit if you want."

Toby's face was to the sun. The sky was still, empty except for one immovable cloud that looked like a boulder. Toby stepped in front of the bench and lowered himself onto it.

"They're going to eliminate pennies." Shelby folded the paper and tucked it under her leg.

"How?" Toby said.

"Just pennies, for now."

"So no more of those little trays: leave a penny, take a penny."

"Those will go to museums."

Toby grunted. He looked at the little girl on the swing.

"That's my sister," Shelby said. "We live through there. You can almost see our house."

Toby looked at Shelby, then back at her sister.

"How was detention?"

"Same as always," Toby said. "I won."

Shelby's sister was swinging higher and higher, getting the chains parallel to the ground. This didn't seem to make Shelby nervous.

"Do you watch Comedy Central?" she asked.

"I don't have cable."

"Is your uncle a hippie?"

"How do you know I live with my uncle?"

"Everyone knows that."

Toby squinted. The sun seemed aimed at him. "His income is up and down," he said.

"They had this guy doing this stellar bit about Hot Pockets."

"I eat those," Toby said.

An active old couple peddled by on mountain bikes. They waved to Toby and Shelby, who watched them until they rounded a thicket.

"What's your sister's name?"

"Kaley."

Kaley held a big toy watch. She wasn't wearing shoes.

"Are you going to be late to tryouts?" Shelby said.

"I'll make the team. Nobody else wants to pole vault. It's not even supposed to be a middle school sport."

"Then why is it?"

"The superintendent. He instated it after he married this lady from Finland." Toby couldn't keep his eyes off Kaley. Her hair was glinting like a fishing lure.

"He did it for love," Shelby said. "He made pole vault a sport for love."

The cloud wasn't like a boulder anymore. It was like a scoop of something. It slid in front of the sun and Toby could see. There was nothing to look at but Shelby and her sister, her sister's filthy feet.

"Would you recommend that island with all the monkeys on it?" Shelby said. "I have to find outings for my family. What's left of it."

"What island with monkeys on it?"

Shelby tipped her chin. "Down by Homosassa Springs. Monkey Island?"

"I don't go on outings."

"You've never even heard of it?"

"Not till now."

"Well, it's there. They filmed a Tarzan movie and left the monkeys."

Toby shrugged. He didn't care about movies or monkeys. He watched Shelby adjust herself on the bench, then push the newspaper farther under her.

"If you ever want to kiss me," she said, "not that you currently want to or anything, I would be okay with that."

Toby felt panic wash through him. He tried to nod.

"I wasn't *telling* you to kiss me. In fact, don't. It would be too weird now. I said that for future reference is all. Just so you know."

Toby stood up from the bench, finding his balance. "Future reference," he said. He stumbled getting back to the sidewalk.

Toby caught the last forty-five minutes of the tryout. It was the first day, so the group had not been broken into events. Toby joined the herd and jogged laps. He did push-ups. He drank from the coolers. He kept seeing Shelby's sister swinging easily up toward the clouds and then losing steam and zipping back toward the mulch, her feet and her hair.

Toby saw himself moving around the field as if from above, as if from a sleepy hot-air balloon. He saw the big girls that threw the shot and the discus. They had bulky upper bodies and lean legs. They wore sweatshirts and shorts and toted a half-gallon of water in each hand. Toby saw Vince giving out Gatorade gum. He saw Coach Scolle, his head of slick curls and his whistle and his distasteful glare. Coach Scolle knew Toby didn't belong at his tryout. Toby felt his lungs burning. Something had occurred. Toby had decided on something. He saw the bare pines jabbing the sky in the distance. He felt the cool, incurious ground when he collapsed on his back after the laps.

That evening Toby skipped dinner and went to the bunker. He listened to his breathing and to busy drones that seemed to come from beyond the bunker walls but that also could have been coming from his mind. For a while, a tint of light came in from above, through a small vent, but once the sun set Toby couldn't see anything. He had candles but he didn't light one. And so he couldn't see the big railroad ties that stood in each corner for support. He couldn't see the spider webs or the pale roots that hung limply from the earthen walls. There was nothing down here but what you brought. Toby thought about the way some of the other kids had looked at him when he showed up for the track tryout. He thought about his hunger, which he could ignore until it went away. He thought about Shelby Register and her little sister, and about their dad who probably patted their heads all the time and watched them sleep and gave them five dollars for each good report card grade.

When Toby was in the bunker, he never knew how much time was passing. He heard voices sometimes, nothing he could understand. He heard whimpering. He heard static. It was all in his imagination. It took hours in the bunker for him to clear away all the chatter from school—blabbing teachers and gossiping classmates and orders from coaches and stupid announcements over the PA.

His back was stiff when he stood up from the folding chair. His sweat had dried on him. He wanted to know who else had been down in this bunker and who had built it. Toby had been *meant* to find it. Toby wasn't another hard-luck case. He wasn't another marauding punk. He'd been acting like one, thus far, but he was destined for higher evil and he could feel that destiny close at hand. He was more terrible inside than every juvenile delinquent in the whole county put together.

Mr. Hibma managed to stretch the genealogy presentations into a three-day affair, giving him a break from lecturing and from compiling trivia fodder. There were only a few kids left who hadn't dispensed the uneventful lives of their recent ancestors. Mr. Hibma was seated low behind his desk, studying the basketball binders. He'd have to rename these plays. Instead of yelling out Ivy League schools, his point guard would bark mixed drinks and famous assassins. Mr. Hibma found a rulebook in one of the binders, and a list of basketball terms. *Pick and roll* he knew. *Backdoor cut*. What the hell was a match-up zone?

Mr. Hibma looked up and called on Shelby. She never volunteered for anything because she didn't want to be a kiss-ass, but she was always prepared. She got up and spoke about her mother's family. Her great-grandparents had owned a cane shop, back in Belgium. Their daughter, Shelby's grandmother, had come to visit the States, fallen in love with a history teacher, and never returned to Europe. She and the history teacher had hosted a series of foster children before finally conceiving Shelby's mother. One of the foster children had become famous in art circles, a woman named Janet Stubblefield who had dropped out of high school to become a hippie. She became expert at constructing mobiles out of old boots, and against her will she developed a following. People from all over began making art out of shoes. The whole business put Aunt Janet off. She moved to rural Tennessee and became a hermit and died in middle age. She had told everyone to stay away, that it was important to her to die alone.

Shelby dropped her note cards in the trash and sat down, light applause playing about the room. She hadn't mentioned her mother. She'd chosen her mother's *side*, but she'd cut the history short. A kid could really get sick of having a dead parent, Mr. Hibma imagined. These kids were all sad or crazy, and most of them had reason to be.

Mr. Hibma asked for the next presenter and a girl named Irene, who'd worn a sweater set and heavy makeup, got up and said some things and retook her seat. Toby was next, the only one who hadn't gone. He'd chosen his father's family, the family whose name he bore: McNurse. They'd moved from Ireland to Canada at the turn of the century, a well-off family who'd chosen to immigrate to Canada instead of the United States because it was harder to get into Canada. Most of them had died in the forties in an accident. An avalanche.

Mr. Hibma was sure Toby was lying. Toby was testing Mr. Hibma, seeing if he would call him on his fake history, but there was also a chance Toby didn't know a thing about his father's family. Toby may never have met the man. Or maybe Toby's history was nothing anyone would *want* to know. Maybe making a history up was the wisest option. Well, Mr. Hibma would give Toby an A+.

"My father was a snake researcher who drove a big Cadillac," Toby said. "He met my mother while driving across the country. He only slept with her because he'd promised himself he'd sleep with a woman every night of his road trip, and she was the only woman not spoken for in Farmington, New Mexico."

Toby sat and Mr. Hibma replaced him in front of the class. He told the kids to give themselves a hand, then to line up and receive a poster.

"I've got *Mermaids*," he said. "*Fletch II*. Except you, Thomas."

Thomas, a kid with a widow's peak whose parents farmed fancy tomatoes, gaped at Mr. Hibma.

"In your notes you had pages printed from the internet. I could see the site info at the top and bottom. You'll be getting a C. Everyone else gets an A-. Toby, you get an A+. Best presentation of the year."

Alone in the classroom, Mr. Hibma returned to his binders. He wondered if they would take the job away from him if the team performed dismally enough. He wondered if he could be stripped of his whistle for encouraging dirty play. He wondered if he was expected to hug the girls, if he was supposed to give pre-game talks in the girls' locker room. He hoped they were all ugly; that would make things easier. He flipped the last page of the last binder, which detailed something UNLV used to run called the amoebae defense. He found a single folded sheet tucked in the binder's pocket. The paper was stiff. In red ink were the words HYENAS & TWIN TOWERS, and a game plan that called for the other team's good player to be triple-teamed while the two remaining defenders stayed under the basket, one on each block, to rebound the misses of the other team's bad players. Hyenas and Twin Towers required two enormous girls who didn't mind being the girls who stood under the basket. Mr. Hibma wondered if the previous coach had ever implemented this strategy. There *were* two girls at the school who fit the bill, the girls who'd failed, who threw the shot and the discus. Mr. Hibma liked the idea of a game plan. He wasn't sure he'd ever had one, for anything.

Toby chose Friday. He wasn't shying away or questioning himself. Friday evening was the correct evening and now it was here and Toby found that he was up to it. This didn't surprise him. In fact, he left Uncle Neal's way too early and had to wander circles around the woods. He put his supplies down and sat near a clotted creek and watched tadpoles dart about. He picked up a handful of dead leaves and smelled them; he didn't know why. Clouds were gathering tentatively. Toby picked some berries off a bush and ate them and they were dry as sand.

He made his way to the railroad tracks and progressed one tie at a time. The tracks went to places Toby would never see. They went past herds of thin, dusty cows who must've believed they were the last of their kind. The tracks wound past landfills swarmed with thousands of vultures. The tracks cut through miles and miles of peaceful palmetto beds. They skirted a subdivision full of gleeful young couples, came together with other tracks, found the shadows of the old factory buildings where stray dogs crossed back and forth. The tracks veered off when they neared the bay and the long bridge where every other week someone jumped off and hoped to die on impact with the water, hoped not to be alive long enough to have to worry about drowning. The tracks went on forever, under eerie lightning unaccompanied by thunder.

As night fell, Toby sat himself down in a copse of struggling cypress trees near the Register house, the dark form of the school looming. Toby hoped it was going to rain. A good rainfall would wash away tracks and obscure scents. It would dampen the spirits of the searchers. The shoes Toby had on were three sizes too big—gray Velcro sneakers that all the stores carried. He was wearing four pairs of socks. He carried a rucksack with air holes poked in it and a roll of duct tape, with notches cut into one edge at even lengths. He had a side view of the house; he could see the front porch, where father and older sister and kid sister were having a grand and cozy old time, and he could monitor the bedrooms, which were in the back of the house. He knew he had to stay open to the prospect that a chance to take Kaley might not shape up. He couldn't force it. He had to keep in mind that the house might have an alarm, or motion lights, or a dog.

It was Register family board game night. It was an adorable little scene and it could have included Toby. He could've been sitting in that fourth chair. Shelby had invited him. She'd matched his stride on the way to lunch and wrapped her thin fingers around his arm and told him that if he came over and hung out and played a few games, then her dad would let them stay up and watch cable. "Cable," she'd said, ribbing him. "It'll be a whole new world for you." She'd told Toby they might be able to take a walk and be alone. Then she'd tossed her hair and shuffled off in her boots, leaving Toby to stand there rubbing his biceps like a little kid who'd just gotten a flu shot, like Shelby's fingerprints had been burned into his tender flesh, like he had no idea who Shelby really was. Toby had felt angry, toyed with. Shelby had been so sure of herself. She'd walked right up to him. Nobody walked up to Toby. It was absurd, the thought of Toby included in this kind of scene, playing board games and giggling, chumming around with someone's dad. He'd done the right thing, telling Shelby he couldn't make it. He had his own porch. He had his own plans. He didn't want to hear anyone's life story or receive any advice. That's what dads did, as far as Toby could tell; they told old stories and dished out advice.

Toby watched the Registers play cards with an oversized deck. They played a game which required them to make sketches, then a game with a plastic bubble that popped the dice. The father was working on a pitcher of something yellow, and kept threading his fingers behind his head like a businessman reviewing robust profits. Shelby was running things. She'd bring out a box and set everything up, instruct Kaley and let her win, place everything back in the box, stand and hike up her army pants, then go in for another game. Toby wished Shelby had never moved to his county. He was too thirsty to spit. He'd filled a thermos with soda but had left it sitting on the kitchen counter. Toby could see his uncle discovering the thermos, taking it out to his rocking chair, and sipping it for hours. Being thirsty was no big deal. Toby could handle thirst. He could handle the nighttime noises of the woods, the spider that had dropped on the back of his neck and had him feeling crawly all over. He removed his shoes and tapped the sand out of them, then put them back on as snug as he could, tugging the Velcro strips. He reached into the rucksack and put his hand on the tape.

The father loosed a yawn. He spoke to Shelby and she took Kaley inside. In a moment, the nearest bedroom lit up. The father, in his seat on the porch, picked up the pitcher and drained the last of the yellow beverage. Maybe he'd stay out awhile, leave the girls sleeping inside. Toby didn't even know if Shelby and Kaley shared a room. His lungs felt made of glass, fogged. He flexed his knees. This was it. Toby felt strange, like he had at the track tryout. He was watching himself from above.

The light in the bedroom died, and after a time Shelby came out onto the porch and handed her father a beer. Kaley was in there, in that dark bedroom. She was in there alone. Toby folded his rucksack under his arm. His courage had flagged and roared back and flagged and now it was back again. He did not feel alone. He felt egged on by something greater. It wasn't Kaley's fault, and it wasn't even Toby's. He would be different now; he would be new. He would possess a secret that put him above his uncle and his teachers and Coach Scolle and all the convenience store clerks and all the nameless punks of Citrus County who thought knocking over mailboxes and stealing cigarettes would save them.

Toby backed into the woods and rounded the house and advanced to the edge of the yard. He would either get caught red-handed or he wouldn't. He stood tall while he strode, bracing for motion lights. A hot coal had been burning in his guts for years and it was about to be doused. He passed a rusted grill that had been turned into a birdfeeder. A kiddie pool. Still no lights. Toby donned his mask and it fit superbly. It made him feel skilled. He watched, through the eyeholes, his fingers come to rest on the handle of the sliding-glass door. He watched, through the eyeholes of the snug black mask, the door budge. Toby slid the door inch by inch. He wouldn't have to jimmy a window. He was going to walk right in. He stuck his head inside first—a flat, oaty smell. It was the dining room. He breathed the baked-hay scent. He could hear Shelby's voice from the porch, but he couldn't hear what she was saying. It sounded like the voices that came to Toby in the bunker. He could hear Shelby's voice and he could somehow hear that the father was listening to her with care, leaning in. One of them could get up to use the bathroom or get something to eat or something to drink or get a sweatshirt at any time. Toby could hear the scrape of a chair on the wood porch at any moment. He could hear it now, or now. But he didn't. He heard the refrigerator humming in the next room. All of Shelby's things were in this house, all her army pants and all the books she read. And her sister. Her sister was in here, eyes drawing closed under her red bangs.

Then everything went fast. Toby slipped down the hallway toward Kaley's room. He hung strips of duct tape from his forearm. If someone came in from the porch now he was cornered. He pulled the door open and Kaley lurched in her bedding. She seemed to know what was happening, that she was becoming part of something. She tried to collect a breath, but it took her too long. Toby had the tape around her head. He had her dumped in the rucksack, her top half first, her kicks thudding mutely against the mattress and then the carpet. She was a real child. She was a person made of flesh, her terror pure and clumsy.

Toby zipped the pack and shouldered it and its lightness exhilarated him. He was strong through the hallway, strong through the dining room. He heard nothing but his own blood. The wholesome smell was gone. Toby didn't bother to close the sliding door. Patio. Patchy lawn. Woods and woods. The breeze was at his back, the ground under him firm. He ran and then he jogged and then he walked and then he felt the gnarled roots under his feet and then, halfway to the bunker, he rested under a giant fern. He had to open the pack and tape Kaley's ankles because she was kicking the hell out of his back. His saliva was foamy. His feet were sloshing in sweat from all the socks. He'd done all of it. He had put a cot and a blanket and a pillow and a bunch of water and snacks and a flashlight and some clothes and a tight-lidded bucket in the bunker and now he'd snatched a little girl. From the moment he'd seen Kaley on the playground to now had been one long afternoon, and night had finally fallen.

Toby strode toward the house on a wanton trajectory. He would be proud, he knew. Soon enough. The mission was accomplished. He was tired in a buoyant way, like for once he would be able to really sleep. He yanked sharp breaths in through his nose, smelling every hidden thing in the woods, trying to get ready to return to his regular life and act regular. All he could think of was lying in bed with his secret. All he could think of was the very near future.

When Toby got to the house, Uncle Neal was on the porch in his rocking chair. He was slugging from Toby's thermos of soda, making calls like an owl. The ashtray on the floor next to him was overflowing. Toby could hear the police radio from inside, the station his uncle listened to at night—the uncondensed blotter, he called it. He couldn't make out the words. His uncle said knowing what the cops were up to helped him relax. Toby had listened to it before, and it was mostly boring. It was a bunch of speeding tickets and the occasional disturbance at a party, and when something important did happen, it was told in codes and jargon, in voices trained to be calm. Hell hadn't broken loose yet, it didn't sound like. It sounded like the same old chatter.

Toby stretched out on a lounge chair with no cushions.

Uncle Neal rotated his head without moving his shoulders. "Hoo," he said. "Hoo."

Toby's eyes wandered to the ashtray.

"Dried banana peels," Uncle Neal told him. He peered into the thermos. "There's something in this shit. Did you put anything in this soda?"

Toby said, "Like what?"

"Something for the memory."

"The memory?"

"You're not poisoning me, are you?"

Toby didn't answer.

Uncle Neal dug something out of his nose. "Some kid introduced me to banana peels when I was your age. I was in gifted. Our teacher was hot."

Toby couldn't imagine Uncle Neal being a different age, being a kid or an old person. He couldn't imagine anyone different than they were. Toby was meant to be in eighth grade, pretty much an orphan. Kaley was meant to be kidnapped, meant to be stashed in the bunker. Everyone he saw every day was meant to be in Citrus County, fated to be carrying out whatever fruitless act they happened to be engaged in.

"There were twins in my gifted class. They teach college now." Uncle Neal hoisted the thermos and paused. "And this ugly Chinese girl, she writes for a newspaper in Boston. This guy Rob said he wanted to be a rocket scientist—works for NASA."

"Can I have some of that?"

Uncle Neal handed the thermos to Toby, who glugged its contents until his throat burned.

"What were *you* supposed to do?" Toby asked.

"I don't know anymore."

Toby took a few more sips of the soda. It was making him thirstier.

He was glad he'd done what *he* was supposed to. He'd filled the bunker. He wasn't like Uncle Neal.

"They kicked me out of gifted," Uncle Neal said. "I got caught leaving fake suicide notes. Kicked me right out."

Toby could still perform his end of a conversation with his uncle. He was the same person, just with a big secret that would give him strength. He could still do everything he had to do. "Were the notes supposed to be from other students?" he asked. "Kids you didn't like?"

"I'd make the person up and leave the note at the bus station or a motel."

"How come? Why suicide notes?"

Uncle Neal cut an eye at Toby. "Think I know? You think that's the kind of thing you do for a known reason?"

"Well, how'd you get found out?"

"Not by telling anybody. The school cop just figured it out. I guess they do that now and again—crack a case."

Tomorrow, Toby knew, every cop in the county would be scurrying around looking for Kaley, looking for Kaley's abductor, and this didn't worry Toby in an immediate way. The cops didn't seem a part of any of this to Toby. They were strangers. What Toby did was none of their business. What came over their radio might as well have been transmitted from the moon.

Toby heard a clap of thunder and then raindrops panned the roof.

He looked over at his uncle, whose shoulders had gone limp. His head was sagging to one side. After a minute, Toby said his uncle's name and got no response.

The next morning, Toby began the walk to the county line, to an immense bookstore where he could watch the news away from Uncle Neal. The few kind slaps of winter had landed and the red marks were fading. Now it would be summer again. Before long, Toby would have to put an air conditioner in the bunker. He'd have to get a little air conditioner and a little generator and he'd have to lug the generator back to the house and sneak it into his bedroom to charge it every, what, couple days? He probably didn't even have enough money saved. Toby's mind was blundering. He'd concocted the kidnapping and looked forward to it and executed it, and now he felt unconvinced that it had occurred. It hadn't sunk in, was all. He felt like if he went down in the bunker right now there'd be nothing but his folding chair. There was weight in Toby's joints as he put one foot in front of the other. He had to grit his teeth and walk through his doubt like it was a cloud of car exhaust.

Toby stayed east of Route 19, tacking northward behind stores selling above-ground pools, used tires. A defunct dance studio. Toby had no clue how Citrus County stayed afloat. The roads were cracking and pine trees were toppling onto buildings. Toby hoped that when the manatees gave up the ghost or a hurricane finally got a bead on Citrus County, trucks of guys would come down from Tallahassee and dynamite the place and slide it off into the Gulf of Mexico to sink.

The bookstore was cavernous and had few customers. It was past lunchtime already, the lazy hours. Toby hurried past the bank of registers in the front, where he was smirked at by a college-aged girl with a dark front tooth. The TV was nestled back among the periodicals and was always tuned to the news from Tampa. Toby positioned a bench. He waited through patter about the nation's top companies to work for, about the poaching of rare orchids. The anchorman grew serious and spoke the words "Citrus County." He spoke Kaley's name. Photos of her appeared next to the anchorman's head. There were those eyes, just as they'd been when Toby nabbed her, round as saucers. The anchorman outlined the search efforts, just getting underway, led in large part by Kaley's father, a mosquito control worker. There had been hopes, when the girl had first been discovered missing, that she'd left the house on her own and wandered into the woods, sleepwalking or something, playing a game, but overnight those hopes had lost steam. Now churches were pledging help, along with Little League teams and off-duty cops from surrounding counties. The FBI bloodhounds were on their way, but the woods were fouled with ATV tracks, the personal effects of vagrants, the droppings of stray mutts, abandoned appliances, the remains of bonfires, beer and liquor bottles. Pictures of Kaley were to be tacked to every power pole for miles. There was talk of roadblocks. Toby didn't know if the response to what he'd done was so swift because this type of thing never happened or because it happened a lot. The kidnapper, according to the authorities, was likely a white male between thirty and fifty-five.

Toby was in one spot, still, while the world rushed around him. He felt powerful. He'd thrown the county into a commotion, had given everyone something important to do. He'd dealt a blow to the wonderful Shelby Register, the only person in the whole county worth injuring. He'd probably made her a different girl. She wouldn't be so sure of herself now. She'd be lost like everyone else. And the searchers were looking for the wrong culprit. They were looking for a dime-a-dozen perverted old man when they should've been looking for an adolescent the likes of which they'd never fathomed.

The bookstore smelled like dust. It didn't smell like books. Racks and racks of magazines stared out at nothing. The anchorman took a moment to regain his solemnity. He informed the viewers that Kaley's father's plea to the kidnapper would be re-aired in a matter of minutes. Toby imagined all the news crews crawling the perimeter of the Registers' property, spying just like he had. He could see the reporters picking at their hairdos in car windows, the women stumbling in their pumps and the men pulling their jackets on and off. It was the news crews, not the cops, who'd found Toby's footprints, the big Velcro shoes. They knew where Toby had crouched. They thought Toby was a dirty old man. They thought he was in Alabama by now. Still, Toby had to worry that through dumb luck someone would happen on the bunker. There was plenty of dumb luck in the world, even if none of it ever alighted on Toby.

Shelby's dad slumped forward, his hands clutched loosely in front of him. He introduced himself as Ben Register. He seemed okay. He was a man in charge of a huge project he strongly believed in. He knew Kaley was still alive, he said. He instructed the kidnapper to drop his daughter at a mall or restaurant or school and speed off, drive somewhere and let the girl go free. She was a problem that was easy to get rid of. Kaley's dad stressed the fact that the kidnapper, at this point, could still get away with this, but the longer he kept Kaley the more chance he'd get caught. Kaley's dad didn't blame the kidnapper for whatever evil he was in the grips of. He took time to look into several cameras. "Every wrong thing you've ever done can be in the past. Now you've got a chance to do something right."

It felt strange to Toby, knowing that this man was talking to *him*. The man didn't know it, but everything he was saying into all those cameras and tape recorders was meant for Toby and Toby only. Ben Register's words were going to float away on the wind and land in the Gulf somewhere. They meant nothing. Every wrong thing Toby had done *was* in the past. He'd finally done something he was meant to do.

The news people, after only a couple days, were showing the effects of spending their nights at the Best Western, eating their dinners at the Chinese buffet, drinking gallons of cheap coffee. Out the window, Shelby caught the cameramen playing cards. They were like actors paid to play cameramen. Nothing Shelby saw seemed genuine. Colors seemed too vivid, the air charged. The sky above was in disarray. There was no sun, as if the sun had been a bomb and it had gone off and blown shreds of cloud into every corner of the world.

Shelby did not want false hope. She did not want to be in shock or denial. She did not want to wait around while her heart hoped and hoped until it was too tired. Shelby wanted to open the front door and scream at all the people out in the road in front of her house. She wanted to tell them to take their decorum and concern and indignation and go the hell home. She wanted the jaded cameramen to go film something else. She wanted to tell the cops who kept coming into her house to check on her and to get themselves glasses of water that they weren't welcome. She wanted to tell all the searchers that her family wasn't one that had a scare and then had it turn out all right. Her family was the type that got it right between the eyes. She wanted to tell the reporters that there'd be nothing further to report, that her father would not do an interview and she would not do an interview and her sister would not be found. Shelby's chest was tight as a fist. She didn't want to be here. She wanted to be out in the middle of a desert, or out on a vast tundra somewhere.

She could already see what this meant for her and her father, but she could not understand that her sister was gone. She could see that for the rest of her life she would be forced to imagine what Kaley would've been like at this age, at this age, at this age, but she could not shake the feeling that her sister was hiding somewhere in the house, that Shelby would open a cabinet in the kitchen to get dishwashing liquid and Kaley would be crouching under there, grinning. Shelby could not grasp that this had happened to her family, her family which, if anything was fair, should've been immune to more tragedy. She would never grasp it.

When Shelby had come in from the porch to get her father some crackers and had walked into the kitchen and opened the fridge, she'd known something wasn't right. Before she'd looked through the archway and seen the open back sliding door, she'd known that something didn't smell right in the house. Smells were missing and there were extra smells. She'd thought of all the mosquitoes that must be coming in. She'd walked over and put her hand on the handle but she hadn't slid the door shut. She had extended her arm out into the humid night air, which was moist but was the exact same temperature as the air in the house. Inside, the house was a wilderness. The walls and roof and foundation meant nothing. They encased a wilderness.

Shelby had been through this in Indiana. She knew that eventually she would go back to school and when she did everyone would be cautious around her, every teacher and every coach and every student. They would all be scared to say the wrong thing. Shelby would be like a bully in the hallways; everyone would hush when she neared. She would be expected to fall back into a regular routine, but her routine would have no chance at feeling regular. And then there was the time *between* now and then. There was today. Shelby wanted to find her sister hiding in the hamper, but her sister was not in the hamper. Shelby wanted to be spared this. She wanted everyone to get away from her house and for the world to be different than it was.

It had quit raining but the sun had not returned. Leftover drops fell ponderously from tree branches and the spider webs looked like strings of dull crystals. Everyone milled about on the edge of the woods. There were a couple bumbling dogs—not trained hounds by any stretch, just lazy mutts who wouldn't know their asses from a drumstick. Toby was going out with one of the baseball teams, a JV team or something, on a search. He wanted to see this firsthand, to see what was working against him. This was what everyone else was doing—the normal people, the innocent. They were helping with the search.

The other kids were about Toby's age. The guy who appeared to be the coach, a guy with long sideburns who wore a jersey that said NEW ZEALAND, stood to the side of the crowd talking in low tones to a woman in fancy shoes. The woman shifted her weight gingerly, her heels scraping into the pebbly ground. No one paid attention to Toby. He stood by and observed as the team, in a graceful fashion that didn't seem intentional, split into two groups. Toby didn't know if it was the infield separating from the outfield, or pitchers from position players, or whether, like a middle school, a baseball team contained cliques. He was surprised at how disorganized and lax an affair this was. He was surprised, also, that the kids were wearing regular clothes. He'd pictured all the baseball teams picking through the brush in their uniforms and cleats. He'd pictured the Boy Scouts, whose searches were being held in a different part of the county, covering ground in those humiliating outfits with the red scarves.

One of the groups abruptly mobilized, and Toby hurried over and joined their ranks. They didn't have an adult with them. They slipped into the woods with no fanfare or goodbyes, leaving the other half of the team and the dogs behind. These kids didn't seem surprised by Toby's presence at the rear of their procession, didn't say anything to him or give any strange looks. There was no plan to the turns the group took, no leader, no discussion. They cut through the woods on the path of least resistance. This was another activity, like church or school, something expected of them that they weren't going to complain about. Toby recognized a few of the kids. He'd gone to grade school with them. He could remember when he'd been more or less the same as everyone else. It seemed a very long time ago. That was before every kid Toby had known became a straight-backed kiss-ass or a troublemaker. These were the choices. They all had to study and eat their green beans and jump back in line at the slightest throat-clearing, like these baseball kids, or they had to vandalize Green Key Beach and shoplift and give old security guards a hard time.

Toby knew this area of the woods, and these kids apparently did not. They were walking in a circle, not a large one. At this rate, they'd be back to the road the cars were parked on in twenty minutes. Toby had wondered what he'd do if he was out with a search team and they started nearing the bunker, but he saw that wasn't a concern on this day, with this group. The searches, in general, seemed to be fanning out in the wrong direction, inland and north. Toby felt disappointed. He wanted the searches to be organized, regimented. He wanted these baseball kids to be consumed with Kaley. They weren't carrying photos of her, weren't even mentioning her. Of all the searchers, they were the nearest to Kaley, yet they had no belief, no spirit for the search.

When the group tightened up, turning a corner, Toby said, "So, where you think this little girl is?"

The group didn't break stride. The shortest one said, "Lot of good guesses, but the best is that she's dead."

"Why do you say that?" Toby asked.

"She could be on a boat to Thailand or in some hillbilly's basement, but probably not. That stuff's for the movies."

"There's no basements in Florida, you dumb Yankee." This kid had a head of bushy curls. "I'm with you, though. She's dead as disco."

"Where'd you hear that? Dead as disco?"

"I'm not certain. I don't always keep track of where I hear things."

"I think she's alive," Toby broke in. "And I bet she's not far away."

"She's dead, but she *could* be close by," a third kid said. This one wore aviator sunglasses. "It's not that easy to get rid of a body."

"Sure it is," said the short kid.

"Whoever finds her will be a hero," Toby said.

"Okay," said the kid with the sunglasses. "How do you get rid of a body?"

"Take it ten miles out in the Gulf and weigh it down and toss it overboard. You can incinerate it. You can feed it to animals. Like pigs. I saw a movie where they fed bodies to pigs."

"You've seen a lot of movies, I bet," said Toby. "I bet most of what you know comes from watching movies."

The kids finally looked at Toby. They kept walking.

"If you guys think she's dead," he said, "you shouldn't be out here."

"We have to be," said the one with the bushy hair. "Our coach counts a search as a practice. You miss a practice, you don't play that week."

"Our coach is a dick," said the kid with the sunglasses. "He always hits on my mom, and if he doesn't stop it he better fucking watch out."

"I don't blame him," the short kid said. "Your mom's hot."

The kid with the sunglasses reached up and shook a branch, soaking the short kid, and the short kid stiffened, nodding in appreciation, water dripping off his chin.

Toby felt like screaming, telling these kids to quit horsing around because Kaley was alive and she needed them. Toby felt slighted. These kids didn't know who he was and were treating him like any old rubberneck who wanted to get in with a search party. And Toby felt annoyed, in a sharper way, at himself. He had the feeling that as long as no one knew what he'd done, it hadn't really happened. He was allowing himself to care about what people knew or didn't know. Toby felt like he could fall asleep in class one day and when he woke up at the end of the period none of this would be real.

Action 7 kept leaving Cracker Barrel on the front walk. The Registers' fridge contained stacks of foam boxes—chicken and dumplings, grits, cheese-topped potatoes. Shelby had eaten none of it except the tiny tubs of apple butter, which she spooned into her mouth with her finger.

The church groups had stopped lighting candles on the front walk. That many candles were probably expensive and it was tough to keep them lit with the wind blowing. Four days in and they'd given up on finding Kaley, whether they knew it or not, and were now going through the motions of church folk, wondering how long faith was supposed to linger in a situation like this, how long faith was supposed to compel you to trip around in the woods getting eaten alive by bugs. It was almost time for them to say something about Kaley being an angel and return to planning their ski trips. The church folk had given up on Shelby, as well. The day before, they'd sent a girl about her age, a squinty thing with a million barrettes, right up the walk and onto the porch with a backpack full of Christian music. Shelby recognized her from school. She stared at the girl through the window by the door and the girl stared back. Shelby eased the door open.

"Here to pray?"

"If you'd like," said the girl.

"Why don't you hand over the bag?"

The girl mustered a smile, picking at a barrette.

"I said hand it over."

"It's stuff for us to hang out."

"I'll hang out with it first," Shelby said. "Then you can hang out with it. We'll see which one of us the stuff likes better."

The girl was about to say something, but Shelby snatched the bag.

"I've got something for you too," Shelby said. "Wait here."

Shelby went to the fridge and pulled out a container of grits. She found a serving spoon. When she returned to the front door, the girl hadn't moved. Her lips were stretched shut over her braces. Her arms hung at her sides, hands resting loosely in her pockets. Shelby drew the door all the way open. She dug the spoon into the grits and flung some at the girl, who was too nervous to flinch. The grits slapped against the girl's forehead. Shelby had never done anything so mean. She heaped up another spoonful and the girl squealed, backing up.

"Watch the step." Shelby unloaded, the congealed grits thudding against the girl's chest, tumbling inside her blouse.

And then the girl stopped backpedaling, suddenly defiant. She closed her eyes and turned her face up, as if daring Shelby.

"I get it," Shelby said. "You're being persecuted. You're enduring whatever trials you have to endure."

Shelby readied her spoon and cocked her arm. She felt low and childish, but that was how she needed to feel. She needed to not be felt sorry for. She thwacked the girl across the bridge of the nose with more grits and then slammed the door. Shelby believed she deserved to act however she wanted. Every hour she had a different soul, and she wasn't going to resist any of them.

Toby didn't know how long Uncle Neal would be out of the house. He rushed from room to room—tissues, bandages, lip balm. Toby had brought trip after trip of supplies down to the bunker beforehand, but there was a lot he hadn't thought of. He'd rushed into the whole thing, he saw, but his mind would catch up with itself. If he could keep eating dinner and keep getting up in the morning and leaving the house, his mind would catch up.

He looked for something other than water to give Kaley to drink, something with flavor, but he didn't want to give her soda and make her that much more unmanageable. He saw her wide, flushed face and her snot-glazed chin every time he closed his eyes. He had decided never to speak to her, never to utter a word down in the bunker. She would settle down. She would see that Toby was a stone and she would settle down.

Toby had to filch supplies from his uncle a little at a time. He took part of a watermelon, and a stack of paper bowls with a picture on the plastic wrap of people having a picnic. Toby needed more buckets but couldn't find any. There were likely a few out in the shed, but the shed was locked up and Toby wasn't allowed into it.

There were two FBI agents, both women. They didn't show up until Kaley had been gone almost a week. They'd been on another case, they explained. Their department had been slashed to the bone. They weren't going to be the primaries for Kaley's case. They were there to help out, conduct some interviews, get the police whatever resources they needed.

The agents had spoken to Shelby's father out in the woods that morning, and now they had Shelby cornered in the house. One of the agents was young. She wore bright sets of jewelry and had tangled, shoulder-length hair. The other was in her forties and had a pixie-cut. The agents interviewed Shelby in the living room. The one with the tangled hair found the remote control and muted the TV. Shelby tried not to look at the screen. It was a cooking program in which ingredients were tracked from their origin at the farm, were monitored as they were shipped to retail stores or co-ops, then finally made their way to plates.

"Maybe you've got some coffee," the agent with the pixie-cut said.

"No," Shelby answered. "We've got beer or water."

"Everybody calls this the *real* Florida," the tangly-haired one said. "I don't understand an expression like that. Is part of the state imaginary?"

"I wouldn't know," Shelby answered.

"And they call themselves crackers. Where I'm from, that's what black people call white people when they're angry."

On TV, an old man was explaining cheese. For some reason, he dropped a package of saltines on the ground and mashed them with his moccasin.

"We've only got a couple questions." The pixie-cut agent reached down and retied her boot, never losing eye contact with Shelby. She was performing her part of their routine. "Does your father have any friends that come around?" the agent asked. "Friends of the family? Drinking buddies?"

"Not down here in Florida."

"Not one friend?"

"Not that comes around."

"Does Kaley have a babysitter?"

"You're looking at her."

"Any prank calls?"

Shelby shook her head. Prank calls seemed like a thing of the distant past, like cotton gins. She reached and pushed the power button on the remote, blanking the TV.

"Did anything of Kaley's go missing?"

"No."

"How do you know for sure?"

"I know how many of everything she has and it's all in there."

"You know exactly how many shirts and socks she has?"

Shelby wondered if these were the same questions they'd asked her father. She said, "The piles in the drawers look the same, and I know because I go in the drawers every morning when I get my sister dressed. When I used to."

After her sister had gone missing, Shelby had inventoried Kaley's room, putting things in their place. The cops who'd come to investigate had been annoyed that Shelby'd disturbed the scene, but Shelby knew they wouldn't have found anything. They were morons. So were these FBI agents. They all asked the same questions. They were all hoping for miracles.

"Should you be writing this down?" Shelby asked.

The pixie-cut agent winked. "I'd rather put it in my head than in a notepad. I could lose a notepad."

"You've never in your life lost your head?" asked the tangly-haired one.

"Why was the sliding door unlocked?" the pixie-cut one asked Shelby.

"I guess we were feeling carefree," she said. "Is that an answer? We'd been out in the backyard earlier, filling the birdfeeder. It was me that forgot to lock the door. My dad told me not to forget to lock it and I forgot."

"Carefree, what a thing to be," said the tangly-haired one.

Shelby wanted to say something cutting to the agents.

"Why do these women keep having all these children?" the pixie-cut agent asked, to no one in particular. "Nothing good comes of it. Why do they keep having them and having them?"

The tangly-haired one raised her eyebrows, an expression that meant she was only the messenger. "Because that's what everybody else is doing, that's why."

Shelby picked her way through the woods at the rear of her house. Toby had PE sixth period and Shelby knew where he went during PE, over by the oversized air conditioning units in back of the chorus room. He always went to the far side and sat against the wall by himself. And there he was. He was reliable. He was where he was supposed to be. Shelby neared the fence, coming out of the woods, and Toby was sitting straight-legged, not more than a yell away from her. Shelby didn't want to make noise. She waved her arm a few times and Toby saw her. He stared at first, like she was a deer that had wandered out of the woods, but then he knew it was her and he walked over toward the fence. The air was still. As Toby got closer, Shelby could hear the dry grass crunching under his sneakers. Here he was. Nothing had happened to him. He was still Toby.

She looked into his deadpan brown eyes and they seemed to know everything. Neither of them spoke. Toby's face was waffled with the fence's shadow. For a moment Shelby forgot to think about herself—about her father, her sister, how she'd left the sliding door open, how she'd let her mother down, how she had to return to school and all of it seemed absurd now. The idea of being graded was farcical. The teachers. The clubs. The buildings themselves, crouched and faded.

The PE coach sounded his whistle. Sixth period was ending. Shelby and Toby knew they had to speak. They had to finish the moment.

"I'm still coming after you," Shelby told him. "I'm going to pick up where I left off."

"I'll be all the places I normally am," Toby said.

Shelby's dad sat at the kitchen table with an open expression on his face, grasping a fork. He wanted coffee but Shelby refused to give him any. She wanted him to sleep.

"The Boy Scouts are the best searchers," Shelby's dad said. "When a Boy Scout searches for something, he falls in love with it."

"That sounds true," Shelby said. Her dad's statements had taken on a philosophical tang.

Shelby had her back to her father. She was picking chicken pieces out of some Cracker Barrel chicken and dumplings, filling a bowl. She would heavy her dad's stomach and give him a shot of whisky.

"This old man from the nondenominational church." Shelby's dad paused. She turned and saw him blinking, something in his eye. He tried to fish it out with his pinkie.

"The old man?" Shelby said.

"He's got this grabber thing and then he brakes the snakes' necks with his bare hands. He collects them in a sack and takes them home and burns them to the heavens."

"You've slept eleven hours in six days."

"I don't feel that tired."

Shelby opened the fridge and shoved aside a mess of boxes, making room to put the dumplings back. She felt a diffuse pain in her midsection. Since her sister had disappeared, all physical pain was diffuse. She placed the bowl of chicken in front of her father. He ate three hunks, then coughed and set down his fork. Shelby went into the next room and put on quiet music. She closed all the blinds. When she returned to the kitchen, her dad had eaten no more of the chicken. He had a hunk on his fork and it was dripping gravy on the table.

"My sister's putting up fifty grand," he said. "A reward for information leading to recovery."

"Her idea?"

"She called yesterday. She'd been in Scotland."

Shelby nudged her dad's hand toward his mouth and he ate the piece of chicken from his fork.

Shelby's aunt, her dad's sister, lived in Iceland. She had a website, popular in certain circles, on which she reviewed books and restaurants and music and entire cities from the perspective of a space alien. The site was called *whatwouldtheythink*. Aunt Dale. She'd been with the same guy for fifteen years but hadn't married him. There was a picture of her in the hallway that led to Shelby's room. Aunt Dale had splotchy freckles and tight braids that stuck out stiffly from her head. She'd been friendly whenever Shelby had spoken to her on the phone, but Shelby hadn't been in the same room with her in years. Shelby had looked at the website before, and it had made her feel lonely. The goings-on of these other people on these other continents were exciting and withering. Shelby had harbored a secret wish, after her mother passed away, that her Aunt Dale would make an effort to be closer to Shelby and Kaley, but that hadn't happened. Aunt Dale was excused from doing a lot of things other people were expected to do. She was an artist, Shelby supposed. Shelby had no idea if she herself was an artist, if she would ever be excused from things for a reason other than that she'd been struck with misfortune.

Shelby's dad looked stymied. He was leaning forward against the table.

"That's good enough," she told him. She removed his chicken and threw it in the trash, bowl and all. She poured a big shot and rubbed her father's shoulders. He took the whisky down in subdued sips, like it was hot tea, then slid the shot glass to the middle of the table. Shelby wanted to sing her father a lullaby. She wanted to make a soothing sound. She rubbed her father's shoulders more softly, found herself humming. It *was* a pretty sound. And it was working; her father was falling off.

Shelby went across the house and pulled the mattress off her bed. She didn't want to have to wake her father and make him stumble to his bedroom. If he took too many steps, he'd come to and head right out the front door. She stood the mattress on its side and tugged it down the hall. It got stuck turning the corner to the living room and Shelby had to bounce it free. When she reached the kitchen she leaned in the door frame and her father was not in his chair. She checked the bathroom, the utility room. She dashed to the front windows and threw aside a curtain. Her father was at the end of the walk. A couple of the reporters spoke and he spoke back. When he was almost past them, a lady reporter wearing a bright scarf, Sandra Denton, stepped from behind a van and stood in his path. The angle at which she held her head was meant to be conspiratorial. Sandra Denton fondled her earrings. She touched Shelby's dad's sleeve. He walked on, into the brush, and she had to watch him go.

Shelby let the curtain drop. She explored the house, looking for something to break. She was going to crumble if she didn't attack; those were her choices. She stomped over the mattress, which was lying on the living room floor, then stopped short in front of the TV. It would make a resounding crunch, the TV against the wall, but she'd regret it. It was good to have in the nighttime. She made a pass through the bedrooms—nothing large enough, delicate enough, nothing calling out to be smashed. She had an urge to trash Kaley's room, to toss the toys everywhere and fling the clothes out of the dresser and flip the little bed over. She couldn't do that.

Shelby rushed back to the window. She brushed the hair from her eyes and went out the front door. Nobody noticed her until she was to the road, then in a blink everyone was staring. She felt like she was on stage, the audience starved. She stepped underneath Sandra Denton's team's camera, which was propped on a tripod, and hoisted it onto her shoulder. It had plenty of weight to it. The tripod didn't fully detach, but hung ungainly, pressing on Shelby's back. The faces surrounding her beamed. Shelby flexed her knees, flung the camera upward with all she had, and shuffled to the side. There was the crunch. The camera, though it remained in one piece, was smashed on the front end. It made garbled noises.

Shelby went back inside and the phone was ringing. Shelby listened to the ringing and then she listened to the machine pick up and then to the crisp, disgruntled voice of the pixie-cut FBI agent. The woman told Shelby she was sorry if she hadn't been professional when she'd interviewed Shelby. She said she usually did not behave like that. Her partner maybe, but not her. They saw cases like Kaley's all the time, and it was hell on the nerves. The agent told Shelby she was a civil servant. She had good days and bad. She coped, like everyone. It sounded to Shelby like the agent was calling from a cafeteria, lots of clinking in the background. She stopped talking just as the machine was about to cut her off.

Mr. Hibma sat through detention, looking over his basketball binders for the sixth or seventh time. That was the thing about detention—when you gave it to a student, you gave it to yourself too. The offender was someone other than Toby this time. Shelby, her second day back, had told her latest trivia partner that he was one of the planet's useless people, that his brain ought to be donated for research. She had done this, it seemed, because the boy was being so polite to her. His parents had likely told him to be extra nice to Shelby Register, and this turned out to be bad advice. Though Mr. Hibma agreed with the assertion that this particular boy's brain wasn't doing him a lot of good, and though the boy hadn't seemed too offended, Mr. Hibma couldn't let Shelby get away with calling someone stupid in front of the class. And he thought she might appreciate being treated like a regular student, might appreciate not being tiptoed around, might like to receive a detention just like anybody else.

Mr. Hibma knew he ought to talk to Shelby about her sister. He was likely the teacher she thought the most of, an adult whom, if she didn't respect, she at least didn't hold in contempt. He knew it was his moral duty to lend her his ear, his shoulder to cry on, but Mr. Hibma could not do these sorts of things. He was deficient. It was one of the many reasons he was not a real teacher. He saw the others do it, saw them take kids under their wings, saw them prod kids into spilling their guts. Some teachers did it for the drama and some because they genuinely cared, but the point was they did it. To Mr. Hibma it was unseemly, insinuating yourself into another person's personal life. That's what guidance counselors and therapists were for. Even the few kids Mr. Hibma enjoyed a rapport with he thought of as work acquaintances. Shelby was one of his favorites, and if he wasn't going to help her now then he never would. He could feel that he wouldn't. It went against his every fiber.

He turned toward the chalkboard and began erasing the vocabulary words. In the interest of burning time, Mr. Hibma gave ten vocab words a week. He had each class's top kiss-ass write the words and the definitions on the board while the rest of the kids copied them. This took up fifteen minutes on Mondays. On Wednesdays, he allowed fifteen minutes of study time. On Fridays, fifteen minutes for the quiz. Blight. Wizened. Ransack.

Shelby had drawn a circle on the back of her hand and was darkening it in with a marker.

"That sort of thing is beneath you," Mr. Hibma told her.

Shelby stopped filling in the circle but did not look at him.

"I've got books you can read, some good Jewish authors. Bellow, maybe."

Shelby seemed intimidated by the idea. She glanced, not alertly, at a Dufy print—a bunch of horses at a racetrack.

Mr. Hibma felt like having a strong drink. If he stayed at this job much longer, he'd become one of those teachers who kept a flask in his bottom drawer. He went to the bookshelf and gathered the Bellow novels and put them on Shelby's desk.

"We never know what's going to screw us up," he said. "We think it has to be glaring tragedies, but that's not always the case." Mr. Hibma wasn't sure where he was going with this. He was, to his own surprise, taking a stab at being profound and helpful.

"Sometimes the tragedies strengthen us in the end. They make us more ourselves, you know—concentrate us."

"Guess I'm pretty concentrated," Shelby said. "I'm like that frozen orange juice."

"Most of your classmates will live their whole lives without anything really good or really bad happening to them. They'll see some funny movies and wait in some lines and maybe get their phones cut off or develop diabetes."

Shelby nodded. Mr. Hibma might have been frightening her.

"I went to one of the fanciest high schools in the country my junior year. That's the root of most of my problems. That and receiving an inheritance."

"Was it a whole school of gifted kids?" Shelby said.

"Gifted." Mr. Hibma shuddered. "Gifted is for chimps. They'll probably ask you to be in that program soon and I hope you'll turn them down. It's a mark of mediocrity, gifted. You'll have a hard enough time without those weirdos."

"Why'd you only go to that school for a year?" Shelby asked.

"Why I got kicked out isn't the important part," Mr. Hibma said. "For seven months I enjoyed an environment of reflection, courtesy, fertilization of any intellectual whim. We had fireplaces to read near. They played Handel during the passing period."

Shelby handled the Bellow novels, reading the spines. The breeze blew something against the window.

"Sometimes good things mess a person up," Mr. Hibma said. He wondered if anything that happened was really *good*. He still hadn't decided, after all these years, what he thought of the fact that he'd been a stolen baby. It had to mean something. It had to have shaped Mr. Hibma. "I'm not making sense," he told Shelby. "I'm lousy at this."

"You're doing fine," she said. "It's not you. I don't *want* to be comforted. I'm not receptive to wisdom or perspective."

"But I'm supposed to be able to break down your walls."

"A fool's errand," Shelby said. "You break down my walls, you're not going to find anything you want to find."

Mr. Hibma was stumped. He wanted to let Shelby know that she was special, that she couldn't let herself be lost to the world because the world needed her. His voice had gone dumb. He'd given Shelby detention in part to test himself, to see if he could get her to confide in him, and he'd failed. Failed to try, really. He stood at the front of the room, lining the erasers up tight and orderly in the tray. He was angry at the world, that it gave the worthwhile people such a hard time. It was difficult for him to even look at Shelby. He dismissed her with a nod, letting himself off the hook.

He sat for a time, part and parcel of the imperfect quiet of the world, and then, when he could, he began drawing up a class rules sheet. He wrote numbers, 1 to 10, and next to each scribbled *see surrounding classrooms.* He taped the sheet to the wall.

Earlier that day, just after school had let out, Mrs. Conner had confronted him in the hall and informed him that it was her duty, as wing chairperson, to enforce the guidelines the liberal arts department had agreed upon. It was mandatory that each teacher post class rules.

"But every teacher has the same ones," Mr. Hibma had said. "And those rules are identical to the school rules."

"Exactly," said Mrs. Conner. "A unified front."

"I hate unified fronts."

Mr. Hibma had never been to Mrs. Conner's home, but he could see it. He saw a screened porch atop a wooden deck. He saw a shed, trimmed hedges. He knew now that he would not kill the husband. He would learn the couple's routine and go visit Mrs. Conner when her husband was off playing golf or shooting woodland creatures or whatever activity he used as an excuse to get the hell away from his wife. Mr. Hibma had already scratched knives or guns, and had considered and thought better of poison. Poisoners always got caught. Mr. Hibma watched the TV shows. Whenever someone bought poison it turned out they'd been videotaped or had left the receipt in their floorboard or the clerk or another customer remembered them. Then the cops went and looked at your computer or library records and saw that you'd researched some topic that was vaguely related to poison. Then everyone said they should've known because you were always a little strange; you'd seemed harmless, though. As careful as you were, there was always something when you used poison. No, what Mr. Hibma saw himself doing was parking in the lot of the nearest strip mall and, in the middle of the night, sneaking onto the Conner property and hiding himself away behind the shed or under the deck, waiting for the husband to leave in the morning, then knocking on the front door and allowing a confused Mrs. Conner to present herself, barging in and throwing her down and smothering her under all his weight with one of her own couch pillows. There would be no blood, no loud noises, no purchases Mr. Hibma would have to make. Most of all, Mrs. Conner would get no last words.

"I'm not *asking* you," Mrs. Conner said. She raked her rust-colored hair. "And I know about the vocab quizzes. Don't try and legitimize your class by stealing from the English curriculum."

"Which kiss-ass is spying for you?"

"Excuse me?"

"Let me tell you something," Mr. Hibma said. "Your shoes are way too small. Your toes flop out onto the floor. Can't you feel it?"

Mrs. Conner had looked down her nose at Mr. Hibma, using the lower part of her bifocals, keeping her composure.

The tryout. Twenty-one girls. Mr. Hibma started them out with stretching, putting them in a circle and having each choose one body part. He backed off and watched the unsteady things roll their necks, bend at the waist, perform jumping jacks. He was more an impostor in the gym than in the classroom. He didn't even know where the locker rooms or the weight room or the coaches' offices were. He'd never, as far as he knew, blown a whistle. He'd never yelled at anyone for that person's own good.

Mr. Hibma closed his eyes and controlled his breathing. He would fake his way through this. If he possessed a talent for anything, it was faking his way through things. This was *his* gym. He was a natural component of this environment. He had boundless energy. Weeks would pass; they had no choice but to pass. The games would come and go and no one would notice that Mr. Hibma wasn't really a coach. As far as these stretching girls were concerned, he was the supreme sultan of basketball.

He held their athletic futures in his hands. Mr. Hibma strode over and stared at the girls and they quit giggling and whispering. They eyed one another.

Mr. Hibma guided himself through a lecture about boxing out. He set up a drill in which he launched errant shots and made the girls slam into each other trying to claim the rebounds. He tried his whistle and rapidly grew fond of it. Mr. Hibma could've picked the team already. It was obvious which girls were afraid of the ball and which weren't. He would keep fifteen; he could keep the three cute girls and never have to play them in a real game. They'd be third-string, morale-boosters, something for the fans to look at.

It occurred to Mr. Hibma to sit all the girls down and speak about the importance of their appearances. In middle school, he reminded them, ugly girls were intimidated by pretty girls. Hell, it was that way with adult women. A team could gain an advantage by keeping tan and having their nails done.

"Do you know what active-length nails are?" he asked. "Spend your allowances on a good haircut, down in Pinellas County. Stop at Macy's and learn a little about makeup."

Eventually Mr. Hibma had to let the girls scrimmage. The short twins with the big teeth could shoot three-pointers. A girl with muscular legs and no eyebrows beat everyone down court each time but was too jittery to complete a layup. One girl, extremely skinny with a bowl cut, could handle the ball. She dribbled between her legs and behind her back and whipped passes here and there. Scoring was at a premium, but the scrimmage had the *look* of a basketball game.

Afterward, the girls huddled again. The twins looked at each other. "Coach?" one said.

"Don't call me coach. Call me Mr. Hibma."

"Mr. Himba?"

"Not Him-ba. *Hib*ma."

"Do we really have to get our hair and nails done?"

"If you want to start."

There was a murmur and then it died down.

"Now," said Mr. Hibma. "Important business."

He explained that it was all of the girls' personal responsibilities to get the two huge girls who threw the shot and the discus to try out for the team. Rosa, the Mexican one, and Sherrie, the other one, had to try out. This was vital.

"Befriend them," ordered Mr. Hibma. "Pressure them. Bribe them. Just get them the hell out here."

Walking onto the school grounds, right up the main drag near the sign that said CITRUS MIDDLE SCHOOL in concrete letters, Toby was called over by two women in a shiny blue car. They were the FBI agents. Their car looked like it had been washed about five minutes ago. The hood was dazzling in the morning sun. They didn't bother to get out. The one talking to Toby was in the driver's seat. She had very short hair.

She said, "Don't worry, sport, we won't make you late. We won't make you tardy."

Toby felt hot. He didn't know if it was because of the agents or because the sun had found him. Toby did not feel worried, in general, about the cops or these agents, but maybe he was just telling himself that. He stood there and partook of quiet deep breaths while the woman asked him questions, mostly about Shelby. Toby answered them honestly. He told them Shelby had come to see him during PE class a couple times before she officially returned to school. He told her they had geography class together. The other agent, the one in the passenger seat, didn't even look over. She squinted out her window.

"Want a bagel?" the agent in the driver's seat said. "Apparently my partner's lost her appetite."

Toby shook his head. He didn't fidget. This FBI agent had no accusation in her eyes. She wasn't trying to make Toby nervous. She was underestimating him, like everyone did. She was questioning him only because she didn't have any good leads, only because he was a friend of Shelby's and she was casting a wide net.

She adjusted her mirror and put on some lip balm. "Is it fair to say you're in tight with all the troublemakers around here?"

"No," said Toby.

"Don't you all run together?"

"I don't run with anyone."

"A lone wolf, huh?" said the agent. "Here's the thing. A lot of these cases crack because people can't keep secrets. There's certain secrets that get heavy and people can't take it anymore and they tell someone. Then *that* person tells someone."

The agent stopped talking. She didn't start again until Toby nodded.

"I want you to be my ears. If any of your buddies say anything I'd be interested in, you let me know."

Toby told her he would and she gave him a staged smile.

"What do you kids do for fun around here?" she asked.

"Fun?" Toby said.

"You've heard of it, right?"

Toby took a broad look around the parking lot, at all the kids getting dropped off by their parents, bags being jerked out of trunks. "I don't know what *they* do," Toby said. "I walk around. I get the lay of the land."

Toby's eyes had adjusted to the gleaming of the car's paint job. He could see into the back seat. There weren't any guns or high-tech equipment. There was a case of bottled water.

"Is she your girlfriend?" The agent leaned out the window. Now there was something in her eyes. "Is Shelby your girlfriend?"

"No," said Toby.

"How about this: Are you her boyfriend?"

Toby took a step back.

"I can see it, the whole goody-goody with the bad boy thing. It's a time-honored tradition."

"Shelby's not a goody-goody," Toby said.

"It's okay to be a goody-goody. I'm a goody-goody and I do all right."

The agent grinned like she'd made a joke, but no one was going to laugh. Especially not her partner. She handed Toby a business card.

"Okay, sport," she said. "I'm going to roll up the window now."

The afternoon hours were the flattest. They were like Citrus County itself, fit only for ambush. Shelby wanted to get higher or lower. There were no basements, no second stories. Her house had no attic. Shelby didn't want to keep walking on the same ground. She was on a dumb plank of land where nothing would roll away. Everything stayed right where it was and festered. Shelby had been reduced to silly fantasies—visions of her and her dad moving off and working a farm somewhere, visions of going to stay with her Aunt Dale in Iceland, of having Aunt Dale show her how to be a rigid, invulnerable woman. Shelby wanted something more dramatic, more honest. She wanted a crashing ocean instead of the wash of the Gulf. She wanted weather that could kill you. She wanted respect from someone who actually knew how to judge.

She walked around the outside of her house, finding no way to get onto the roof. She ended up in the backyard, lost. She lifted the kiddie pool and flipped it over and curled underneath it. The sounds in the air, the accidental noises of the world, were different under the plastic shell. They seemed to come from a long way off, from the bottom of some blue sea. Shelby felt animalistic. She detected a strength, a madness, a rogue element inside her that would help her shape the days of her life. She wanted to determine herself. She wanted to force her way into an open destiny.

On his way to track practice, Toby walked up on Shelby at the playground. She had a newspaper, like the first time he'd talked to her here, when Kaley had been swinging. She held the paper at arm's length as if it smelled bad. Toby didn't know what she was doing at the playground. She ought to be avoiding this place. Toby kind of missed the old Shelby, the regular Shelby. It was disorienting to be around someone bleaker than himself. And Toby still had a slight fear that Shelby would detect his guilt with some sisterly sixth sense. He sometimes suspected she could read him like a book, that she would look into his eyes and see Kaley slumped against the bunker wall on her cot, her dirty feet smudging up her sheets, her ears red and teeth gnashed. Shelby wasn't looking for clues, though. She had never been part of the search. She was just trying to understand what it meant that her sister was gone.

Toby sat down on the end of the bench. Shelby wore a thin T-shirt that revealed the soft form of her breasts, which shifted each time she moved her arms to turn a page.

"They're opening a jazz bar in Crystal River," she said. Nothing was happening in her face. "Have you ever heard anything more pitiful?" She folded the paper, taking the time to follow the original creases, then flung it under the bench. "They say music soothes the soul."

"I haven't heard much music." Toby found that he wanted to say something to make her feel okay. He wanted to see some hope in her.

"How come you still haven't asked for my phone number?" Shelby said.

"Because I don't have a phone," said Toby.

"In your house, you don't have a phone?"

"Never have."

"Your uncle again, huh?"

Toby shrugged. The swing set looked lonesome. Toby wished they'd come and tear it down already, get rid of this old playground that didn't belong here.

"Can I ask *you* something?" he said. "Did you really throw a bunch of

Cracker Barrel on a girl?"

Shelby's lips pinched. "All that stuff is still in the fridge. My dad won't throw it out because that would mean admitting how much time has passed." She looked at Toby flatly. "I don't know what we eat anymore. I really don't."

Toby tried to keep his eyes from darting to Shelby's chest. He felt sick. He felt like he might throw up and he never felt like that. Shelby rested her arm down the length of the bench. She touched Toby's ear.

"What the hell are you wearing?" she asked him.

Toby had on skimpy green shorts and a tank top that read GREECE.

"You're shallow," he said. "Making fun of someone's clothes is shallow."

"You haven't been to Greece, have you?"

"I haven't even been to a Greek restaurant."

Shelby drew her arms to her chest and shuddered, startled to be cold.

"I know it's going to be okay," Toby said. "We'll be okay."

"You don't have to try to be a good guy." Shelby drew a breath. Thunder could be heard, far off. "We won't be okay, you know that."

"I don't. I don't know anything."

The thunder was steady and not very threatening. If it did anything harmful, it would be to other people. Toby, out of nowhere, could feel his courage gathering. His stomach didn't feel bad. This wasn't the dashing focus his evil sometimes provided him, but his own simple, native courage. Shelby considered Toby the one good thing about Florida and Toby knew it. He slid down the bench toward Shelby and heard the newspaper crumpling under his feet. He could smell Shelby's hair. She had goose bumps but to Toby she was warm. Suddenly she hopped up, startling Toby, her boots making a chirp. She strode past the swing set, leaving muddled tracks in the sand. As she passed, she pulled one of the swings in the air and released it and it was still swinging when she disappeared around the corner. It was the swing Kaley had been in that day. Toby couldn't raise himself off the bench. He watched the swing. He watched it until it stilled, until its slight movement was the work of the breeze.

When Toby got to practice, Coach Scolle was herding everyone into a circle. He said they had to move ass because if he felt one drop of rain he was clearing the field; no one was getting struck by lightning on his watch. He went around and made everyone name their goals for the season. Vince, the kid who tried to buy friends with gum, wanted to clear six feet at the high jump. Rosa and Sherrie, the enormous girls, wanted to beat Pasco High, a black school that, with the exception of girls' volleyball, dominated all sports within the district. When it was Toby's turn, Coach Scolle complained about having a pole-vaulter on the team, about having to lug the apparatus out every day, about the high-jumpers sacrificing valuable mat time, about worrying that Toby would break his neck on Coach Scolle's watch. The coach informed Toby he would waste no energy instructing him.

"You better check that book back out and do some trial and error," Coach Scolle said.

"I still have it," Toby said. "I'm on chapter two—conditioning."

"Could be a long chapter for you."

Toby shrugged. Plenty of people on the team were in worse shape than he was, overweight even. Coach Scolle asked Toby's goal. Because pole vault was a middle school sport only in Citrus County, Toby could not hope to win a state title, possibly not even a district title. "To learn to pole vault," he said.

Coach Scolle huffed. "Believe it when I see it."

This was the point at which, normally, Toby would've been a smart-ass. He would've asked the coach if the real reason he was afraid of a few clouds was that his man-perm could get damaged. If the real reason he was afraid of rain was that one of the windows of his Firebird was busted out and covered over with a plastic bag. But Toby said nothing. Being seen as a bad seed would only hinder him from here on out. He didn't want that kind of attention. Though he hadn't realized it when he'd tried out, he saw now that he'd joined a sports team to appear average, and showing up the coach and getting booted from the squad would defeat the purpose.

On his way to the taco place, Toby made another stop at the big bookstore. He dropped his bag off at the front and maneuvered back to the TV. The national news had abandoned Kaley, and Toby found that the Tampa news had let her drop off, as well. He figured out how to change the channel and watched for almost an hour. The weather in St. Petersburg. Sports in Tampa. A drowning in Lutz. Someone had driven an El Camino into the side of a flower shop. A girl at the university had blackmailed her poetry professor. A cemetery was being sued. These people didn't give a damn about Citrus County. They didn't give a damn about Kaley. They would if they knew she was alive and who had her. They'd give a damn then. Toby sat there before a bank of magazines—motorcycles, health food. All these interests. Everybody had all these interests.

The shop that sold used hardware and appliances was right up near the Chinese buffet. It was about a mile from Uncle Neal's, which was a long haul with Toby toting a wide two-wheel dolly behind him the whole way. And he was going to have to drag it the whole way back, but loaded, right along the roadside, right through the weeds.

Most of the store's stock was out front, sprawled over the yard, but Toby needed a stand-alone air conditioner and the lightest generator he could find. That sort of stuff would be kept inside. He rested his dolly on a refurbished pulpit and entered the store. The old woman who ran the place nodded at him and he nodded back. He went to the back aisles and quickly the items he was seeking appeared before him on the shelves. He felt grateful. They were right next to each other, kind of a set. It felt like an endorsement, finding exactly what he needed so fast.

Toby carried the items one at a time to the front counter and waited for the old woman to ring him up. He saw now that the woman had a little girl with her. She was hidden behind the counter, at the old woman's knee. The little girl kept thrusting her fists into her pockets then slowly pulling them back out.

"Not taking no chances," the old woman said. "I'm keeping my grandbaby right here. Her mama goes to work, this little one's right here with me, not at the daycare with some pot fiend watching her."

Toby dug his bills out and started straightening and sorting them. The old lady's eyes were on him. She had ratty hair, but her eyes were clear and her posture was straight.

"What do you think of this one?" she asked the little girl, jabbing a thumb toward Toby.

The girl shrugged.

"I don't know either," said the old woman.

Toby dragged his stuff home and stashed it and then turned right back around and headed back to the dirt road. He'd forgotten. He'd meant to go to the drug store. He had to walk all the way to Route 19. He needed hair clippers. Kaley's hair was riddled with knots and snarls and Toby couldn't begin to loosen any of them.

The next day, Toby found a note on his dresser: *See me in the shed*. Toby had never been allowed in Uncle Neal's shed, but he knew from looking in the window that it contained a stove and a bunch of potted plants that were likely some backwoods hallucinogen. Uncle Neal kept the place off-limits with a padlock. He went out there each Sunday, even in the crush of summer, and did a bunch of snipping and boiling.

Toby pushed the shed door open and found Uncle Neal standing before a mess of purplish stalks and a steaming stew pot. He wore rubber gloves and wielded a pair of tongs. An open bag of uncooked tater tots sat on the counter, and a forty-four-ounce soda with a long straw. There was a bowl of lemons. A bag of sugar. Cutting board.

Uncle Neal raised a heap of stalks over the pot and let them fall.

He bent down and slurped some soda. "Drop one of those tots in my mouth."

Toby reached into the bag and fed his uncle.

"Are you getting high?" Toby said.

"This isn't drugs, it's hemlock."

The stalks were giving off an acrid aroma. Toby pulled the door open all the way.

"I keep a gallon in that fridge for one week," Uncle Neal said. "Then I throw it out and make more. It's the secret to my success." His forehead gathered in appraisal.

Toby began coughing.

"The steam can't hurt you," said Uncle Neal. "Might make you happy. I used to look forward to breathing it, but I guess I built a tolerance. I built a tolerance to most things that might make me happy."

Toby cleared his throat and wiped his eyes.

"This stuff wouldn't really kill you," Uncle Neal said. "If you drank the whole gallon it might maim you." Uncle Neal sipped more soda. "Quarter those lemons."

Toby stepped up to the counter and positioned the cutting board. He was already getting used to the stench. Now he recognized it from Uncle Neal's clothes, the clothes he always wore to do his Sunday chore in the shed—the faded blue T-shirt and worn jeans. The stuff *was* doing something to Toby. He felt light.

"Hemlock is potent when it's young," Uncle Neal explained. "The plants get over five feet tall, I get rid of them. They grow little white flowers sometimes." Uncle Neal handed Toby a miniature spoon to dig out the lemon seeds, then he went about watering the plants, fondling their leaves.

"I don't get this," Toby said.

"Well, that's because you're a little slow on the uptake." Uncle Neal smirked. "You'll understand one day. Maybe one day soon."

Toby waited.

"I got a .38 snub in the house. Every morning, I have to decide to let it rest or decide to take it out where the light can hit it."

"So, the hemlock is—"

"The hemlock is to remind me of the choice I have to keep living or to stop. If I choose to keep living, I have nobody to blame but myself. Anything that happens to me, I signed up for it." Uncle Neal set a mug in front of Toby. "Put the seeds in there. I'm going to plant them, in case I keep deciding to live."

"Can't the gun remind you? You always know it's there."

Uncle Neal looked disappointed. "How long does it take to pull a gun out?"

"Not long," said Toby.

"What does it smell like?"

"What does a gun smell like?"

"Yeah."

"Not like this."

"That's right," said Uncle Neal. "Nothing smells like this." He ground up a leaf in his hand and then sniffed his fingers. "Doesn't matter what I'm doing out here. I could be playing solitaire. The point is to think about living and dying. If you don't make yourself think about it, you won't. It's not in the nature of a human being to step back and consider big choices."

Toby kept working at the lemons, wondering if Uncle Neal really had a gun, wondering what would happen to him if his uncle killed himself, where he would end up. Toby considered things. He considered things all the time.

"That's some haircut," Uncle Neal said. "You joining the service?"

"It's for pole vault," Toby answered.

"You're still doing that?"

"Of course."

"There's a haircut for it?"

"There's a haircut for everything."

Uncle Neal helped Toby squeeze the last of the lemon quarters, then he pulled out a wastebasket and brushed the carcasses into it with his forearm.

"Do I get a key to the shed?" Toby asked.

"Why not?" Uncle Neal said. "I'll have one made."

Toby turned to leave but Uncle Neal called his name.

"One more thing. I'm going to start giving you an allowance—thirty-five dollars a week. In case you want to start… I don't know, spending money. I can't take it with me."

Toby had never thought of getting an allowance. He'd always gotten by on his lunch money, but now, with Kaley, he had expenses. This felt like finding the bunker, like the rains that had fallen the night Toby took Kaley, like the air conditioner and generator. Something was on his side.

"Make it fifty," Toby said, joking.

"Deal."

"Just like that?"

"I never negotiated anything in my life," Uncle Neal said. "I'm not about to start with a little shit like you."

The churches, the Boy Scouts, the Little League teams—everyone had finally quit. Shelby's father was losing weight and looked like a version of himself from fifteen years ago, a version Shelby had only seen in photographs. He was a boxer again, swinging and swinging because that's what he knew how to do. He was growing a beard. The hair on his head was limp, but his beard was vital, aggressive in its takeover of his face. He stuffed flyers in the same mailboxes. He posted Aunt Dale's $50,000 reward wherever he could. He joined an organization that raised money to publicize abductions and another that raised money to hire bounty hunters.

The police had tracked some guy to Alabama and, though he had nothing to do with Kaley's disappearance, were able to arrest him for animal cruelty. They'd poked around a small trucking company based on the other coast of Florida. The last bit of aid the police department could offer came in the form of a therapist, a black man who hailed from New Mexico. Instead of business cards, he carried books of matches with his name on them: Cochran Wells.

"How long does this session have to take?" Shelby asked him. "Is there a certain amount of time?"

Cochran tipped his head at her. He looked like a stately, full-blooded dog. He had a controlled afro and wore a light-colored suit.

"Not long," he said.

Shelby's father looked like he was falling asleep. She touched his shoulder and he yawned.

"I'm taking diving lessons," he said. "The police have no budget for divers, so I'm going to search all the springs myself. Is that something I should tell you?"

"You said something there." Cochran had to push back from the table to cross his legs. "You said you'd search *all* the springs. That means you don't expect to find anything."

"I don't," Shelby's father said.

Shelby had hardly slept the night before. She'd stayed up watching comedians. One of the comedians would get her laughing and the next thing she knew her face would be slick with tears. Last night it had been a nasally guy who told jokes about the state of Texas. Shelby had felt light and giddy for a moment and then she was muffling her sobs so she wouldn't wake her father. *This* was her therapy, she supposed, not anything Cochran Wells could tell her. He was explaining something about emotional perseverance to Shelby's father. She interrupted him.

"I have a question," she said. "What's the difference between therapy and psychotherapy?"

"Psychotherapy is the Jewish word for therapy." Cochran allowed himself to laugh.

"Do you dislike Jews?" Shelby asked.

"I don't like or dislike anyone. I apply my empathy one case at a time." Cochran paused. "I evaluate circumstances, not individuals."

"Lucky us," Shelby said. "We got plenty of circumstances."

"I finally had a dream," Shelby's father put in.

Cochran bellied up to the table and uncapped his pen.

Shelby's father's dream took place in the woods, at night. He couldn't see anything but he could smell the woods, could smell tree bark and old breath. He was lost. Sometimes he smelled car exhaust or meat grilling. It was almost dawn. Suddenly, all the scents were blown away and bright artificial light flooded down. Shelby's father had wandered into a small, shipshape warehouse. It was full of damp socks. They were Kaley's socks, hung to dry on clotheslines.

Shelby's father returned to the mosquito control offices on a Monday. Shelby fixed him a lunch and saw him off, then she watched a documentary about fighter pilots. The narrator was English and favored English pilots. Shelby enjoyed knowing that her father wouldn't bust in at any moment, vine wrapped around his ankle. She had the house truly to herself. The sun was up, finding its way through the blinds. First period would begin in seven minutes. Shelby drank some orange juice and found her school bag. She sat on the couch. She pictured her father at work, doing familiar things with his hands, driving familiar roads, filling out paperwork. It would be good for him. People would walk on eggshells around him for a couple weeks, as they continued to do around Shelby at school, but in time his work-life would be monotonous and consuming and his sleep patterns would return to normal and his crazed gloom would break like a fever, would turn to a reasonable sadness. That's what happened. Eventually your gloom listened to reason.

The next show was a history of the World Cup. They had grainy footage of Pele and they kept replaying one of his moves. First period was starting. Shelby let her school bag slide to the floor and stretched out on the couch. She wasn't prepared to gaze at chalkboards and projector screens, to hurry from place to place so she wouldn't be late. She especially wasn't prepared to explain to earnest-eyed teachers why she wouldn't be participating in their spring clubs. She'd been all set to go around with Interact, painting houses for poor people. She'd been set to join and possibly captain the debate team. The lady who ran the French group had made her silky overtures. These were possibly the three things Shelby felt least in the world like doing: painting, debating, pronouncing.

Shelby watched the soccer players. They had wonderful hair. She muted the commercials and she could hear the faint shouts of the kids who had PE first period. It was an enchanting, crushing sound. Maradona's hand-of-God goal. Maradona was very short. Shelby knew she would skip the whole day. She would skip and tomorrow none of her teachers would say a word about it.

She went to the pantry and found nothing—healthy cereal, tuna. She knew she didn't want to eat anything out of the fridge but she couldn't stop herself from opening it. Shelby thought of her father again. She could not keep up this petty grudge—leaving the Cracker Barrel food in the fridge as it molded. She set the garbage can near and began dumping the foam boxes into it. She tied the bag up, put in a new one and continued, a sharp stink escaping each box as she transferred it. She fetched disinfectant and scrubbed the shelves of the fridge. She saw, sitting on the floor of the pantry, the bag of religious teen paraphernalia that girl had come to the door with, and she dropped that in the trash as well. She took the garbage bags outside, then lit a candle in the kitchen.

She went into her sister's room, plucked a coloring book off the shelf, sat down and flipped the pages. She imagined Kaley at the kitchen table. Kaley never paid attention to the lines. Or sometimes she colored only one object, a hat or something, and deemed the page finished. One coloring book would last her months; she'd keep going over certain pictures, making alterations. She was really gone. Shelby's sister's absence was a physical law of the universe. Shelby tore each page out of the coloring book she was holding, building a stack of pictures, then she dropped the empty binding in Kaley's Manny the Manatee wastebasket. She picked up each sheet, one at a time, and tore it into small, even shreds. After a few minutes, the wastebasket was full of busy confetti.

Shelby left Kaley's room, went up the hall, and paused at the sliding-glass door. She leaned her front against it, tired of being afraid, and surveyed the backyard. She tried to feel lordly. It was time to get rid of the kiddie pool. That was a chore she could do. None of the memories of Kaley playing in it meant anything and it was time for the pool to go. All Shelby thought of was curling underneath it that day. She would wait for garbage day, after her father had left for work, and drag it out to the road.

A thin, black snake lounged on the patio, still, half in the sun. She wanted to see it move, wanted to see how it slithered. She pressed herself harder into the glass and watched. She closed her eyes, hoping that when she opened them the snake would be sneaking off. Shelby didn't want to cheat, didn't want to slide the door open and poke the thing with a stick. She could hear a clock in another room ticking dutifully. Shelby watched the snake, the line the shade made inching over it, until it was fully in the sun.

The phone rang. Shelby went to the kitchen and plucked the receiver off the wall. It was the FBI agent, the one with the pixie-cut.

"Why aren't you in school?" she asked Shelby.

"I come home for lunch."

Shelby went to the living room and sat. She was in the same spot as when the agents interviewed her. "Your investigation hit a dead end?" Shelby said.

"I talked to your dad. We shook down all the sex offenders in the region."

"How many are there?"

"Sex offenders? About eighty in Citrus County."

Shelby didn't know if the number sounded high or low.

"They split us up," the agent said. "My partner and I."

"How come?" Shelby asked.

"They said it was poor performance, which was hard to argue, but really it was because we were involved."

"You were her girlfriend?"

"You could say that."

"So now you have a man partner?"

"That would've made sense."

"Why are you telling me this?" Shelby asked.

"Oh, sweetie. A lot of people are going to tell you a lot of things. You're like me. You understand everybody but nobody understands you."

Shelby looked at the phone a moment.

"There was talk of us quitting the bureau," the agent said. "Opening a shop somewhere."

Shelby got up and went back to the sliding-glass door. The snake was gone. She covered the mouthpiece of the phone and said the word "fuck."

"I called in order to give you the last word," the agent said. "I'm an adult and I realize that you deserve to have the last word with me."

Shelby stayed quiet.

"I want you to tell me what you think of me, then hang up. I want you to be honest."

Shelby held perfectly still.

"Shelby?" the agent said. "I know you're there. Take a minute to think and then say whatever you want. I need some truth. I know there are things you want to say to me."

Shelby closed her eyes.

"Please, Shelby. Don't play games. Don't be a jerk. Shelby? I'm being an adult here."

On the way out of Mr. Hibma's class, Shelby had whispered to Toby that she was going to find the old lost tennis court after school, that Toby should meet her there and keep her company, so once the final bell had sounded he headed out through the pastures behind the football bleachers. The tennis court couldn't have been more than a mile away, but there was no trail. You had to walk through the pastures and then over a high spot in the swamp and then it was in among a bunch of spindly pine trees. It was in the middle of nowhere, a full tennis court.

When Toby arrived, the court was empty. He walked up to the fence. The surface of the court was cracked with weeds. The net was sagging. There was an aluminum bench with algae or something growing on it. Toby started as a ball flew over the fence and bounced into the corner. He turned and saw Shelby coming out of some high grass.

"I can tell you by the way you walk," Shelby said. "Even with your hair short, I could tell it was you."

Shelby was wearing sunglasses. They made it look like she had a hangover.

"What do I walk like?" Toby asked her.

"You have a hitch. You leave room in every step to change direction, to change your mind."

"I hardly ever change my mind," Toby said.

The sun was hitting Shelby. Her arms and legs were bony. It seemed strange that she could walk around and throw things, as bony as she was. Toby felt he was betraying himself, being out at this tennis court. Betraying the bunker. Even betraying Kaley. The courage he'd felt that day at the playground was gone. Shelby seemed dangerous, but not because she could find Toby out. For some other reason, she seemed like a trap.

"Help me," she said.

She waded back into the tall grass and Toby followed. They dragged their feet and shook the underbrush and whenever Toby found a ball he handed it to Shelby and she threw it back over the fence. She seemed charmed that people used this court. Someone had dragged racquets and dozens of balls through a half-hour of Florida wilderness in order to play on a dilapidated court with a rotting net.

"People get really bored," Toby said.

The two of them worked their way through the grass and then around some cypress knees. They found eight or nine balls, all new, bright in color and rubbery in smell. They looked absolutely fluorescent against the dingy court. Toby asked Shelby how she knew about this place and she said she'd heard some of the searchers talking about it.

"A while back a millionaire lived in Citrus County," Shelby said. "His mistress loved tennis, so he had this court built out in the woods so they could play in secret."

"Wow," Toby said. He knew this story was false. This tennis court, along with a half-built golf course Toby sometimes walked through, were remnants of an unfinished development. Nothing romantic. And he wasn't going to tell Shelby but her mysterious new tennis balls were probably the work of drunken teenagers. Most mild mysteries in Citrus County boiled down to drunk teenagers.

They made it around to the opposite side of the court, where the pines were. Toby had no idea why they were doing this. They found a couple more balls and then when it seemed there were no more Toby spotted something down under some thick brush, down in a little ravine that must've been formed by a sinkhole.

Toby held onto a vine and lowered himself. He mashed a bush over with his foot and reached down and grasped the ball. He cleaned it of clumps of dirt and an insect or two, put it in his pocket, and climbed up to flat ground.

He presented the pale, bounceless orb to Shelby, and she didn't hurl it over the fence. She held it in one hand and with the other she drew Toby in by the elbow. She was kissing him. Shelby's mouth was moist and assertive and Toby could feel the world's vastness. He knew there were oceans out there that made the Gulf look like a puddle. There were places covered in snow, places where people ate snakes for dinner, places where people believed that every single thing that happened in their lives was determined by ill-willed spirits. Shelby tasted like nothing. She smelled like freckles and she was making sounds, but she didn't taste like anything. Toby didn't know whether his eyes were open. His feet were planted and he was keeping his balance as Shelby leaned against him.

When Toby thought of his hands, he began to panic. The point of the kissing had been reached where Toby was supposed to do more, something with his hands. Shelby's fingers were up under Toby's shirt in the back. He could feel the old bare tennis ball rubbing his skin. Toby took a step backward and Shelby almost fell. He said he had to go. Shelby looked at him like he was a silly child. Toby did have something to do. It wasn't a lie. He always had something to do.

The flashlight had broken. Maybe Kaley had broken it on purpose. It was hard to say. Toby didn't want her down there in the pitch dark, so he had to go back to the used hardware store. Kaley wasn't coming around to Toby, but she did seem to be considering the idea that the masked figure that tended to her was as much a victim in this as she. It was undeniable that Toby was her servant. When he bathed her, his eyes averted, it was clear that hers was the position of strength.

Toby went into the store and grabbed a flashlight at random from the bin. His mouth still felt numb, hours later, from kissing Shelby. The nothing her mouth had tasted like had gotten into Toby's mouth. He had no appetite.

When he got to the counter the old lady said, "You're in the very early stages of becoming a regular. You're meaning to become a regular and get special treatment and have me know your name."

Her grandbaby was with her again, standing back there behind the counter. A disposable camera hung around the child's neck. Her eyes were closed.

The old woman held a bowl of candy out toward Toby and he declined.

"That's smart," she said. "No candy from strangers. You're not a regular yet. We're still strangers."

"I'm not big on candy," Toby said. "I'm not a candy person."

"See that?" She was addressing her grandbaby now, who reluctantly opened her eyes. "You could learn something. He knows enough to turn down strange candy and he knows enough to make a polite excuse when he does it."

Later that week, Shelby skipped school again. She didn't want to go to school and she didn't want to sit in her house. She ordered a cab and waited on the front steps, staring as a hulking bay tree dropped its white bulbs and they parachuted down. Another floated down, and another, until a big crow plopped down in the yard and Shelby saw the cab at the end of the drive, its dust settling. The driver had done a turn and had the car facing the main road. The car was about a hundred feet long and had no hubcaps.

Shelby got in the back seat and told the driver she wanted to go to the Crystal River Outlet Mall. He didn't have a meter. He had a laminated chart full of starting points and destinations. Shelby's ride was $23, one way.

"I suppose you need me to wait while you're in there," the driver said. "You need a ride home."

Shelby nodded at the mirror.

She was headed to the mall, she decided, to search for a present for Toby. She had $300 from years of birthdays and holidays and she was tired of saving it. She wanted to buy an item priced around $200. That, plus the cab, plus lunch at the food court, would pretty much rid her of her money.

Shelby gazed out her window at the ponds, the smug vultures.

"Look at those pitiful creatures," the driver said.

"The vultures?"

"The cows, if you want to call them cows. Have you ever been to Ireland? The cows are like elephants."

Shelby nodded, aware that the driver could not see her doing so.

"It's a whole different world over there. The green grass goes right to the ocean. The farmers wear sweaters. The women smile and talk to you."

Shelby traced the stitching in the seat with her finger.

"In this country, if you hold the door open for a woman, she just brushes by. Over there, they look you in the eyes and say 'Cheers.' They touch you on the arm."

They passed a sprawling lot that sold pickup truck toppers and then the roadsides became undeveloped, jungle-like. Shelby wished the driver would be quiet, but he went on and on about Ireland until his long car rocked to a stop in the parking lot of the mall. He sank into his seat and tuned into a talk radio program on which everyone was laughing caustically.

Shelby followed a tile walkway through JCPenney and found the mall proper. Jovial organ music was piping in. A calendar kiosk. Shelby came to a stop. The kiosk had no attendant. Most of the calendars Shelby saw seemed good to buy as a joke—pro wrestlers, soap stars. The company that made the calendars depended on people buying them as a joke. And then there were puppies and wineries and one of foreign city scenes—colorful doors and bicycles and fountains. There were no pictures from Iceland. That was why Aunt Dale lived there. It wasn't a nation that had its photograph taken for silly calendars that ended up in a second-rate mall in Citrus County, Florida. There was no silliness in Iceland.

Shelby walked on until she ran up against a stout, venerable odor. The scent was at once inviting and sickening. Shelby took a few blind steps into the shop and found herself in a maze of glass cases. There were cigarettes from many countries, pipes, ashtrays carved from marble. Toby didn't smoke, as far as Shelby knew. Maybe he should, though. She could encourage him to take it up. She could show him she wasn't somebody he had to be careful with. She wanted the Toby she'd first known, the alarming Toby. She wasn't getting that anymore. If she could get the genuine Toby, then she could be the genuine Shelby. And why couldn't she? Why couldn't they let their guards down and just *be* with one another? Shelby could go with Toby on all his interminable walks. He could carry a pipe and Shelby could carry matches and the two of them could carve a place for themselves in the Florida afternoons. Shelby went near the register and the clerk poked his head through a wall of displays and said, "No way."

He was a small man who wore loose clothing. "Don't bother with a fake ID," he said. "I've seen them all."

"I don't smoke," Shelby said.

The clerk withdrew his head, disappearing behind the cases. "I used to pretend I couldn't tell the IDs were fake, but they changed the law. I had to sit through a seminar."

Shelby looked at her reflection in one of the cases. "I don't have a fake ID to show you. I don't even have a real ID."

The clerk sniffed.

"How much is this humidor?" asked Shelby.

"With the green trim? Two-twenty."

"Really?" said Shelby.

"If you have your parents' credit card, I can't accept it. You could have stolen it. The charges will be unauthorized."

Shelby didn't get the feeling the clerk was doing anything in particular that was keeping him hidden in his fortress of cases. He was back there picking at his sweater.

"I have cash," Shelby told him. "I have a pair of hundred-dollar bills and then another hundred bucks in smaller denominations. It's rolled up in my pocket."

"I cannot sell you that item. It comes with sample cigars; they have to be sold together, per the manufacturer."

"This isn't an easy store to shop at," Shelby said.

"Not an easy store to own."

Shelby left. She walked the remainder of the mall, her determination melting off like Florida frost. It was a silly notion, she supposed, that you could communicate something important through a gift from the outlet mall. There were pet stores and stores that sold suits and a store full of pianos, and Shelby didn't want to step foot in any of them. She crossed over to the food court, where she ate a frozen yogurt, listening to a shoe salesman dole out compliments to a woman who did people's nails. Shelby didn't want to be in the mall for another minute. The mall couldn't help Shelby. Her mother and her sister were gone and her father was broken and the boy she liked was afraid of her. Shopping wasn't an answer.

Shelby went back through JC Penney and out into the parking lot. The cab was still there, the driver slumped behind the wheel. Shelby hopped in the back and pressed her legs down onto the warm vinyl seat and the driver sat up straight and got them speeding down Route 19, wind whipping in the window. Shelby turned her face to the fresh air and shut her eyes, but soon enough the driver was at it again—roasted lamb, beer with character. Again with the women.

"Let me out here," Shelby said.

The driver squinted in the mirror. "Sorry if I'm boring you, princess."

"You're not sorry. You would've stopped."

"Is that a fact?"

"This'll do," Shelby said. "Right next to this expansive field."

The driver took his foot off the gas pedal.

"How much do I owe you?" Shelby asked.

"I wouldn't take money from a little princess like you. I knew you were stuck-up the minute you got in my cab."

"You're not charging me anything?"

The driver didn't respond. He looked straight ahead. The car rumbled onto the shoulder and came to a halt. Shelby got out and shoved the door shut and strode past the cab in the direction of her home, the sun bright but not heavy on her. The cab stayed put. Shelby didn't look back, and the noise from the engine was soon too faint to distinguish.

Another flashlight broken. She was doing it on purpose and it wasn't a battle of wills that Toby would let her win. He wasn't going to leave her in the dark. He wasn't going to let her believe that her behavior had any effect on anything. She was banging up her elbows and knees, making them bleed and scab. She had dumped all the water out on the floor and Toby had stolen towels from the house and mopped it all up. He acted like it was a game, like it didn't bother him. It was nothing but work, and Toby was okay with work. What he was doing wasn't supposed to be easy. It wasn't supposed to be simple. He'd done easy and simple all his life.

The old woman's grandbaby wasn't with her. She was with her mother, Toby was told. Without the child, the old woman was listless. She was doing a word search of Mexican cities.

Toby handed her the flashlight he'd chosen, a big rubberized one this time.

"Other one didn't work?" the old woman asked.

"No, it was a dud."

She made a face. "Well, I won't charge you for this one. The owner says no returns, no refunds, no mercy, but there's right and there's wrong."

"I appreciate that," said Toby.

"Don't get the wrong idea," she said. "This doesn't mean you're a regular."

Uncle Neal left for a long job in Largo. For several days, Toby subsisted on corndogs, honey sandwiches, and a bin of cashews. He mixed up pitchers of punch, never finding the correct sweetness. He spent time in Uncle Neal's rocker, waiting for the evening air to lose its heat. He went to track practice, where Coach Scolle, bored with Toby because he wouldn't take the bait of the coach's taunting, let him go his own way. The baby grasshoppers appeared, millions of them, black with bright stripes down their backs. They'd be everywhere for three weeks then promptly disappear, not showing themselves again until they were brown and thorny. The dishwasher broke and Toby found that he enjoyed doing dishes. He hung out in Uncle Neal's shed for the heck of it, because he could, breathing the fumes of the hemlock.

One night, Toby dug some cans of beer out of the pantry and poured one over ice. He went to the back corner of the house and pulled himself onto the roof. He ran his palms over the shingles, took his shoes and socks off and then his shirt. He basked in the moonlight, slugging the old watery beer, until he abruptly climbed down from the roof and went to his room and dug out his mother's hand mirror and clutched it to his chest. The mirror was the only thing of hers he had. He'd found it at the bottom of a box of his warm clothes, years after his mother had died. He squeezed the mirror in his fingers until he thought he might break it. Kidnapping Kaley, thus far, was not saving Toby from anything. He had performed a great act, but where were the great consequences? Everything was the same. Whatever had been wrong seemed more wrong now. For him *and* for Shelby. Why had he thought it would be a good idea to damage her? She could have been something good in his life. That's why she was so scary. Maybe she still could be. Maybe Toby could manage all this. Just the day before, Shelby had walked Toby to track practice. She had dragged him around a corner, put her hands under his shirt and opened her fingers onto his ribs, had run them, prickly hot, up to his chest. She'd held him there until he had no choice but to kiss her again. They would kiss anytime it struck Shelby's fancy. Toby supposed that was the deal. This time, he'd noticed that her thin lips did not feel thin at all. He'd pushed forward and she'd pushed back, pinning him against a wall. One of the sprinters had walked by then, and a hurdler, and Toby was relieved. Shelby withdrew her hands and backed up. Coach Scolle was approaching. She ran her hand over Toby's buzzed head and strolled off into the dark shade behind the gym.

Toby pressed his mother's mirror to his cheek and then stashed it back in the closet. He didn't want to start up with the mirror again. If he needed the mirror he was in trouble, and maybe he wasn't in trouble.

As the week wore on, Toby resorted to homework to distract his mind. He had plenty of math exercises to copy down, and a biology chapter to look at. He had to give a presentation on South Africa in Mr. Hibma's class, so he checked an "S" encyclopedia out of the school library and lugged it home. To his disappointment, it contained nothing but straightforward facts—agriculture, population, land area. Mr. Hibma wasn't interested in those things. He would want to know what country South Africa had a rivalry with, what illegal activity it was known for, who had been assassinated there. Toby had to incorporate food into his presentation. He had to get a South African song. Toby needed a good score, at least a B. He did not intend to fail a class or be subjected to summer school. Forging his detention slips, staring at the wall, *getting* detention at all—these were no longer part of the program. He wanted not only to continue being underestimated, he decided, but to start being ignored. He wanted to meet his obligations at school and with Kaley in the bunker and with track and field, and maybe if he did all that he'd know what to do about Shelby. He just needed to meet his obligations. Kaley would be fine. She could be somewhere else or she could be in the bunker. Toby looked at it that way: You don't always get to choose where you are. Toby sure as hell didn't.

PART TWO

Mr. Hibma had watched the half-hour loop of Headline News three times, staring at a story that had to do with insurance companies and all the recent hurricanes. He drank a glass of warm chocolate milk. He read two chapters of *To Kill a Mockingbird*. He could yawn, but not sleep. Glen Staulb had died. Glen Staulb was a New England playwright Mr. Hibma had been enamored with while in high school. Each of his plays was written according to a certain constraint; none of the characters could speak, or the lines had to be lifted from another play. Mr. Hibma, at the time, had considered Glen Staulb the height of brilliance, and though Mr. Hibma had since outgrown the gimmickry of the plays, he still valued the excitement they'd brought him, valued the time he'd spent alone with the pages feeling superior to the rest of the world because it was full of people who were lukewarm toward Glen Staulb, who hadn't heard of Glen Staulb and didn't care to. Mr. Hibma missed his youth in general, he realized, back when the knowledge that he was different from other people filled him with pride, not dread. Mr. Hibma was almost thirty. His mind was growing stale, his body stiff, but mostly he was exhausted by the idea of remaining in his life for another fifty years, for another five. He wished his life were a terse novella. He wished he knew how long he was destined to live. He wished he knew whether he'd be murdered or killed by a venomous snake or just waste away of old age.

He turned off the TV, set his dinner plate in the sink, threw out a tabloid he'd purchased that afternoon, and sat in front of his computer. He got himself onto the Internet and began poking around. The Internet, for Mr. Hibma, was a guilty pleasure. He missed no chance to publicly rail against computers, forbade his classes to research their presentations on the Internet, refused, no matter how heartily the other teachers urged him, to keep his grades and attendance and lesson plans on the computer, bragged about the layer of dust that blanketed the keyboard of the Gateway in his classroom.

He found his way to a site for a suntan lotion company, then a gambling site. When Mr. Hibma used the internet to masturbate, he did not allow himself to visit porn sites, finding it more rewarding to troll for incidentally sexy images. He didn't want the women posed in ways expressly meant to make men masturbate. Mr. Hibma hit a travel site which featured a hot mother sprawled on the beach with her children. He found a site for women's tennis. He undid his pants and slouched in the desk chair, awaiting an erection. Here was something, a French airline—stewardesses.

Mr. Hibma jumped in his chair, the breath startled from his lungs. It was the neighbor's dog, with its piercing barking. It was like an old man hacking in your ear. Mr. Hibma's heart was thumping, his penis as flaccid as it could be, a slick of jello in his palm. He shut down the computer, then sat in silence a minute until the dog started up again. It was a collie mix whose owners, about a month ago, had moved in two villas down from Mr. Hibma. They always left the dog on their porch, and it barked most every night. Mr. Hibma had complained to the owners, a fortyish couple who both wore flip-flops and both had dyed yellow hair. They weren't going to do anything about the dog. The dog was something to be lived with. Like everything else.

Before each season, it was customary that the middle school and high school girls' basketball teams scrimmage. It was thought that the high school players would receive a boost in confidence by pounding the smaller, younger team, while the middle school team, after being routed by older players, would find it easy when they played girls their own age. Little did the high school coach know, Mr. Hibma's front line weighed a combined four hundred and fifty pounds—a wild guess—and they looked even bigger when you got them out of their sweatshirts and into tank tops. Mr. Hibma watched the other coach's face when the girls thundered onto the court for warm-ups. The high school coach was an older fellow with a Long Island accent who wore those stretchy, snug shorts favored by PE coaches. When he saw Rosa and Sherrie, all he could do was stand there and stare at them, his whistle clenched in his teeth.

There had been two failed attempts to bribe Rosa and Sherrie onto the team. One of the cute girls who sat the bench had offered them honorary student government positions, which they declined, and the second-string small forward offered them $10-an-hour jobs at her father's aluminum warehouse, also declined. After that, the good players began an unfocused program of sitting with Rosa and Sherrie at lunch and asking them questions about their pasts. They did this for a week, neglecting the topic of basketball, and though the humongous pair were vague about their histories, one thing became clear: These two were deeply racist against black people. At this juncture, the point guard, as a good point guard should, had an idea. She plied Rosa and Sherrie with the sweet fantasy of defeating Pasco High at basketball, of vanquishing a black school at a black sport. The Lady Spiders had not beaten Pasco in nineteen years. How much this had to do with the girls agreeing to join, Mr. Hibma did not know, but here they were, the immovable object and the other immovable object.

While his team was running layup lines, Mr. Hibma noticed Toby and Shelby in the stands, the only spectators. They sat side by side, each reading a book. Shelby's looked like one of the Bellow novels, Toby's like that pole-vaulting manual. Toby wasn't really reading. He had a bothered look on his face and kept watching Shelby out of the slats of his eyes. Toby looked tired. It was surprising, these two together, but it also seemed inevitable. Mr. Hibma was struck with jealousy. It could've been because Toby and Shelby were reading and he had to coach a basketball game. It could've simply been because they were young and still capable of having all the feelings you could have when you were young.

The game commenced and the high school girls quickly scored six points. They had a way of getting themselves open from about ten feet and sinking bank shots. Mr. Hibma called a timeout and suggested to his team that it might not be the worst idea in the world to begin playing defense. He told them they shouldn't feel any pressure because they were *supposed* to lose, and when they retook the floor they indeed hardened the soft spots in their zone. Rosa and Sherrie got every rebound. The rest of the first half, there was little scoring. Mr. Hibma's perimeter-shooting twins threw up airballs. The fast girl with no eyebrows reverted to missing her layups, something Mr. Hibma thought she'd been cured of. Free throws were bricked, inbound plays botched.

Mr. Hibma looked up into the bleachers and Toby and Shelby were gone, off to a more secluded spot, he figured. Mr. Hibma wondered what Shelby and Toby thought of him. They probably didn't know enough about life to feel sorry for him. They probably didn't realize Mr. Hibma wasn't a teacher—not like the other teachers. He was more similar to Shelby and Toby than he was to Mrs. Conner. He felt grateful that neither of them had Mrs. Conner for a class. They were vulnerable and Mrs. Conner would see that and move in and ruin them. Whatever any kid was going through, they were better off without Mrs. Conner. They had to survive their adolescences without resorting to religion or meth use. They had to remain themselves; this, for some reason, was important to

Mr. Hibma. Whether or not they ever knew it, people like Shelby and Toby and Mr. Hibma were allies in the world, allies in spirit, and Mr. Hibma, despite himself, cared what they thought of him. He wanted them to feel desolate, at least for a moment, when the news reached them later in life that Mr. Hibma had passed away.

Mr. Hibma had brought iced tea and lemon wedges for halftime. He let the girls fill their cups and find places to sit, then he relayed his plan: Chapman. They wouldn't run their standard offense, Wilkes-Booth, any longer. They would slow it down. There was no shot clock in middle school basketball, so if the high school girls wanted to ever get the ball back, they'd have to extend their defense. When they did this, Mr. Hibma's point guard, the girl with the bowl cut, would slither around until she found an open teammate. The plan preyed upon the impatience of the opponent, who would surely not have the discipline to sit back and watch the entire sixteen minutes of the half tick away.

And it worked. The high school girls were confused. Mr. Hibma's point guard sliced and diced. The twins hit a few three-pointers. The fast girl banked in a layup. Rosa and Sherrie got rough, sending any high school girl who ventured into the paint sprawling across the hardwood. The high school coach walked over and complained to Mr. Hibma about his decision to employ a time-killing strategy during a scrimmage. "My team's had five possessions since halftime," he whined. Mr. Hibma, in a low tone, asked the man to kindly return to his own bench before he found himself with a black eye, and the man, looking scandalized like an old woman in a Victorian novel, shuffled away. Mr. Hibma was shocked with himself, not for telling the guy off but for out-coaching him. Mr. Hibma was faking being a coach, but his faking was better than this guy's real thing.

In the end, Mr. Hibma's team lost by four points. He gathered his girls up. "There's still one area that greatly concerns me," he said. "Only a handful of you have made any discernible effort to improve your appearance."

The girls looked at the floor.

"I don't want to have to bench anyone over this, so here's what we're going to do. I'm appointing the three cute girls, since they have a workable grasp of cosmetics and hygiene, as beauty captains. They're in charge of making each of you over, and you better do what they say. We have eight days until the first game, so I'm going to spring for self-tanner out of my own pocket."

The starters were dazed. The twins looked at their nails then hid them in their fists.

Shelby slapped at mosquitoes, observing her father as he directed his glare into the hissing grill. He seemed transfixed. It had almost suited him, becoming a single dad. He was a man who liked a challenge, who liked having his work cut out for him. Being a single dad had, in a way, settled him. He could run everything in the household just the way he wanted to. He'd been content, knowing he'd never marry again, knowing his daughters would be his life's work. He'd done it all—grocery shopping, cooking, cleaning, helping with homework, the banking, driving Shelby and her sister to doctor's appointments and birthday parties.

"A big steer got electrocuted," Shelby's father said.

She sat up straight.

"Somebody left the gate open at one of those substations. The thing was chewing a vine that was wrapped around a cable." Shelby's father sniffed his forearm. "And then I find these kabobs on sale at that Weeki Wachee Market, in those bins at the front of the store. I wonder if there's a connection."

Shelby noticed all the twitchy muscles in her father's calves and biceps. He looked like he'd gone ten rounds, puffy under the eyes, spaced-out.

"What is this we're listening to?" Shelby asked.

Shelby's father set down his tongs. "Lady that works in the mosquito lab gave it to me. She got the songs off the computer."

The song that was playing was a garage-load of groggy guitars, the lyrics unintelligible but clearly longing.

"I never wanted you to be an only child," Shelby's father declared.

Shelby said, "I'm not an only child."

"Only children are deprived." Shelby's father turned a knob on the grill, tapping it with his thumb. "All the only children I ever knew had something wrong with them."

"Everyone ends up with something wrong with them."

"I never see *my* sister, but we were always fond. My sister is the type of person people are jealous of."

"I'm contacting her for my Iceland presentation," Shelby said. She'd found a reason to get in touch with her aunt, an excuse, and now she felt embarrassed for *needing* an excuse, a ruse, a school project. It didn't make sense to Shelby that she was still afraid of things, that anything could make her nervous. Fear was an emotion that did not add up. It was her aunt, after all. She would be glad Shelby was old enough now that the two of them could get to know each other.

Shelby's father plopped the kabobs onto a platter. He went in and got beers, handed one to Shelby. She took a swig and the flavor was bracing. The beer didn't smell good, but it tasted like something that could cleanse you. It was the time before night, when the air was perfectly still and didn't want to be breathed.

Another song began. White rappers. They emphasized the last word of each line, the word that rhymed. Car horns and whistles were mixed into the music.

"Did they just call the devil a trick bitch?" Shelby asked.

Shelby's father shrugged.

It was Christian music. Shelby hit the stop button and her father didn't protest. The woman in the mosquito lab had outsmarted them. She'd smuggled her beliefs into their home—contraband. She thought she knew what Shelby and her father needed. This house was a place people snuck things out of and into. They snuck little sisters out and snuck music in. Maybe Shelby needed a big, obvious enemy. A specific enemy that could never be defeated.

Shelby watched her father slide a hunk of beef off his skewer and cut it into pieces with his fork. She had more of her beer.

"Are we going to move again?" she asked.

"Do you think we should?"

"I just want to know."

"Where would we go?"

Shelby had no idea. She didn't think it mattered. It wouldn't matter where they were going, only where they were leaving.

"I don't think I have the energy for it," Shelby's father said. "Selling the house, finding a new job, packing up." Shelby's father pushed his plate aside and brought his beer in front of him. "We're buddies," he said. "Anything we do, we'll discuss it."

Shelby pressed her bare feet into the wood of the porch. She didn't know if she wanted to be buddies with her dad. She knew she wanted him to shave his beard. She could never tell what he was really thinking, because half of his face was hidden. She wondered if her father would ever go on a date, go on vacation. There were a lot of things besides moving that he didn't seem capable of.

"I almost left your mom," he said. "And you."

He set his beer bottle down, farther away than he'd pushed his plate. Shelby had seen the words issue forth from his beard, but she couldn't immediately grasp them.

"I wasn't in love with her," he said.

Shelby sat very still. She kept her eyeballs still, her organs.

"I didn't want to give up the fighting life," her father said. "She didn't cost me a great career or anything. I wasn't *that* good. But the life."

"So I was an accident?" said Shelby.

"No, you weren't an accident. We talked about getting married and when your mother got pregnant we were happy. A couple months later, before the wedding—"

Shelby's father reached over and grabbed his beer and finished it. Shelby touched hers; it was warm. The things her father was saying were whipping past her.

"The night before the wedding, I started driving south. I had a bunch of clothes packed and I remember I packed a spatula. I didn't know where I was headed. I drove half the night and then turned around and drove back. I never forgot the exit, either. This many years later, when you and me and your sister passed it in the car on the way down here. I remembered that exit where I turned back."

Shelby wasn't angry. If this was being a buddy, she didn't like it, but she wasn't angry.

"I'm glad you did," she told her father. "I'm glad you came back."

"*You're* glad?" Shelby's dad chuckled. "I thought I was doing that because I was a decent man, like I was making a sacrifice, doing the right thing. I was real impressed with myself. I saved my life, coming back. I saved my own life. For whatever it's worth."

Shelby passed her beer to her father. He wouldn't mind that it was warm.

"It's worth something to me," she said.

Toby accompanied Shelby to the public library. He knew she had something he needed, something that would fortify him, but he didn't know if it was something she could offer or that he could accept. He didn't know how to mine another person for something good. To Toby, Shelby was the opposite of the bunker; she was a bright kind of worry. In the bunker, Toby had to rely on his evil to lead him, but with Shelby he had to rely on his everyday self. When he thought about her, he felt he could toughen up and go about his normal business and keep his bunker business out of the rest of his life.

The library was open till nine on Wednesdays and Shelby wanted to e-mail her Aunt Dale. It was not fully night. The woods felt cramped. Shelby walked beside Toby, loosely grasping his elbow.

"My dad used to be an optimist." Shelby halted. "And *I* used to be a realist."

They'd reached a fork in the trail. Toby nodded to the left. Shelby was sweating, her skin lustrous.

"I guess I'm a pessimist now," she said. "My dad says he hates pessimists."

"You can call yourself whatever you want," Toby said. "The same things are going to happen to you."

"The bad things, anyway."

"Especially the bad things."

"What happened to your mom?" Shelby asked.

Toby felt how soft the sand was under each of his steps. In this part of the woods, it was like beach sand. He didn't look at Shelby.

"You were young when she died, right?"

"I didn't know her and neither did my uncle."

"Why not?"

"I was too little. We lived far away from here."

"Where?"

"Another part of the state."

Shelby was still holding Toby's elbow. "Is your uncle your dad's brother?" she asked.

"I don't talk about this stuff," Toby said. "It really doesn't matter whose brother anybody is."

"Well, what did she look like, your mother?"

"I don't have any pictures of her. I think she had long hair."

"Can't you see her in your mind?"

"What does it matter what she looked like?"

"I think it matters," Shelby said.

"I don't think it matters at all," Toby said, sharply. He guided his elbow out of Shelby's grip.

She got the hint. She didn't ask any more questions. The trail hardened and then, near a buzzing power substation, turned to a gravel road. The library came into view, its parking lot swarming with old people and high school kids who couldn't yet drive.

Inside, an elderly gang barked questions about their tax forms. The librarian held a tolerant look on her face and repeated the statement, "I am not an accountant." Shelby waded toward the computer lab and Toby went to the periodicals. He perused the wall of magazine covers and chose something about animal psychology. He found a cushy chair. He was still upset over Shelby grilling him about his family. Next thing, she'd want to come over for dinner or something. Toby's family was his own business. He rubbed his eyes. The front of the magazine he'd chosen featured a shark relaxing on a dock, a radio nearby, a bottle held in its fin. Toby opened to the table of contents and couldn't make sense of it; it was just a bunch of words. There were so many magazines, and none of them were meant for Toby. He didn't belong where he was. He didn't belong in the library, or in Citrus County. He didn't belong in this padded, institutional chair. It wasn't right that he was a human being on planet Earth. A mistake had been made.

Toby felt a tap on his shoulder and started. Shelby was done already.

"That was quick," Toby said.

"E-mail. That's kind of the point."

Shelby pulled Toby out of the chair and they filed through the old folks and made their way past a faction of listless skateboarders. They took the frontage road instead of the woods.

"I have to tell you something," Toby said. "You can't ever come to where I live. My uncle can't handle visitors. It could be bad."

"Is he crazy?" Shelby asked.

"Certain things set him off. New people are a bad idea."

"You know where I live and I don't know where you live. Seems like that gives you an advantage."

"Believe me, my uncle isn't an advantage."

"Does he have a job?"

"He works alone."

"Is he dangerous?"

"Mostly to himself," said Toby. "I can't have anyone know he's not well. They might lock him up or ship me off somewhere."

Toby did not deny that Uncle Neal was crazy. But Shelby's aunt sounded crazy. Her dad was crazy, now. Coach Scolle was an asshole. Mr. Hibma was a weirdo. In the northern part of the county there were churches full of Pentecostals who handled snakes.

Toby and Shelby headed down the frontage road, mincing their steps for potholes. Meaty insects hovered. Toby and Shelby walked past the back of a restaurant, where a bunch of smoking waitresses with big purses smiled at them. They strolled beyond the Goodwill and into the parking lot of a strip mall. Every store was closed but one, a flag shop. A bell dinged as they entered. A thin man wearing high-tops and a bandana came out from the back and said he was doing inventory.

"Please don't steal anything," he said. "You look like good youngsters, so I won't check to make sure you have money." He sighed theatrically and returned to the back room.

"I bet that works," Toby said. "Begging every single customer not to steal."

"Could backfire," Shelby said. "Could put the idea in someone's head."

"You going to take something?"

"Not today. I have money."

Toby had noticed that Shelby was never without a small amount of cash. She was a prepared chick. She had everything she needed, which wasn't much, parceled throughout the pockets of her shorts. Toby watched her. The flag shop was lit with weak lamps and a large fan was set up in the corner which managed to ripple the merchandise and dance wisps of Shelby's hair around. She bit her bottom lip as she browsed, working her way through the flags of many nations, through twenty variations of the

Confederate flag. Universities. Mottoes. Cartoon characters.

"Found one," she called to the guy in back. She yanked it off the rack, unfurled it on a counter near the register, and stood aside. It was brown and white, about 6' by 4'. In the center, toward the bottom, was an official-looking seal, and in each corner was the print of a palm and fingers. The greater part of the flag was occupied by regal letters which spelled out LICENSED HANDJOB ACCEPTANCE STATION. This made Toby nervous. He wondered what the clerk would think.

"You look flustered," Shelby said. "Before I knew you, I never took you for such a flustered dude."

"Before I knew you, I wasn't," said Toby.

"I'll touch your penis in a couple weeks, okay?"

Toby didn't force a laugh or pretend he hadn't heard Shelby. He stood there.

The guy in the bandana emerged, a tape gun in one hand.

"What happened?" he asked.

Shelby paused. "I zeroed in on the goods I wish to purchase is what happened."

The guy edged closer. When he saw that Shelby had a flag on the counter and cash in her hand, he relaxed his grip on the tape gun and stood up straight.

"Wow," he said. "You two aren't nomadic vandals. You're a nice young couple."

Shelby took Toby's hand. The clerk proceeded to ring up the flag without seeming to notice what it said. He folded the flag into a snug triangle and wrapped it in paper like a deli sandwich.

"Shipment next week," he said. "You should stop back by."

"Count on it," Shelby told him.

"More humorous sexual stuff."

Shelby handed over the money and told the clerk to keep the change. She forced the packaged flag into one of her pockets.

"Please be safe," the clerk said. "You two are the best youngsters I've ever had in here."

Toby moved toward the door, not sure if he was pulling Shelby or she was pulling him. As they passed back into the night, the bell on the door dinged. They regained the frontage road, a stretch that had no light at all. The stars were out. They weren't twinkling.

"Where you going to fly that?" Toby asked.

"I'm going to nail it to the front doors of Central Citrus Baptist."

"What for?"

"It's a musical issue," Shelby said. "Some offensive music was snuck into my house."

"Offensive?"

"It's hard to explain."

Shelby was getting ahead of Toby and he sped up.

"You could just keep the flag. We could get it out sometimes and look at it."

Shelby stopped. It was too dark to know what was on her face.

"You don't get it," she said. "I'm embroiled in a contest of pranks that has gone on for thousands of years, between people long before me, and if there's a God then he's been watching the whole thing and laughing. Someone stole my sister. That was a hell of a prank, don't you think? A lot bigger than hanging a flag."

"I see," Toby said. He didn't. He didn't see what the church and its music had to do with Kaley. He almost wished he could tell Shelby where her sister was, so she knew who was worth being afraid of, so she wouldn't waste her energy on a false enemy. The only thing to be scared of in this county was Toby, and he wasn't going to hurt Shelby anymore. He hoped he never hurt anyone anymore.

Toby started the two of them walking again. "A hammer and nails will be too noisy," he told Shelby. "If you're going to do this, you need a staple gun."

The classroom kept dimming then flooding with light as masses of clouds passed in front of the sun. Mr. Hibma pointed at a kiss-ass and ordered her to close the blinds. It was the last day of the foreign nations presentations. Mr. Hibma asked for a volunteer and here came Toby, a box of visual aids in his arms. Toby's eyes were puffy, pinkened. He competently pushed his way through a bunch of obscure facts. He played a South African pop song. He gave everyone a serving of some canned root in a sugary sauce.

Next Shelby got up. No props. Iceland: puffins, aurora borealis, the Sugarcubes, Irish monks. Shelby had an aunt there. She ran a website, which Shelby promised she had not looked at in researching her presentation, a website called *whatwouldtheythink*, on which the aunt reviewed things. This aunt, Aunt Dale, had been with the same man since Shelby had been alive, but refused to marry him. Shelby's aunt didn't care for the United States. She refused to put ads on her website, and was compensated instead by the government of Iceland.

"Hold up," Mr. Hibma said. He knew Shelby's aunt's website. He went on it from time to time and read reviews of performance artists. He hated performance artists.

"So you had that Stubblefield lady as one aunt," Mr. Hibma said. "The lady in Tennessee, in the barn. And then you have expatriate Aunt Dale as another aunt."

"Right, but Janet Stubblefield wasn't my real aunt."

"And both of them are nuts in a pleasing way."

Shelby looked skeptical.

"Oh, Aunt Dale's nuts," said Mr. Hibma. "She's dedicated her life to conjecturing what impression Martians might have of Earthly customs."

"Abnormal," Shelby conceded.

"Do you know how many people are abnormal in a way that pleases me?"

"In the world?"

"Let's estimate."

"Four hundred?"

This seemed a perfect guess. "And you have two of them for aunts."

Mr. Hibma wondered if Aunt Dale had ever visited Citrus County. The area seemed ripe for *whatwouldtheythink*. It was unimpressive in a noteworthy way. Mr. Hibma could see Aunt Dale at the Best Western lounge, chatting with the mermaids. He saw Aunt Dale down at Hudson Beach—a scatter of damp dirt and a burger bar with Calypso music. Mr. Hibma saw himself serving Aunt Dale dinner in his villa. "The drywall is all original," he would tell her. He would serve calzones, baked by the Long Islanders down the street.

Mr. Hibma dismissed the class, allowing each kid to grab a poster on the way out, something they now did out of obligation. He'd broken into a long patch of straight-to-video action movies—beefy, confused-looking men and women with shiny cleavage.

When the last kid was gone, Mr. Hibma shut the door. He stared at a Bosch print. Grotesque birds. Women with bonnets. Demons hiding in big eggs—or were they being born? Bosch had captured the horror so deftly that it seemed to echo. Mr. Hibma felt he might find himself in the painting, walking around lost with chalk in his pockets.

He was very jealous of Aunt Dale. He was meant to do few things, and what Aunt Dale did, criticize, was one of them. She'd made better decisions than Mr. Hibma and had ended up in a better life. That's what Mr. Hibma should've done with his inheritance: started *whatwouldtheythink*. He never should've ended up throwing a dart. He should've *chosen* his life.

He sat down at his desk and squared a sheet of paper in front of him, readied a pencil, then wrote the following letter:

D,

I plan to kill a fifty-something-year-old woman in early June, an English teacher, and I would like to invite you to review the murder, to evaluate it as a work of art. I will smother this woman with a couch pillow. I have told no one of this but you.

Mr. H

Mr. Hibma did not feel in possession of himself. He didn't know why he'd written this letter. He felt again like a character in a novel. Not a passive character, though—not at the moment. His story was going somewhere.

Mr. Hibma wasn't going to mention which county he lived in, certainly wasn't going to mention Shelby. In fact, he would drive to the middle of the state, somewhere near Orlando or something, so the postmark wouldn't give him away. Mr. Hibma was going to go home and dig up the address of *whatwouldtheythink*. He was going to get an envelope out and slip his letter inside and he was going to drive to Clermont or wherever and pay whatever you had to pay to mail something to Iceland. First he was going to get a PO Box in Clermont, and he was going to use that PO Box as his return address. And he was going to have his mail from that PO Box forwarded to his villa. He was doing something. He was taking part in his life.

Toby had received, on his locker, a card informing him that his pole-vaulting book was overdue. The fine was a quarter a day. There was no mention of a maximum fine the book could accrue, of a retail value the library put on the book. Toby didn't know if he could simply re-borrow the book, or if the library would take it away from him and put it back on the shelf, in case another student wanted a turn with it. Toby wanted to keep the book till the end of track season. He was going to keep it and then pay the fine. He had an allowance now. He could afford it. Not that the book was helping a great deal. All Toby could claim to have mastered, so far, was his natural fear of hurtling through the air. His grip and his stride were coming along. Except for the moment when he was supposed to gain altitude, to shoot upward, he could approximate the *look* of a pole-vaulter. He was a member of the track team. He was *on* the team. That was the important thing.

The first meet was upon him. Toby rode the bus with his teammates out to a complex that bordered the rock quarries, near the grounds of Lecanto Middle School. There was no crowd, not even parents. Toby drank a soda then jogged a lap around the track. There was only one pole-vaulter on the opposing squad, a sturdy Asian kid who wore a visor. Toby went over like a stand-up sportsman and shook the kid's hand, and the kid wished Toby luck in claiming one of the two all-county spots. There were six pole-vaulters total, the kid explained. He, himself, would have one of the spots, and the other one was up for grabs. He told Toby one of the most pivotal parts of pole vault, this season at least, would be the coin flips. It would be crucial to never go first, because if you went first you didn't know what height you had to beat. Pole-vaulters were supposed to alternate turns, but last year two kids had kept bumping shoulders as they crossed paths and they ended up getting in a fight. One of the kids got his tooth knocked out, the Asian kid told Toby, so now one vaulter went three times, then the other went three times.

Toby couldn't quite follow all this. "The coin flip?" he said.

"I've got it mastered." The Asian kid had a twinkle in his eye. "I've been practicing for months."

"You can be good at coin flips?"

"Same as anything: practice."

"When you practice, do you flip the coin yourself?"

"That wouldn't do much good."

Toby went off by himself to stretch. His team was designated the home team, so he would be the one to call the flip in the air. He wanted to call this thing right and tell the Asian kid that he hadn't practiced a bit, that he was just a fortunate person. Toby drank some water, sized up the bar, and threw himself on the mat a few times. The 400 started. The runners flew up the straightaway, then bunched on the curve. When they passed Coach Scolle he ran with them for a stretch, grunting. Rosa and Sherrie sat in the direct center of the field, back to back, eating fries one by one. The female long-distance runners perched themselves atop the big coolers and painted their nails. When the 400 ended, there was no cheering. The runners slapped each other's arms and climbed into the bleachers.

Here came the pole-vault official, silver dollar resting in his palm. He told Toby to call it, then tossed the coin and retreated a step. The silver dollar seemed huge. It somersaulted unhurriedly in the air.

"Tails," Toby said.

The coin did not bounce. It was cradled by the grass, heads up. Toby looked at the Asian kid, who wasn't bothering to gloat.

"You didn't do anything," Toby scolded him. "I'm the one who called it."

"You went with your gut, didn't you?"

"Flip it again," Toby said to the official. "Just for fun. I want *him* to call it."

"What will that prove?" said the Asian kid. "It's a meaningless flip."

"Pretend it has meaning."

"Pretend?"

"Nice and high, now," Toby said.

The official was amused. He flipped the coin.

"Tails," the Asian kid called.

Up went the coin and down it fell. "Tails it is," said the official. He picked up the coin and ambled off.

Toby took his three tries, not clearing more than eight feet, while his opponent serenely ate a container of cut melon.

Toby rode the bus back to school then walked home through the woods, passing close to Shelby's house. The night he'd taken Kaley seemed distant, like a part of history. All the secrecy and intrigue had staled. Toby no longer got a charge from seeing an old man wearing those gray Velcro sneakers. Thinking about Kaley while he was at school didn't buoy him, didn't make him feel important. He wondered what he ever thought was special about her. She was fussy and messy and even without an appetite she managed to burn through food by leaving the containers open. She spilled half the water Toby brought down there. She was starting to smell in a way Toby couldn't wash off. Toby still hadn't uttered a word to her. If he did, it would be to yell at her.

When Toby got to the house he went in his room and took out his mother's hand mirror. He'd told Shelby the truth when he said he had no pictures of his mother, but he had the mirror and that was all he needed. It had a faded, oriental-looking pattern on it. Its weight always surprised Toby. It felt good to hold. He squeezed it by the handle, cooling his palm. Toby sat on his bed, keeping his head stationary and angling the mirror so as to examine the corners of his room. He wondered if his mother had ever used the mirror, if she'd held the mirror in one hand and a brush in the other and sat erect on a chair near a window, if she'd left the mirror on a stand near her front door and checked her makeup in it. Toby doubted it. It had been a gift, probably, from someone not very dear. It had collected dust over and over and been wiped clean over and over. It had been unwanted, but too nice to throw out.

Toby forced himself to stand. He put the mirror back on the shelf and went outside, headed for a little gas station that mostly sold cigarettes and beer and lottery tickets. It was night. The wind singing in the tops of the pine trees irritated Toby.

At the gas station, he loaded up on junk food—packaged cakes full of creams and custards, cookies, candy bars. Kaley had to eat *something*. She didn't like fish sticks or chicken patties or apples. Her cheeks weren't plump anymore and you could see her spine right through her shirt. He had to give in and let her have soda too. She wasn't drinking water.

Toby had to keep lugging the generator back and forth. He had to keep washing Kaley's bedding and emptying her buckets. She wasn't the least bit afraid of him. She could sleep. She wore that shrewd look, seeing through the dimness like a cat. The bunker smelled like Kaley and Kaley smelled like the bunker. The bunker was becoming her home, Toby a visitor.

Shelby wore yellow rubber gloves. She'd lathered up the bathtub, had bleach and glass cleaner and some brand-new sponges. She was resting, sitting on the toilet bowl. She had already vacuumed all the carpets in the house, dusted the tables and dressers. She didn't feel like they'd lived here long enough for it to get dusty. It had been someone else's dust, the previous owners' dust. Shelby arched her back to make her spine crack, relishing the scouring, chemical air.

She had a little radio with her, tuned to an AM station on which a very old man was relating stories about the past. Shelby felt like she was the only person listening to the station, like the old man was talking only to her, but she supposed that was how everyone felt. The old man was speaking about the establishment of the first national parks, about how men in need of work had come from all over the country to blaze trails and put in signs and build ranger stations. There were no commercials. When the old man went to pee, you had to wait for him to come back.

Shelby wondered if she was sanitizing the bathroom of Kaley. Shelby had given Kaley a hundred baths in here. She was scrubbing the last traces of her sister out of this room. She ought to be doing something constructive, like homework or like cooking or maybe exercising, but those things seemed so difficult. They required so much faith. Shelby felt comfortable on the hard, flat cover of the commode. She wished her father wouldn't come home, that night wouldn't fall. She could stay where she was and think of her sister calmly and honestly—just think of *Kaley*, not about whether or not Kaley was with them, whether she was gone forever. Kaley was not like other kids. It was a fact. She wasn't like other people. Kaley never held onto anything, not grudges or promises. It was a type of toughness Shelby did not possess. Kaley could forgive. She was a person who could forgive the world and forgive the people closest to her.

The old man on the radio cleared his throat and broke it to his listeners that it was time for him to wash up for supper. Shelby heard his chair creak and then the swishing sound of his slacks.

The porch. Uncle Neal had *his* generator out, testing it—the same brand as Toby's, but bigger. Uncle Neal had examined the roof, he told Toby, and stocked canned goods. Hurricane season was around the corner again.

"Maybe this is the year," Toby said.

"This place ain't worth a hurricane's time. I'm doing this stuff because it's the kind of stuff I like to do."

"Preparing?" said Toby.

"No, wasting time. I like to waste time." Uncle Neal massaged his nose and snorted, trying to dislodge something. "I made a to-do list, that way I can waste the whole day."

A stinkbug landed on Toby's thumb and he carefully brushed it away.

"I've been meaning to ask you if you got a tapeworm, because we need to get to the doc and get rid of it before I'm out of house and home."

Toby shook his head.

"We've been going through snacks and drinks like I-don't-know-what."

"I'm growing," said Toby.

"Going through toilet paper too. I guess the two go hand in hand."

"Maybe I do," said Toby. "Maybe I have a worm."

"I think I lost my to-do list," Uncle Neal said. "I'm going to sit in my rocking chair until it turns up. If you go in, bring me one of those cloves."

Toby went in and choked down a few cold nuggets. He spotted a pack of black cigarettes and assumed these were the cloves. He pulled one out, went back to the porch, set himself up in a low chair, then passed the clove to his uncle, who pulled a match from somewhere and struck it on the porch floor.

"Think I'll *make* it to hurricane season?" he asked.

Toby looked out in front of him, at nothing.

"I'd say it's a coin flip." Uncle Neal held his clove away from his face. "Did you grab the mail?"

"I didn't."

"I'm watching for the county newsletter. They're trying to put in a putt-putt on Route 50. I'm going to speak against it."

"Do you mind if I smoke one of those?" Toby asked.

"I won't stop you."

Toby fetched the rest of the cloves. When he returned to the porch, Uncle Neal struck another match and held it out toward Toby. The smoke was bluish. It filled Toby's skull and sat in there. As soon as Toby had his clove going good, Uncle Neal looked at the one he was smoking, a dreary expression on his face.

"On second thought, let's put these out," he said. "This isn't the mood for clove smoking. Cloves are for when you're worn out but hopeful."

Uncle Neal blew most of the burning ember off his clove, then tamped it out patiently on his knuckle. One of his knuckles was gnarled.

"I guess we're not too hopeful," Toby said.

"I should say not."

Toby spun the lit end of his clove into the floor. He slipped what was left of it behind his ear. He didn't want to be sharing a mood with Uncle Neal, but it seemed he was.

"What do you smoke in this mood we're in now?" Toby asked.

"Don't know," Uncle Neal said. "Something we ain't got."

A little girl's body was found in a scrub habitat across from Buccaneer Bay, a small water park located in the next county south. The girl had gone missing years ago. She'd been left in a shallow grave and little more than bones were left of her. Her parents now lived in Jacksonville and had been flown over to identify her hat and fill out paperwork. She'd been buried in high-heeled shoes someone had put on her.

All this had happened in the course of a single day—the body being found in the wee hours by an old-timer training his terriers, and the parents, at about two in the afternoon, making a statement to the press. When Shelby had arrived home from school, she'd known nothing about it. She'd found her father in the kitchen, mumbling in front of the sink, leaning on the counter in a way that made him look crippled. He refused to sit. He gave Shelby a summary, his voice stiffening on the phrases he quoted from the news. He told Shelby that he considered this little girl's family lucky. He was facing Shelby now, leaning on the counter with his forearm.

"Stand straight," Shelby commanded.

He did so, sort of propped himself. Shelby noticed a garbage bag on the floor, full of pamphlets. She nodded toward it and her father said he'd made an error joining all those, whatever they were—clubs. They couldn't help him. They were support groups, that's all.

"Is that so bad?" Shelby asked. She didn't know what to do about this other little girl, what to say or think about it. It had nothing to do with her and her father. That wasn't true, though. It was an insult. Shelby felt disrespected.

"I think it is bad," Shelby's father said. "I think being in all those groups will keep me from—" He didn't finish.

"Maybe you're right," Shelby said.

"You don't keep getting mail about it, do you?"

"You're leaning again," said Shelby.

"Why did I bring us here?"

The simple answer was that a job had been waiting for him. There was a guy high up in mosquito control that he knew from his boxing days. Shelby knew what her father meant, though. In any other county, none of this would've happened. Kaley would still be with them.

Shelby bent so she could catch her father's eyes and he aligned himself. He did something with his jaw and drew an enormous, wheezing breath. "Are you going somewhere?" he asked. "You're always going somewhere."

"I am, aren't I?"

"Toby? Is that where you're headed?"

"Not today. He's always busy."

"What's his deal?"

"What do you mean?"

"I'm not sure I know," said Shelby's father. "I don't know what questions to ask anymore."

"I don't think Toby has a deal. I don't think he wants one."

"Is he okay, though? Is he okay for you to hang around with?"

"I'm not sure," Shelby said. "I think that's what I'm trying to find out."

"You will then," said Shelby's father. "You'll find it all out."

Shelby held her arms out, but did not move any closer to her father. She made him stand free of the counter, made him lead in the hug, provide the firmness. Her and her father's lives were a series of injuries and insults to those injuries. Shelby wanted to see that little girl's bones. She wanted to know every single thing that had happened to her.

"Was that some kind of prayer you were saying?" she asked. Her father's arms were clamped around her, pressing on her ribs. "That mumbling when I walked in—was that a prayer?"

Her father squeezed tighter, almost stopping her breath.

Shelby dumped the contents of her book bag and replaced them with the handjob flag, a pack of snack cakes, and a staple gun she'd dug out of the utility room. Since her sister's disappearance, no one—with the exception of Mr. Hibma, from whom she'd drawn a couple detentions—would dare discipline her. She'd been given a free pass on skipping school. She'd been caught stealing a cookie in the cafeteria and nothing had happened. She'd thrown her PE coach's whistle in the toilet.

She followed the path she and Toby had taken to the library, then cut to the right at the fire road and shuffled through a corridor of spaced myrtles. She neared Central Citrus Baptist and took a moment at the edge of the woods. A painting crew was packing gear into a van, three guys all wearing denim shorts. Shelby watched as they slid a ladder into an apparatus on the roof of the van, dug bottles of sports drink out of a cooler, then crept out of the lot.

Shelby advanced to the front steps of the church, which were cordoned off with tape. The painters had done the steps, the front porch, the shutters. Shelby ducked under the tape and stepped up to the door, the soles of her boots sticking with each step to the newly painted wood, leaving imprints of her treads. It felt to Shelby like she was taking sides. She wasn't sitting on the fence. She was doing something Toby would appreciate, no matter how he'd acted when Shelby first mentioned it. Shelby was doing something her Aunt Dale would approve of. She was doing something, she believed, that she *herself* could get behind.

She hung the flag, three staples across the top and three across the bottom, then dug a marker out of one of her pockets. On an open space on the flag, she wrote:

> I, Shelby Register, hung this flag. I did it in the early evening, April 4. The prints in the paint will match my boots. I purchased the flag at the shop in the Sunray Shopping Plaza. I do not have a receipt, but the owner liked me and will remember me.

The opening game of the season was a breeze. After the final buzzer, the other coach approached Mr. Hibma affably. He was encouraged by how good Mr. Hibma's team was, optimistic that they could beat his rival, the coach at Springstead Middle.

"Hell," Mr. Hibma said. "We're going to whip Pasco."

"I can't beat him myself," said the other coach. "I'm writing this year off. I'm starting a lawn service."

"How does one go about starting a lawn service?"

"You need a big truck and an open trailer. Then you need the mowers and shit. You need a couple guys to work in the sun."

"And this will enable you to quit teaching?"

"That's the fantasy. Yesterday I picked up the magnet for the truck door: Sunrise Lawn Management."

Mr. Hibma stepped over to his team's cooler and filled two cups with iced tea. He handed one to the other coach. Mr. Hibma knew there were ways out of teaching, but he'd never pursue any of them. That was part of what he had to admit to himself, that he wasn't the kind of person who started his own business or went to night school. He didn't hustle.

"Let me ask you something," Mr. Hibma said. "You don't seem interested enough in girls' middle school basketball to have a rival."

The guy swished some tea around in his mouth. "Has nothing to do with basketball," he said. "The coach at Springstead is an old friend of my wife's, and he told her about some of us going to a strip club on teacher planning day."

"What a dick," Mr. Hibma said.

The guy nodded, downing the rest of his tea, getting slightly worked up. "He's the one who invited me. You know? *He* invited *me*."

"We'll shut them out," Mr. Hibma assured him. "We won't let them score a point."

He held his cup aloft, though it was empty, and the other coach matched the gesture.

Mr. Hibma went to the locker room to address his team. Not much needed to be said. He told them not to get tendonitis patting themselves on the back, that their fitness still wasn't up to snuff. He explained to them, because something had to be said about Rosa and Sherrie's disregard for his rules concerning personal appearance, that he was instituting a double-standard: Rosa and Sherrie could look however they chose. Life was full of double standards, he told the girls. They should get used to it.

On the way home, Mr. Hibma stopped at the video store. He wanted a porn movie. He'd been unable, lately, to masturbate, and he'd decided to leave all subtlety by the wayside, to stare at slick bodies as they slapped together, to listen to heavily eye-shadowed women shriek. He'd crank the volume on his TV until the shrieking drowned out the barking of any dogs.

Mr. Hibma proceeded to the back of the video store. He nudged through a pair of saloon doors and into the adult room. He'd never been in it before. There was no one else in the room, so Mr. Hibma took his time, skimming synopsis after synopsis. The saloon doors weren't tall, so people that walked by could look in and see Mr. Hibma. He didn't believe he should be ashamed, didn't believe anyone had the right to judge him, but still, he was a teacher. He was in a strip mall with a toy store and an arts-and-crafts shop in it. It was about a hundred degrees in the adult room. Despite its rattling, the fan built into the wall did nothing. Mr. Hibma could feel the blood in his cheeks. An older man came through the saloon doors, whistling to himself. He didn't acknowledge Mr. Hibma, simply went to the movie he wanted, plucked it off the shelf, and was gone. A lady with a gaggle of kids tottered by outside. She paused and gave Mr. Hibma a look. He had to get out of there. He picked a movie, one about a women's football league. He steeled himself and emerged into the main room, breathing the fresh air, walking with his movie pressed against his leg. He turned up an aisle and stopped in his tracks. A girl from his first period—Karen was her name—was behind the register. What was she, fourteen? Maybe her parents owned the place. Mr. Hibma ducked into the war section and stalled for a minute, wondering if he should wait for

Karen to go to the restroom or take a break, but he knew he couldn't get his porn movie. He rested it on the shelf behind a Vietnam documentary and slipped outside.

He drove two miles up the road, to a restaurant with a separate bar that was usually empty. He would salvage the night. He would drink a series of gin drinks and eat something fried and go home and collapse. In the morning, if he still desired straightforward porn, he'd drive to another town. This bar made strong drinks. It had a jukebox full of forgotten music. It smelled like smoke, but nobody was ever there to smoke in it.

When Mr. Hibma pulled into the lot, he saw a fleet of cars adorned with Citrus Middle School parking stickers. He stepped around a bush and peeked in a window. Librarians. They'd bunched the tables together. Assistants. Even volunteers. There were maybe nine of them, sipping determinedly at pink wine. Mr. Hibma knew when he was beat. He leaned against his car, face upturned toward to the sky, racking his brain for something else to do, some other way to salvage the night.

He had to change himself. The world wasn't going to change to suit him. He tried to see himself as he would be after he murdered Mrs. Conner, but all he saw were faint, unclustered stars. He could see the act, the smothering, Mrs. Conner's flailing limbs, but he couldn't be sure what it would mean for him. He didn't *want* to kill anyone. He didn't hope for it to come to that. And neither did anyone else. Dale wasn't going to answer his letter. No one was going to help Mr. Hibma. He was flying uncharted skies.

Shelby had her father's checkbook out and a book of stamps and a pile of statements and envelopes. She had electric bills, water bills, trash pickup, cable, phone. Half of them were late. Shelby went through and stamped all the envelopes. You didn't have to lick stamps anymore. She remembered always wanting to lick stamps for her parents when she was little. Now they were stickers. She picked up a pen to date one of the checks and it wouldn't write. It scratched against the soft surface of the checkbook. Shelby shook the pen and licked the point and still it wouldn't perform its function. She didn't have another one handy. It felt like a colossal chore to get up and find another pen. She ran her fingers against the fine grain of the table.

Shelby imagined walking around in the summertime and seeing her breath, the billboards in an unimaginable language she would never try to learn, every meal centered on fresh fish, every cabinet full of vodka. The sun setting at eleven at night. She imagined flying in a jet, and acting like she did it all the time. Shelby would point at menus. She would have the best guide. She would stay in the best part of the city, in an apartment whose balcony probably looked out over the morning bustling of shopkeepers.

Aunt Dale had finally answered Shelby's e-mail, and in a sincere tone that wasn't stiff in the least. Shelby and her aunt already had a rapport, as much as was possible over a computer. They weren't estranged relatives, they were Shelby and Aunt Dale. Shelby wasn't going to come out and write what she wanted, but it ought to be obvious. She wanted to be invited for a visit. She wanted to go to Iceland for the summer, or for a week, a long weekend—a chance to be far from the shadows of her real life. Breathing foreign air for even an hour, she knew, would help her. She was going to hint and hint. She was going to win Aunt Dale over. Aunt Dale knew what she was doing in the world and she would share that with Shelby. Shelby would return from her trip tough and levelheaded. Shelby had already e-mailed back and forth four or five times with her aunt. Now it wasn't taking longer than a day to get Aunt Dale's responses. Aunt Dale had already quit asking Shelby how she was doing, had already dispensed with pleasantries. And for Shelby's part, she posed question after question about Iceland, about the people and the TV shows and the government. It wouldn't be long before Shelby would see it all herself.

Toby made the walk to Wal-Mart. He found the Home & Garden section and within that, past stacks of hoses and fertilizers, found the pest control aisle, the ant killer. Every time he went to the bunker, Kaley had more bites. She had no concept of using the trash bucket and keeping the lid on it. She did as she pleased and hummed in Toby's face and got skinny. And ever since that girl had been found out by Buccaneer Bay, Toby felt he had no chance of getting caught. The cops and the FBI thought it might be the same assailant. There was no end to this in sight. The authorities had made nothing but wrong assumptions the whole way through, and they were only getting wronger.

Toby got the attention of an employee, a guy with lots of stuff on his forearms—spiked leather bracelets, a watch, a key on a rubber coil, wristbands.

"Which is the strongest ant killer?" Toby asked.

"They're for different situations."

"What about for, like, a cabin way out in the woods?"

"A cabin?"

"Well, say a barn."

"A barn with what in it?" The guy's hair all laid one way. It went the same direction from one ear to the other.

"Do you have anything that's not harmful to humans?"

"None of them are harmful to be around. You can't ingest them, though."

"What do you recommend? I can't make another trip out here."

The guy put his hand through his hair, sweeping across with the grain. "They're all good quality. If you don't like something you buy here, you can always bring it back. Return it to customer service. That's our policy."

"I don't want to return it to customer service," Toby said. "I want to kill ants with it."

Another presentation. Toby's topic was pole vault. Shelby watched him as he handed out headbands and stuttered through a brief physics lesson he'd found in that library book of his. He capped his talk with a biographical sketch of the man considered the greatest pole-vault talent of all time, a man who'd quit the sport at age twenty-four to become a sculptor. For political reasons, he'd sat out the Olympics. At his funeral, eight women, all claiming to be the love of the pole-vaulter's life, showed up stunned and weeping.

"*Just* the eight women?" Mr. Hibma asked.

"I'm not sure."

"It's better if it's the eight women and no one else. It should be the women and a priest, and then you find out the priest is in love with him too."

Toby shrugged. His involvement with the story of the great pole-vaulter was over.

Mr. Hibma released him back to his desk. The following two presentations chewed up most of the period—one about iguanas, one about glass-blowing. Mr. Hibma craned his neck to see the clock and decided there was time for one more. Shelby raised her hand. She went to the back of the classroom and removed a stack of quiz maps from the seat of a stool, then dragged the stool to the front of the room. She pulled a small bottle of ginger ale from one pocket and a highball glass from another, opened the soda and poured it. She dove into the informational portion of her presentation, rushing through the various styles and shticks. She named the great comics, mentioned the hallowed clubs. She wanted to make sure she had time for the demonstration, during which she would concentrate on a particular genre: insult comedy.

"The comedian comes out and chooses people at random to make fun of," she said. "The fear of being singled out is what makes this type of comedy thrilling."

Shelby took a sip of her ginger ale. She glanced at Mr. Hibma, who was looking at the floor, his mind somewhere else. She gestured toward a big kid named Luke. For a moment, it seemed, he thought he'd won something.

"Holy hell," Shelby said. "A cowboy."

Luke's wardrobe consisted of boots, jeans, T-shirts from country music concerts, and a beat-up ball cap with a fishing hook on the brim. Between classes, he dipped snuff.

"Boy, the closest you been to a steer is burger day in the cafeteria."

A chuckle or two.

"You may be a butt-ranger, but you sure as hell ain't a cowboy."

Shelby was winning the class over. She moved on quickly, hoping to get a couple more shots fired before Mr. Hibma stepped in. Maybe he'd let the bell stop her.

"Grady, my man." Shelby hopped up from the stool. "Pussy-whipped by a seventh-grader. Ain't that something?"

Shelby felt Mr. Hibma's grip on her shoulder, not firm but cold.

"We get the idea," he said.

Shelby took a last sip of her soda and set it on the stool. Grady was smarting, relieved Shelby had been reigned in, his face mired in mirth. Shelby did not feel shaky. She felt sturdy.

Mr. Hibma looked at her. "Stay after class, please."

The bell sounded and the kids formed a scuffling procession. Toby grinned dumbly at Shelby as he left, a look she couldn't interpret. When it was only Shelby and Mr. Hibma, he came and sat next to her, in a student desk.

"I think you said some stuff that needed to be said."

"Am I getting another detention?"

Mr. Hibma shifted in the smallish desk, making room to straighten his legs. "You're not in trouble, but I had to keep up appearances. If anyone asks, I was frightfully angry."

"Should I apologize to those kids?"

"I wouldn't."

Shelby nodded.

"You didn't go for the easy targets. You didn't go for the kiss-asses or the fat kid or Vince."

"Writing jokes is difficult."

A car with a loud stereo passed outside the window. Its thumping faded but didn't go away completely.

"What kind of graffiti is this?" Mr. Hibma was tracing something on the desktop with his finger. "It's a lost art, rebellion."

Shelby felt closed in. She stood up and went to the window.

"I don't want those Bellow books," she said. "I can't read them right now." She tipped her head toward her desk. The books were stacked sloppily underneath it.

"Leave them right there when you go. If you tried, you tried."

"I didn't, really."

"You carried them around for weeks, and they're very heavy."

Shelby, once again, was not in any real trouble. Maybe Mr. Hibma was onto something. Maybe discipline did not suit Shelby and everyone knew this but her. Maybe getting in trouble was a poor goal for her. The cops and the church people knew it, and that's why Shelby had heard nothing about her flag. The incident had been covered up.

Mr. Hibma sometimes stopped off at the cluttered drug store down the street from where he lived for no other reason than it was the last chance to delay his arrival at Sun Heron Villas. Sometimes he just wasn't ready to drive into that weedy parking lot of long, low cars and walk past his neighbors' little statues and put that heavy key in that flimsy front door. Today, though, he had purpose in the drug store. A greeting card for Mrs. Conner. He had decided he was no longer going to indulge in fantasies of killing this woman. Mr. Hibma felt ashamed for sending that letter to Shelby's Aunt Dale. He wished he'd never driven to Clermont, wished he'd never stood in line at the post office for ten minutes behind that Mexican man who was wearing slippers and a robe. Dale had likely never even seen the letter. She probably had screeners for her mail. She probably had a dozen stalkers. Mr. Hibma didn't like having that letter out in the world, having it sitting in some foreign stack on a foreign desk in a foreign nation.

Mr. Hibma was going to put it out of his mind—the letter, the feud, all of it. He was going to start being friendly to Mrs. Conner. Becoming a regular teacher was the only thing that could save Mr. Hibma. He had to stop faking everything. After he faked something, even if he was successful, as with coaching the scrimmage against the high school, he always crashed and ended up feeling lower than ever. Perhaps he had never given himself a serious chance to be a real teacher. He'd been setting himself up to fail. He had to, first off, comply with Mrs. Conner's latest memo and host the next wing meeting in his classroom. That would be a start. He'd never hosted a meeting and, in fact, most of the other teachers had only glimpsed his classroom from the hallway. He would provide refreshments and hang a map or two. Maybe he could start smiling and gossiping. Maybe he could begin taking his lunches in the teachers' lounge.

He approached the automatic doors of the drug store and they lurched open, scraping the ground. Mr. Hibma deserved a farmers' market—products hand-carved, hand-blown, hand-sewn, shade-grown espresso and fireweed honey and artisan cheeses—but what he had was Thomason Drug. He entered and was slapped from all sides by chatter, voices refusing to blend, shrill calls jumping up into the light, competing. The place was packed with fifty-year-old women. The other times Mr. Hibma had stopped at the drug store, he'd been the only customer, but today it was lousy with not-old, far-from-young women, ten to an aisle, all turning item after item upside-down, looking for price tags. There was a sale taking place. Maybe the store was going under. Mr. Hibma was not going to be chased off. He was going to get his card.

He waded into the morass, no idea which direction to go, and drifted toward a rack of sunglasses. He tried on a pair, made of electric blue plastic, like for water sports. They looked comical on Mr. Hibma. He didn't return them to the rack. They helped with the low fluorescent haze. Mr. Hibma located a central cross-aisle and read the hanging signs. Perfume and T-shirts, almost given away. Candy. Baseball mitts. Mr. Hibma felt safe behind his sunglasses. They somehow put a buffer between himself and the fragmented warbling. These women were deciding which snack foods could be frozen, whether a certain blouse was purple or more of an eggplant, whose ex-husband was the most despicable, which purses matched which jackets, whether Bailey's Irish Cream went bad. It was liquor, Bailey's Irish Cream, but it was also dairy.

A lot of the women were nurses, and it made Mr. Hibma wonder if the nurse who'd kidnapped him had been one of these. Not *all* women became these. Maybe becoming one of these was what that nurse had been trying to escape. She wanted a two-person family out in the desert, down in the mountains in Mexico. The only chatter would've been the chalky, disarming trills of the birds. Probably not. Probably she was a nutcase, and not an interesting one. A regular old nutcase.

Congratulations. Condolences. Mr. Hibma slid farther up the aisle. His eye was caught by a card revealing the top half of an almost-nude woman. She looked like she was having fun. The woman was about Mr. Hibma's age and a lot of care had been taken with her hairstyle. Her sexy birthday wishes were going to make Mr. Hibma feel a way he didn't want to feel, so he quickly moved on, advancing sideways through plump nurses and very skinny ones. Apology—the smallest section, five cards in total. Mr. Hibma didn't want to apologize. He wanted to reconcile, maybe. Not even that. He wanted to make a fresh start.

He slipped the cards out of their slots one by one, narrowed it to two. One of the finalists was adorned with perched doves, the other had a couple of cartoon Indians dropping their hatchets in a hole they'd dug. The two nurses next to Mr. Hibma were almost screaming at each other. To stem the tide of their voices, Mr. Hibma displayed the two cards in front of them and asked which they'd prefer to receive. They were his target audience, about the same as Mrs. Conner. They seemed not to notice his outlandish sunglasses.

"What'd you do wrong?" one of them asked.

"Nothing specific," said Mr. Hibma. "I was being myself."

"You should never apologize for being yourself. I learned that after I got divorced," said the second woman. She had bags of flavored coffee clutched to her chest.

"Doesn't that depend on what kind of self you have?" Mr. Hibma said. "What if your self has something wrong with it?"

"People don't change. They try to but they can't. That's speaking from experience."

"You're probably right. I probably won't change."

"I hope not," said the woman with the coffee. "I'm never going to change for anybody ever again."

Toby rose early Saturday morning and dragged more supplies out to the bunker. He brought a dustpan and also another pillow, because Kaley had torn the stuffing out of her old one. He'd been keeping her for two months now. What, nine weeks? What did weeks and days matter? Toby didn't want to keep track of time. It meant nothing. He went down and did what he had to do, thankful that Kaley was ignoring him this morning, then marched back to the house.

When he opened the front door, Uncle Neal was sitting in a chair staring at him. Odorless smoke hung about the room. Uncle Neal reached back and set his pipe down. His eyes were bloodshot and the corners of his mouth were sharp.

"Seen the nail clippers?" he asked.

"I have better things to do than keep track of your nail clippers," Toby said.

"That's a debatable claim," said Uncle Neal. "Not that I care to debate it, but it's a highly debatable claim."

Toby took a step toward his room and Uncle Neal stood and asked if Toby was hungry. Toby looked at the table and saw slices of white bread with butter, some kind of meat patties, and peaches in a bowl. Uncle Neal never buttered Toby's bread, but today he had. The meat patties were arranged so they were slightly overlapping, like in an advertisement.

"My breakfasts don't suit you anymore, do they?" Uncle Neal said.

The food had no aroma. It was like the smoke.

"I'll heat up a plate in a little while," Toby said.

He again started toward his room and this time Uncle Neal stepped right in his path.

"I feed you for years," Uncle Neal said. "All of a sudden you're too fancy. All of a sudden I got to eat alone. You got some little girlfriend you're always going and eating fancy with."

"I don't have a girlfriend," Toby said.

"Oh yeah? What do they call them these days if they don't call them girlfriends?"

"You don't need to worry about calling her anything. She's never coming around here."

Uncle Neal was still standing in front of Toby. He seemed engaged in the moment in a way that wasn't usual. He still had his lighter in his hand and now he slipped it in his pocket.

"I know who she is," he told Toby. "The girl whose sister got snatched. You got some sick fascination with her because her sister got snatched."

"I'm not sick," Toby said. "I'm just fine."

"I used to think I was going to raise you." Uncle Neal gripped Toby's shoulder. Toby finally smelled something—Uncle Neal's shirt. He'd been wearing the same clothes for days. "I used to think we could help each other."

"Well, we can't," Toby said.

"I know what you're doing, you little thief."

It felt like Uncle Neal could've broken Toby's shoulder. Toby tried to move. He said, "What am I doing?"

"You're stealing from this house and selling the stuff at that rat-ass flea market. You're a businessman, a little merchant. I brought up a boy who would rob his own flesh and blood. A little fucking capitalist."

Toby didn't feel like answering to this accusation. He *had* been stealing. It was a lot easier to get things from the house than to keep making extra trips to the grocery store or the drug store. And it was free. What could his uncle do about it?

"I'll tolerate disrespect," Uncle Neal said. "I'll tolerate thinking you're something special. I tolerate that stuff all the time. But there has to be a line, and I'm the one who has to draw it."

Toby kept quiet. He felt each of his uncle's fingertips digging into the bones of his shoulder. Uncle Neal hadn't laid a hand on him in years—hadn't pushed him around or even mussed his hair, hadn't dug Toby in the ribs after making a joke, hadn't slapped him on the back when he was coughing. Uncle Neal looked at his hand and flexed his fingers. He inhaled greedily.

"And I gave you a fucking allowance. That was *my* choice. That was my own poor rearing."

Uncle Neal hit Toby then, a kind of open-handed punch. He rushed it and it didn't land squarely. He hit Toby a second time. Toby wilted, but not out of pain. Uncle Neal seemed surprised that his blows were having an impact.

"I want it to hurt me more than it hurts you," Uncle Neal said. "It doesn't, though. It doesn't hurt me."

"It doesn't really hurt me, either," Toby said. He didn't look up, but he had the feeling his uncle was staring at his own hand.

"I can't be hurt anymore," Uncle Neal said. "I'm that low."

"You're tough, is all," Toby told him.

"I'm not even ashamed."

Toby kept crouching there, still. He couldn't tell exactly where Uncle

Neal's blows had landed because his whole head felt hot. Somewhere inside, he was glad Uncle Neal had hit him. It was a relief. Uncle Neal backed away, his shadow lifting. He walked out the front door and Toby got himself standing. He heard Uncle Neal's footfalls across the porch and then his truck starting up with the wail of an old frail dog. Toby went to the bathroom and took a look. He was going to have a bruise on his neck and a mark on his forehead, but they wouldn't last. He shook his shoulder out. That was probably the last time his uncle was going to touch him. The man was desperate. Something in him was rancid and weak. He and Toby had to put up with each other. Kaley and Toby had to put up with each other. Shelby had to put up with the whole world. How did *anyone* keep from going rancid? How come everyone wasn't like Uncle Neal?

Toby's nose was running but his eyes were dry. He ran the hot water and got out a washcloth. He let the water turn steamy and then he let it run and run until he could no longer see himself.

Toby and Shelby had agreed to meet on Sunday, and Shelby decided they should go for a ride on the old folks' trolley, a stout yet aerodynamic-looking bus that, three times a day, drove a big loop that included a pharmacy, a supermarket, the movie theater, the county offices, and a cafeteria-style restaurant. Shelby gave the driver two crisp dollar bills and she and Toby took the back row. There were only two other passengers, a frail old woman adorned with jewelry and a younger guy with a box of T-shirts on his lap. They sat in the middle of the bus, across the aisle from one another. The woman was hugging herself, shivering. The driver, a lanky black man, had the trolley's air conditioner pumping.

At the first stop, the pharmacy, no one got on or off. Same thing at the supermarket.

Shelby elbowed Toby and he looked away from the window. She got a good look at his face. She could tell he was dreading being asked about it, so she decided she wouldn't. She didn't like people in *her* business. She knew how he felt. If his dings had been the result of a fistfight with another kid or a pole-vaulting injury, he would've said so. Something had happened with Uncle Neal.

"When's the last time you let someone be your friend?" Shelby asked.

Toby thought. "Last year."

"What happened?"

"He transferred to a middle school in Gainesville so he could play basketball there."

"Still friends with him?"

Toby shook his head.

"Why, because you guys don't have a phone?" Shelby draped her arm across Toby's lap.

"Even if we did, probably wouldn't still be friends."

Toby fidgeted into a straighter posture. Shelby's hand was resting flat against his thigh. He didn't notice, or else he was acting like he didn't notice. The mark on his neck almost looked like a paw print. Shelby was going to make him forget about his uncle, for a while at least.

They pulled up near the movie theater. There were a few people standing outside, but none of them made a move toward the trolley. It was a two-screen theater, showing a horror flick and a kids' movie. A poster of a bald guy hanging upside-down, one of his eyes bulging out, hung next to a poster of cartoon automobiles.

The old woman turned in her seat. She cleared her throat, and this action sent a chill through her.

"Excuse me, sir," she chimed.

The guy with the box on his lap looked at her.

"I'd like one of those T-shirts, one of the long-sleeve ones. Would you entertain a trade?"

"I might *make* a trade."

"A bracelet?" The old woman hoisted her arm. "They're real." With her finger, she separated one bracelet from the others. "This one's worth sixty bucks."

The guy looked in his box. "A small, I guess."

The two of them exchanged their goods. The guy dropped his new jewelry into his shirt pocket and the woman slipped the T-shirt on over her head. She tugged it this way and that, getting it straight, a faint smile on her face.

The trolley jogged into motion.

"I had lunchtime friends last semester," Toby said. "Dina and Tom."

"Who are they?" asked Shelby.

"They're that couple. I wasn't really *friends* with them."

"What couple?"

"Dina and skinny Tom. The two that say they're going to get married when they turn sixteen?"

Shelby was at a loss.

"I used to sit at one of those four-person tables with them. We'd pile our stuff in the fourth chair."

Shelby pressed her palm against the inside of Toby's leg, squashing the notion that it was resting where it was resting on accident. Toby talked more quickly.

"I've never seen much reward to friendship," he said. "Starts as an interview and ends as a job."

"Where'd you hear that?"

"It's part of a toast."

Shelby moved her hand until it rested against a lump that could've been what she was looking for or could've just been a fold of Toby's bunched-up shorts. The trolley pulled up to a cluster of two-story glass buildings. There were spindly oak trees everywhere, newly planted. It was the government offices. They were closed today. The old woman and the guy with the T-shirts exited the trolley and went their own ways. Shelby had no idea where they might be going. The driver got off for a moment and spoke on his cell phone. When he got back in, he adjusted his rearview mirror and put drops in his eyes. He held his hand in front of a vent, making sure it was blowing cold air.

As soon as they were back on the road, Shelby unbuttoned Toby's shorts and burrowed her hand. Toby made a deft adjustment of his hips, making it easier for Shelby, and then he stilled, eyes forward, back arched off the seatback. Shelby's hand was hemmed in so she took short strokes, trying not to squeeze, trying not to hurt Toby. He was motionless. Shelby ceased her stroking. Toby's legs were shaking. She didn't want him to finish already. She resumed, slower, working her hand luxuriantly. Toby was holding his eyes open. The next stop was in sight. Shelby executed some rough jerks and a small sound escaped Toby. He fumbled with his shorts, yanking them down, exposing himself to the air and the light. Shelby watched Toby's face, on which still rested a bland expression, and felt cheated. She wanted to see some exaltation. She wanted to see him reel into another, better state. Toby put his hand on Shelby's, aiming himself toward the seat in front of them. The stuff ran most of the way down the seat and then lost its liquidity. It was unmistakable. Anyone who saw it would know what it was.

Shelby looked at Toby. His hair was growing spiky from when he'd buzzed it. Shelby couldn't tell if anything had happened, if their souls had scrubbed against one another. The trolley stopped and Shelby tugged Toby out of the seat and guided him to the front. Shelby's eyes met the driver's and he winked at her, but not in a knowing way. The driver didn't know a damn thing. Winking at young people was something he always did, part of his procedure.

Shelby and Toby ventured inside JB's Cafeteria and filled trays with meatloaf and sweet potatoes. As Shelby sat across from Toby, both their mouths full, she was struck by a fresh and potent curiosity. She wanted to know, now, not only Toby's darkness but where he slept and what he ate and what his favorite type of weather was and what made him sneeze. She wanted to know what he dreamed of at night, what was going on in his mind when he stared at the wall during class. Shelby was fascinated with the efficiency of her hormones. She had engaged in a sex act and now, what, she was in love? She had caused a male of the species to blow his load and now, what, she wanted to be his little girlfriend? Astonishing. Shelby tried to enjoy the feeling. She felt lush.

Before basketball practice, Mr. Hibma rushed over to the common area in the main building of the school and approached the carnation booth. It was manned by a younger girl, not an eighth-grader, a tiny thing wearing a suit. Her pumps were like a doll's shoes. She was probably a replica of her mother. Her mother had dressed her this way and pulled her hair back like that because her daughter was going to be in the public eye, a saleswoman. Or the girl's mother was a slob and the girl was rebelling.

"Where is the money going?" Mr. Hibma asked her.

"A field trip," she said. "Washington D.C."

"That's a lot of carnations."

The girl's back was straight and her hands rested on the tabletop. "I've already got Publix to match our funds, and we're going to get a big discount from Amtrak. We have a quarter of what we need. We project to hit our mark by the end of the semester, then go on the trip this summer."

"Do you want to be a politician one day?" Mr. Hibma asked.

"No, I want to work for a politician."

One of the girl's eyes was off, aimed slightly to the side. It made the rest of her look that much more put-together.

"My name is Gina Lampley," she said. "You're Mr. Hibma." She shot her hand out toward him. "I can't wait to take your class. I've heard you get to do a lot of presentations. I don't get nervous talking in front of people."

"I look forward to having you." Mr. Hibma had to grow comfortable with the kissing of his ass. It was one of his problems, he knew. The other teachers enjoyed kiss-asses and he didn't. He had to start valuing each student for what they were. Some kids were just kiss-asses and they couldn't help it, no more than one can help being Samoan or allergic to celery.

"I like your shoes," the girl said. "An *old* teacher would never wear those shoes."

Mr. Hibma looked at the girl, kindly he hoped. He knew she had completed all the necessary paperwork allowing her to be out of class this period. She'd chosen this spot for her booth because of the heavy foot traffic. She'd stenciled a flower on each order form, stacks of them. She was going to grow up and thrive in the world of red tape, fine print, licenses, sales, arts and crafts—the world everyone was forced to live in.

"Can I specify which color?" Mr. Hibma asked.

The girl nodded pertly. "Red or white."

"Better go with white."

"How many should I put you down for?"

"One will do the job."

The girl got an order form and started filling it out herself. She asked if the tag on the flower should say who it was from, and Mr. Hibma said it should. The carnation was to go to Mrs. Conner, room 142. Mr. Hibma reached in his pocket and pulled out a wad of bills. He gave the girl three of them.

"Oh," she said, like an honest mistake had been made. She held the limp, gray money in her fingers. "Do you have any crisper ones? I like them to lay flat in the envelopes, then I can fit the same amount in each."

"Crisper bills?"

"If you don't, that's okay."

Mr. Hibma looked around the common room. This girl was only being herself, like everyone had a right to.

During a pop quiz in American History, Toby was called to guidance. He left his quiz paper face-down on his desk and walked to the office, where he presented himself to the kiss-ass who manned the reception desk. He was directed down a hallway, to the sixth door on the left. Toby had never been called to guidance. He knew this was not supposed to mean one was in trouble. Maybe the counselor was curious about Toby's plans for the summer, or which classes he wanted to take next year in high school.

The door was open. The counselor, behind her desk, looked up at Toby, almost smiling. Toby recognized her. She used to be the resource officer, the school cop. She nodded at the chair in front of Toby and he sat. The counselor looked odd wearing a blouse with a scarf around the collar instead of her blue uniform.

"The old counselor wrote a book," she said.

Toby felt like he was wearing a blown disguise. He didn't know why. No one was going to find out about Kaley. Those FBI agents had never contacted Toby after that day in the parking lot. If they couldn't sniff anything on him, this lady sure couldn't.

"I have to call you kids out of class," the counselor said. "You never come down on your own."

Toby had to piss. He'd had to piss during his pop quiz and had forgotten to stop at the bathroom on his way to guidance.

"I take the files home on weekends and browse—see who might could use a nudge in the right direction."

"You think I could?" Toby said.

"You were on a watch list coming out of grammar school." The counselor leaned forward, pressing her shapeless front against her desk.

"Can I go to the bathroom?" Toby asked.

"Do you happen to know how many detentions you've compiled here at Citrus Middle?"

"None," Toby said. "My record is clean."

The counselor chuckled archly. "You've had twenty-nine. And that's without all the undocumented detentions from Mr. Hibma."

"How do you know about those?"

"I believe you met Cara, the receptionist. This place is full of spies."

"I've never been expelled," Toby said. "That's something to hang my hat on."

"Why don't *you* tell *me* why you're here?"

Toby was sweating. It wasn't nerves. He really had to pee and it was hot in the office. He hoped this woman wasn't going to start asking questions about his uncle, about his home life.

"I'm thinking of a flag. I'm thinking of a church. I'm thinking of a mild-mannered, straight-A student, a lovely girl, who now runs around with a scowl on her face."

Toby tried to look out the window but it was covered over with newspaper comics, with dogs and cats thinking human thoughts.

"I had nothing to do with the flag," he said.

"I know that. What I'm wondering is whether Shelby's behavior is a result of her sister going missing—I don't think it is, entirely—or a result of her being bored because she's too smart for this place—I doubt that, too—or whether she's under a good, old-fashioned bad influence. I'm wondering if someone's taking advantage of her while she's going through a tough time."

"Everyone gets taken advantage of," Toby said.

The counselor closed her eyes a moment. "I don't claim to be great at this job, but part of the description is looking out for the well-being of the students, and that's what I'm doing. Shelby's well-being, not yours."

At that moment, the bell rang, startling Toby and also startling the counselor. Toby could leave now and piss.

The counselor took a look toward the hallway. "Don't think you're slick," she said. "Don't for a second think you're slick."

That evening Toby had a meet. It was a home meet, at Spider Field. Shelby attended, sitting herself neatly in the bleachers like a seasoned girlfriend, her hands wrapped around a big cup of soda. Toby still hadn't figured out what he needed from Shelby. Since the old folks' trolley, Toby had felt in debt, like he owed Shelby something, and he didn't like owing anybody. Someone doing something generous for Toby, showing affection—he didn't understand that. He didn't understand the math of it. He felt queasy when he thought about what had happened on the old folks' trolley. It was childish—people running around trying to touch each other and suck each other and everything else. Toby was as bad as anyone. He looked up into the scattered crowd and there was Shelby, straw between her lips, waving.

Toby's opponent this night was a wiry kid with bitten fingernails. The kid had a small radio on which he played manic-sounding music at low volume, and also a journal, which he flipped open from time to time and jotted things in. Toby's opponent won the coin flip, then, inexplicably, perhaps to show how confident he was, chose to vault first. Toby stood by and watched as the kid faulted on his first vault. The kid turned off his radio and blew into his hands. His second vault, he faulted again. His third attempt, no chance. His steps were all wrong. The kid flopped down roughly in the grass and threw back the cover of his journal. All Toby had to do was clear the minimum height and he'd win. He was going to win. He glanced up at Shelby and she stood and let out a cheer.

At home, Toby took out his mother's mirror. He breathed on the mirror and buffed it with his T-shirt. He'd had a new thought, and he had to shine a light on this thought. The thought was this: He could leave Kaley in the bunker and quit taking care of her, quit feeding her, let her bones be found in ten years like that girl near Buccaneer Bay. This was the thought. There it was. This was an easy way out. It would set him back to nothing, set him free. He'd have a clean record then, like he'd told the guidance counselor. He could go straight to school and straight home like a regular kid. He could worry about his grades, things like that. He could probably sleep. He would sleep if he knew that in the morning he didn't have to go to the bunker. He hated the bunker. It was his to find and wasn't it his to give up? It was Kaley's now. If Toby left her to go permanently quiet down there, then he could do whatever he wanted in the afternoons, whatever he wanted with his weekends. He could let Shelby have him. Kaley would fade. Toby would forget her, almost. Kaley would be another mistake, like the rest. People made mistakes all the time. Toby could welcome the days instead of bracing for them. He'd never welcomed days before, Kaley or not, but he'd never had a reason to. He'd never had Shelby.

Toby pressed his hand against the mirror's glass, leaving a print. He couldn't look at his face. His face was full of guilt and weakness, and abandoning Kaley would require more strength than taking her had, more strength than keeping her. Toby was unworthy. He had to get control of his mind. He was being a crybaby because his evil wasn't spoon-feeding him instructions every two minutes. He had to listen harder. He had to feel his instincts. He couldn't, though. All he could feel was what the future might be like.

Shelby took an elevator and found the passport office. She'd been to the drug store for her photo and she'd dug out her birth certificate. All she had left was the paperwork. She wasn't sure if she was going to have to forge her father's signature. She was prepared to. He wouldn't have minded her getting a passport, but Shelby didn't want to tell him why she needed one. She didn't want to tell anyone anything until she'd actually been invited. Aunt Dale had sent Shelby e-mails complaining about that guy she'd never married, and complaining about traveling and about people she had to work with, the kind of complaining one did to a friend, to a confidant. It was a relief to Shelby, hearing about someone else's problems instead of being asked about her own. At this point, it took Shelby longer to reply than it did Aunt Dale, because Shelby couldn't always get to a computer. Shelby was a little surprised that her aunt hadn't suggested they talk on the phone, but for someone like Aunt Dale phones were dusty old history. Phones were for regular, slow people.

There was one lady working in the passport office, no other customers. The lady had high-waisted pants and a big wooden hair clip. Shelby told her what she needed and the lady began compiling forms.

"Shouldn't you be in school?" the lady said.

"Yes, I should." Shelby put her elbows on the counter. "But you guys aren't open on weekends."

"So you're running some errands today?" The lady was good-natured. She used a blunt, manicured fingernail to flip through the forms.

"I love errands," Shelby said.

"Where's your accent from, sweetie?"

"I don't have an accent," said Shelby. "I pronounce the words correctly. *You* have an accent."

"Everybody has an accent."

"That's what people with accents think."

For the wing meeting he was hosting, Mr. Hibma brought in strawberries from Plant City along with a jug of Romanoff sauce he'd cooked up. He brought a twelve-pack of cream soda and some tamales a woman outside his villa complex was always selling.

Besides Mr. Hibma and Mrs. Conner, there were nine teachers in the East Liberal Arts Wing. Of those nine, seven blended together—dumpy but not disheveled, out of shape but not fat. The other two were young. One was Pete, a guy who taught advanced English and on weekends played in a punk band. Mr. Hibma had been inside Pete's classroom only once, back when Mr. Hibma had first come to Citrus Middle. Pete had shown Mr. Hibma all his Sex Pistols and Ramones posters. He'd confided to Mr. Hibma that all the old teachers were against him, and seemed to think he and Mr. Hibma were going to be friends. He'd kept asking

Mr. Hibma to come see his band play for months on end, before finally giving up. Now their interaction consisted of nods in the hallway and the occasional strained chat.

The other twenty-six-year-old was a round-faced girl who held advanced degrees in Spanish. She drove down to USF several evenings a week. She was a master of Latin linguistic study, but couldn't leave Citrus County because her husband ran a river rock company that serviced the entire Nature Coast. And she apparently had no problem with this. She had no problem with working at Citrus Middle rather than at the UN or an embassy in Madrid.

Mr. Hibma waited by the door as his guests arrived, offering greetings and indicating the refreshments he'd put out. Pete ate a tamale. Nobody touched the strawberries. Mrs. Conner patted Mr. Hibma on the shoulder and he gave her his most congenial smile. She set up shop at the front of the room and everyone else settled into the students' desks. The social science teacher, a woman with an expansive forehead who wore a Spider Pride T-shirt every Friday, excused herself and returned with a Snickers. She explained that her diet allowed her one serving of candy per week, and this was when she was choosing to have it.

The meeting began with an update on the progress of a new remedial program, updates about former students Mrs. Conner remained in touch with. Reports were exchanged about problem students. There were kids who needed drugs and weren't on them, kids who were on drugs and didn't need them, kids with overbearing parents, kids whose parents were never around. Mrs. Conner also had two staff petitions for everyone to sign, one backing the idea that students not be able to miss class for sports-related activities, the other backing a ban on the books of Kurt Vonnegut. Not one teacher in the school assigned Kurt Vonnegut. It was a preemptive strike, probably an order passed down from the headquarters of Mrs. Conner's church.

"I ain't signing it," said Pete. "Unless you help me get my shows approved as music extra credit, I'm not helping you do anything.

Gathering around a flagpole to pray is extra credit and witnessing the creation of live music ain't?"

Mr. Hibma had noticed that, for effect, Pete sometimes said the word *ain't*.

"Your shows are in bars," Mrs. Conner said.

"Not all of them. You know that."

Mrs. Conner's face was bothered yet composed, like she'd breathed in a sour smell and was waiting for it to blow away in the wind. "You're comparing prayer to rock music?" she asked Pete.

"I'm comparing prayer to *punk* music. They both enhance your soul. They're both things to believe in."

The sour smell had not blown away from Mrs. Conner. Mr. Hibma could tell she wanted to say a million things to Pete. Mr. Hibma's gut impulse, despite himself, was to stick up for Pete, but Mr. Hibma had a fence to mend and he didn't mind sitting this one out. He'd left behind that ridiculousness about killing Mrs. Conner, had left behind that stupid letter he'd written. It was history. He was glad Dale hadn't responded.

Mrs. Conner sighed and something gave way in her eyes.

"Let's hear it," she said. "Let's hear the music."

Pete zipped out of the room. The other teachers looked at one another, listening to the slaps of Pete's converse sneakers fade to nothing. The slaps returned, grew louder, and here was Pete again, boom box in hand, searching for an outlet.

To Pete's credit, he did not identify his muse or expose symbolism in his lyrics. He pressed play and backed away from the boom box. At first there was only hissing on the tape. In a stifled voice, someone counted off, and then noise filled Mr. Hibma's classroom. The noise was not fettered by a melody. Each member of the band was playing as loudly as possible, forcing the maximum yield out of his instrument. Occasionally, confoundingly, the sound intensified. Someone was singing, but only because someone had to. When the noise ceased, it was just as startling as when it had begun.

"Okay, okay," said Mrs. Conner. "All right." She waved her hands, imploring Pete to stop the tape before the next song began.

He lunged forward and smacked the panel of buttons.

"I guess it doesn't matter what you're singing because no one can understand it," Mrs. Conner said. "Draw up a petition and I'll sign."

Pete was confused. He was supposed to be held down by Authority. Authority was not supposed to be reasonable. Pete seemed to miss the irony: Mrs. Conner, to spare *herself* from hearing any more, was willing to petition that the students be subjected to Pete's music; because the music was unbearable, it had gained support. Maybe Pete had just lived the first punk moment of his life. Mr. Hibma knew he shouldn't hate Pete. Pete and the Spanish expert had done him no harm. Mr. Hibma despised them, he understood, because he was no better than they were. Despite arriving at Citrus Middle from vastly different paths, he and Pete and the Spanish expert were all here now, all willing to stay.

Shelby received a note instructing her to skip PE and report to room 171E to meet with Mrs. Milner, the gifted teacher. She found the room and pulled the door open, and Mrs. Milner was sitting on a padded chair in front of a large table. The room was huge and carpeted. Against the back wall, in shadow, a bunch of half-built or half-destroyed mechanical devices crowded one another.

"You're late." Mrs. Milner threw her head so she could look at Shelby.

Shelby advanced a step or two before she realized there was no chair for her. This was a sort of test, Shelby figured. Shelby was supposed to employ her problem-solving skills. She was supposed to explore the junk in the back of the room and fashion a chair herself, or turn the table upside-down so she and Mrs. Milner could sit in it like a canoe.

"I'll stand," Shelby said. This was the most trouble Shelby could manage to get in: being invited to join gifted. "I don't have much time."

"Something life-altering going on in PE?"

"Why don't you pitch me?" said Shelby. "I'll stand here and you give me the pitch."

"I'll start with the price. The price is your beloved PE." Mrs. Milner pushed up the sleeves of her sweater. "This room is a free zone. Explore, don't explore. Interact, don't interact. That kind of freedom sells itself. This is a place where chariots are built, where naps are taken."

Shelby now saw that the junk against the back wall was meant to become a Roman parade float.

"Gifts can be scary," Mrs. Milner proposed. "A lot of people are afraid of their gifts. Don't you think that's true?"

"I'll reserve all comments for when the pitch ends," Shelby said. "Is it over?"

There was a glint in Mrs. Milner's eye. By being difficult, Shelby was making herself more attractive. "Higher mathematics are here," said Mrs. Milner. "Reading Tolstoy in Russian. We have a guest lecturer once a month."

"What's that crunching noise?"

"Our ice machine. The Best Western donated it."

"Why do you need an ice machine?"

"I would've asked the same question—in fact, I did. But now I don't know how we ever got along without it." Mrs. Milner pushed up her sleeves again, this time tucking them into themselves. "We have a blender, too."

Shelby was tired of standing. She had an urge to accept Mrs. Milner's invitation, ask her to leave the room, and go to sleep on the tabletop.

"I know there was some ugliness between you and Lena, and she wants me to tell you she holds no hard feelings. And there's no preaching permitted in this room. It's a free zone, and to me that includes free of religion."

Lena was the girl Shelby had pelted with grits. "I didn't know she was in gifted," Shelby said.

"She's very bright and very sincere."

"I'm going to respectfully decline," Shelby said.

"Tell me the reason."

"I don't want to be sequestered with kids who think they're exceptional. I prefer kids who are a tiny bit smart and don't know it."

Mrs. Milner cleared her throat. She was not impressed. "Gifted gives you options."

The idea of options sounded odd to Shelby. Options in life. She had no idea what she'd opt for. She had never needed dreams, hopes even. Maybe now she did. Whatever her dreams might be, they'd have nothing to do with being in gifted.

"The real reason is this," Shelby said. "Someone I trust told me not to join."

"Who?"

"I won't say."

"That person is ill-informed. I take ten students in my class and most of them enrolled in the second or third grade. The only reason a spot is opening is Daphne Biner is moving. If you get in now, you'll be grandfathered in for high school. You're going to *need* gifted."

"Why am I going to need gifted?"

Mrs. Milner looked astonished. "Friends," she said. "These will be your friends. Do you think those regular kids out there have any idea how to be friends with someone like you?"

"I've never seen a lot of point to friendship," Shelby told her. "Starts as an interview, ends as a job."

Mrs. Milner turned sad, a woman crumbling under the weight of her unheeded wisdom. She rested her hand on Shelby's forearm and Shelby gently peeled it off and whispered the word "No." Shelby stood above Mrs. Milner like a holy person over a disciple, the icemaker humming like a distant choir.

Shelby and Toby followed the main trail to the public library. They walked quickly, outpacing the mosquitoes. They heard the robotic xylophone music of an ice cream truck. The music grew distant, then close, then trailed away altogether.

In the library, Toby went into the computer lab with Shelby and they shared a chair. She saw him reading along as she relayed bits of light gossip from school. Aunt Dale liked middle school gossip. Shelby wrote that she wondered if Icelanders used ketchup, if they went skiing a lot, what the drinking age was. After sitting stumped for a moment, staring at a poster of Mel Gibson reading a book, she pecked in:

> I'm dating a boy named Toby. I think about him all day. He's got a little boy belly but his arms are as hard as a steering wheel. He smells like wet logs and doesn't have one freckle. He's not like anyone else. I'm waiting for him to work up the nerve to put some earnest moves on me. I would like one adult in the world I can speak openly to and who will speak openly to me, and I choose you.

That would get Aunt Dale's attention. Aunt Dale had been sharing plenty about herself, answering all Shelby's questions. It was time Shelby shared.

She hit SEND. She let her eyes drift around until she was looking at Toby. He'd read her message and was making such an effort to be blank-faced, he appeared grave. Nobody else could unnerve Toby, but Shelby did it every other day.

"You look insane," she told him. "You look like the person that wrote the ice cream truck music."

"*I'm* insane?" Toby asked.

Shelby logged out of the computer and slipped her library card in her pocket.

"Don't tell your Aunt Dale anything about me," Toby said. "I don't want to be included in this experiment. Being honest with adults?"

"Aunt Dale isn't a normal adult."

"And I'm not a normal kid. Hard as I try."

Toby picked up a basket on his way into the grocery store. He put some ground beef and a tomato in the basket, to seem normal. He stood in the medicine aisle. There was a section for upset stomach, and he grabbed something from there. There were pills especially for nausea, and he grabbed those. There were a bunch of boxes with coughing children on them. Toby hadn't been to the bunker in three days. The sun was going to keep setting and rising. Toby wondered what Kaley was thinking. Toby had skipped a day before, but never two and certainly not three. She would run out of food today or maybe tomorrow. After that, Toby had no idea how long it would take. She was sleeping in her own filth, trying to become as much of a mess as she could, knowing Toby would have to clean her up. Her wounds were getting infected—her elbows and knees. The water and the jug of iced tea and the juice packets wouldn't last. Toby wondered at what point she would stop expecting him, at what point she would know in the pit of her stomach that she was absolutely alone in the world. She had no allies and was losing her only enemy.

Toby had glimpsed it. While walking alongside Shelby, he'd seen how things could be, how they *would* be, when Toby had nothing to hold him back, nothing squeezing his soul like a terrible vine. He could do it. He could leave Kaley down there. Toby didn't have to answer to his evil. He could do what was right for himself and for Shelby. The sun kept going down and it kept coming up, and if Toby could keep clear of the bunker then one of these days when it came up it would find Toby unfettered.

Toby told himself he wasn't in the grocery store to get medicine for

Kaley. He was getting medicine in order to restock Uncle Neal's cabinet, before Uncle Neal noticed and went nuts. Uncle Neal wouldn't notice, though—not at this point. Toby looked at the ground beef and the tomato in his basket. He got more medicines, not any of the boxes with children on them. There was something meant to boost your immune system. Regular old multi-vitamins—couldn't hurt. Toby got lip balm and antibiotic ointment. He kept looking at the coughing children on the boxes of kids' medicine. They were trying to look sad, trying to trick Toby. They weren't real children.

Springstead's coach, the rival of the coach who was starting the lawn service, had beady eyes and neck muscles. Mr. Hibma did not go over and speak to him before the game, as was the custom among coaches, and the guy seemed not to notice, wrapped up as he was in the fact that his point guard had a bad ankle. He kept making her try it out, hoping she could play.

The first time Springstead had the ball, Mr. Hibma put on Earl Ray, a half-court press, throwing Springstead's shaky backup point guard into a profound fluster that remained with her the rest of the game. The poor thing dribbled off her shin, threw the ball in the stands. Meanwhile, Mr. Hibma's point guard got into the paint whenever she felt like it. She was a magical sprite who'd cast a spell on the ball. She'd also, Mr. Hibma noticed, cast a spell over a spindly boy with long hair who now sat in the second row at each game. Since Mr. Hibma's regime of beauty had begun, the team had gained four boyfriends, which, added to the three it'd already had—the pretty benchwarmers'—gave the Citrus Middle girls' basketball team a not-too-shabby following. If Mr. Hibma wasn't mistaken, he was doing a serviceable job coaching. Maybe he *could* be a teacher. Of course it couldn't be that hard; look at all the people who managed it. Mr. Hibma had just been lazy. He'd been daunted by the idea of selflessness, of commitment.

His team won, 29 to 5. Mr. Hibma wanted to criticize them, to prevent them from growing complacent, so he raised his voice and informed them that they'd made a liar out of him. He'd made a promise. He'd given his word that they would shut Springstead out.

Mr. Hibma set himself up on his couch and began filling in a fresh grade book. He had a list of all the assignments he'd given and printouts of his class registers. He had to start from scratch. He'd turned his classroom upside-down, but the grade book was nowhere to be found. It had made its way into the wide world and Mr. Hibma would never hear from it again. He could handle it. Every job had difficulties. Everyone's time got wasted.

Mr. Hibma listed the kids' names, then the assignments and dates. He had this grade book crisis under control. He could estimate, by this point in the year, what each student would score on each assignment. Once in a while, though, an A student bombed something or a D student cobbled together some lucky guesses. The safe way was to make sure each kid ended up with a higher average than expected. Mr. Hibma plugged away at the grades for over an hour, until his eyes began to feel strange. Very strange. He set his grade book work aside. He felt like he was stoned, except he wasn't hungry, didn't feel lazy. It was like being stoned in way that sharpened one's mind rather than dulling it. Mr. Hibma could smell the garbage in his kitchen trashcan. He could see magnified details from the Springstead game—the mole on the opposing center's shoulder, the scuffs on the players' shoes. Mr. Hibma's identity felt shifty. The vocab words he'd assigned that week ran through his head. Reductionism: *the theory that every complex phenomenon can be explained by analyzing its simplest physical mechanisms*. Reechy: *smoky or sooty*. Mr. Hibma wanted the television on. He dug the remote out from under the couch cushions and hit the power button. Professional wrestling. The wrestlers preened around the ring. One of them luxuriated in the upper hand, tossing his hair.

Mr. Hibma took out the garbage and replaced the bag, then he began dusting. He shoved several rags in his pockets and carried a can of Pledge. In high corners he found cobwebs. He dusted every flat surface he could find, working up a light sweat, then returned to the kitchen and threw out all the rags, clean or dirty. He dug out butter, flour, milk, sugar, eggs. He banged around in his drawers until he found a yellow sheet of paper on which was written a recipe for rugelachs. It was the old man's recipe, the man who'd given him the inheritance, the man whose inheritance he had blown. Incredibly, Mr. Hibma had all the ingredients he needed.

Preparing the rugelachs did not help. Mr. Hibma got them into the oven, set the timer for twenty-five minutes, and began pacing laps around the inside of his villa. Everything he looked at annoyed him. He fetched a garbage bag from the kitchen and took it to his CD rack. He dropped new wave CD after new wave CD in the bag, until the plastic began to tear. He got another bag for rock, another for classical. He tied the bags and rested them near the door, then advanced to the bedroom and dealt with his wardrobe. His socks had holes in them, T-shirts had pit-stains. He stuffed two more garbage bags. He went to the kitchen, where the rugelachs were almost ready, and disposed of old vitamins and spice bottles and coupons, musty macaroni boxes. He took the rugelachs out of the oven and placed them on a platter to cool. He grabbed all the trash bags he'd filled, heaving them over his shoulders, and lugged them in one load out to the dumpsters.

On the way back, he stopped at the mailboxes. There was a letter, forwarded from Clermont. D. Register. Mr. Hibma rubbed his thumb over the return address. His ears began to buzz. Holy shit, Dale had written him back. Mr. Hibma's forehead tingled. He had no idea who he was. He was in the middle of Florida, at a bank of mailboxes. He sniffed the envelope and it smelled salty. He wasn't going to fumble ripping it open. He was going to tear it evenly across the top.

Mr. H,

I have decided to respond to you even with the risk that your plan is not in earnest, because if you fail to do what you propose, your letters themselves may constitute some sort of art. I understand that this is probably a hoax, but the world needs all kinds of people, even perpetrators of hoaxes.

Mr. Hibma didn't feel stoned anymore. When a stranger from another continent challenges the validity of your very self, you are no longer stoned. Dale had written him back. His letter hadn't been redirected by handlers. Dale was interested in Mr. Hibma. She *wanted* to believe he could kill someone. She wouldn't say that, but Mr. Hibma knew. Inside, she was rooting for him. She believed in his old self, the self from before he'd started trying to change. She wasn't a stranger. Mr. Hibma had something like a friend. For him, this was what a friend was.

Mr. Hibma felt like a con man and he felt gullible. He'd conned himself with this plan to mold himself into a real middle school teacher, a monitor, a mentor, and he'd fallen for it. What was he trying to do to himself—hosting wing meetings and buying greeting cards and forcing his smile on everyone and carrying his burritos across the hall to the lounge to sit in there with the rest of them? He'd seen this as his future and it was coming apart in a matter of moments. He was ashamed. He'd been trying to make things easier on himself, as if they ever could be.

Mr. Hibma went inside and gorged himself on the rugelachs, stopping every couple minutes to read Dale's letter again. It was handwritten. Mr. Hibma had Dale's handwriting and she had his. He was getting grease smudges all over the paper. He didn't care. He had no idea what Dale looked like, and he wished he could picture her at her desk, overlooking Reykjavik, a begrudged grin on her face as she wrote Mr. Hibma's reply. He had no idea if he was conning Dale as he'd conned himself. He had no idea if he could follow through on his proposal, and he didn't expect to know. It wasn't something you guessed at. Mr. Hibma was going to find out if he was indeed a perpetrator of hoaxes. He was going to find out if he could change the basic fabric of his life. He was going to call his own bluff.

PART THREE

His evening free, Toby took a walk with Shelby after track practice. The days were getting longer. The woods were producing that ticking sound that came with heat. They walked alongside a straight country road on a trail beaten into the weeds. They neared the post office and could hear that something was happening on the other side. It was a fundraiser. Toby and Shelby listened to some people talking and understood what it was for. The last train that would ever push itself through Citrus County was scheduled for next Thursday, and after that the tracks would have no use. These people had gathered with the intention of turning the tracks into a bike trail. They *looked* like bikers, most of them. Toby could imagine them wearing fingerless gloves and bright helmets.

"I don't know how I feel about this," Shelby said. "Walking along train tracks is important for little kids."

"I used to do it," said Toby.

They did a lap around the gathering. There were T-shirts, bumper stickers. Someone from a bike shop had a table set up. Everyone was united.

"I'm not going to worry about it," Shelby said. "I'm going to support this." She took a five-dollar bill out of one of her pockets and dropped it in a big jar. "It's not my job to protest things."

"We're entitled to a hot dog," Toby said.

They moved to the refreshment table and picked up hot dogs and cans of soda. There was a backhoe sitting on the edge of the post office lawn, and Toby and Shelby went and sat in the yellow scoop, in the shade. The backhoe was enormous. It was hard to say if its presence was related to the fundraiser.

Toby sipped his soda. He unwrapped his hot dog from many layers of limp tin foil. He felt comfortable with all the people around. He liked being with Shelby when there was no chance of them making out. He watched her open ketchup packets and mustard packets and squeeze them.

"My mom used to take these from places," she said.

Toby didn't really want his hot dog, now that he smelled it. The soda was enough.

"Fast food places," Shelby said. "Even something like this. She'd clean them out. We had buckets of sweetener."

"Were you poor?" Toby asked.

"Not really. *She* was, growing up."

"I don't consider that stealing," Toby said.

"To this day, when I use a big ketchup bottle it feels like a treat."

Shelby stacked the empty packets in the tin foil and balled the foil up. She took a bite of her hot dog. Dusk was coming on, but there were no crickets out or anything. People were still showing up to the gathering, hardly anywhere to park.

"Look at that little thing," Shelby said.

Toby craned his neck. It was a tree frog, right next to Shelby's leg.

It looked frightened. It didn't belong in the scoop of the backhoe, shady spot or not.

"I used to have one of those as a pet," Toby said.

"Did you catch it and keep it in a jar?"

"He appeared in my shower one day. Every time I went in there he was in a different spot."

"Did you name him?"

Toby shook his head. He watched Shelby wipe ketchup off her lip.

"He kept losing color," he said. "See how that one's so green?"

Shelby didn't move away from the frog, but she didn't try to touch it either.

"There was nothing for him to eat. I had to let him go."

Shelby looked at Toby before she finished her hot dog. "That counts," she said. "That's a story you shared with me."

Toby shrugged.

"I'd like to see somebody say it wasn't."

Toby looked over at the crowd. The edge of the backhoe scoop was digging into his legs. He had given Shelby something of himself, but he felt like he'd *gotten* something. He'd given and now he had more. That was the trick. The thing he'd been trying to get from Shelby, whatever it was, he could only get by giving. He could smell Shelby. She smelled like clean, clear water. He moved his hot dog farther away from him. He didn't want to leave the backhoe scoop. In the scoop, he didn't have to think about anything he didn't want to think about.

That night, Toby got his mother's hand mirror and carried it out of his bedroom, out onto the porch, where he sat heavily in Uncle Neal's rocker. He set the mirror in an empty chair, the chair he usually sat in. He wasn't sure how to proceed. He grasped the mirror and looked at himself. His hair had grown to the point where he looked wild, disgraced. Toby had been thrown into the wrong life. He wanted a life where there was nothing between him and Shelby. He wanted to have that life without having to strand Kaley in the bunker. He was a kidnapper and might soon become something worse, but he was still a kid too. He could feel himself as a kid with a ripening heart who looked forward to things, who borrowed his schemes from the same old shelves as everyone else, who loved dumbly like people were meant to.

He would've given anything to go back to the beginning of the semester. There'd been nothing wrong with his old self. He'd been blind, about a lot of things. He saw now that he'd needed Mr. Hibma's detentions. He missed them. In detention, he was a kid. Mr. Hibma was the closest thing Toby'd had to an adult who gave a shit about him. He'd made it seem that Toby's actions had consequences. He'd sat there with Toby, just the two of them, instead of going home, and sometimes the silent air of the classroom had been tinged with relief—Toby and Mr. Hibma, the both of them, relieved to have a part to play. And look at Toby now. He'd been away from the bunker for five days. He could barely get a bite down. He didn't sleep, didn't dream. He knew Kaley was out of food. She was starving and he couldn't eat. As bad as Toby's life had been, he'd never seen a situation as desperate as Kaley's was right now. She was alive, but her thoughts had run out. She probably had no more emotions, not a trace of anger.

Toby looked in the mirror and he couldn't see anything. He had no idea what he felt toward Kaley, if he would be proud of her if she fought for her life. Toby left the mirror and walked into the woods. Sap oozed down the pine trunks and the azalea patches ogled one another. The only clouds that could survive were the nimble, vicious ones. Toby sensed a disturbance above his head and saw a broad web and a spider with yellow stripes. It had caught some hefty, armored, buzz-sawing beetle from somewhere more tropical than Citrus County. It was amazing that the beetle couldn't break the web. It was as caught as caught could be. Every couple minutes, when the beetle stilled, the spider shimmied down toward it, knowing it had to do what spiders did, had to wrap the big sucker and administer the poison. When the spider got close, the beetle would flail for all it was worth, quaking the web, almost flinging the spider to the ground. The spider would retreat, wait a minute, then try again. Retreat. Try again. This went on and on.

Shelby had been enjoying a dream about gangs of sly otters who could convince women to do anything. But then she smelled something and the otters were gone. It was morning. The smell wasn't part of the dream. There'd been a scent in the dream, but not a savory one. There'd been the scent of wet eyelashes. Shelby didn't know where this new smell was coming from. She kept her eyes shut, didn't look at the clock. Bacon and maybe something baking. She heard footsteps up the hall and a knock. The door creaked open. Shelby knew it was her father. She rolled and let light into her eyes, her hands shooting down instinctively to make sure she was decent, that she hadn't writhed her pajamas up or shucked them off. She looked at the head poking into her doorway and it took her an exhausting moment to know that it was indeed her father. He'd shaved his beard. Clean-shaven, Shelby's father looked vulnerable. The skin on the bottom half of his face was gray, unseasoned.

"Be in the kitchen in five minutes," he said, and Shelby could see the words being formed in his throat and born out his lips. He made a frisky motion with his eyes, then withdrew his head.

What now? Shelby thought. He'd cooked breakfast, like the old days. No one had cooked breakfast in their kitchen in forever.

Shelby slipped on a pair of her army pants and a tank top. There was so much to shelter her father from, so many threats to deflect. She wasn't sure she had the energy.

In the kitchen, Shelby saw five or six waffles piled on a plate, more on the way.

"When did we get a waffle iron?" she asked, taking a seat.

"Wedding present," Shelby's fathered answered. "It was in the attic."

"This house has an attic?"

"It's more of a closet in the ceiling." Shelby's father moved the syrup from the counter to the table, pulled two short glasses from a cabinet. He was jittery, as if afraid to lose momentum. He poured Shelby some juice, and then she noticed the juicer and a stack of grapefruit carcasses. There was bacon, too. He pushed a plate of it toward her.

"I didn't know we had a juicer, either," Shelby said.

"I got it when we moved down here." Shelby's father picked up a napkin and wiped his mouth, though he wasn't eating anything.

Shelby sipped her grapefruit juice. She squeezed syrup onto her plate and dipped a strip of bacon in it. She ate that strip and then another and then another. She grabbed a waffle. Her father was staring at her—a heavy stare, full of blatant pride.

"I'm going to ignore my real feelings," he said. "I'm going to make my real feelings think they're barking up the wrong tree."

Shelby's throat was thick with bacon. She wanted to hug her father or say something supportive. She saw herself doing it, hopping up and giving him a big squeeze around his trim waist and saying just the right thing, but she couldn't get out of her chair. She couldn't do more than sit there, cutting up her waffle.

"I'm taking you to St. Pete," he said. "The Dalí museum, then an early dinner at the pier."

Shelby pushed her plate away, suddenly full. "An outing," she said.

"That's what it'll be."

Shelby rose and went to her room. She put on lip-gloss and a lime-colored dress, then she brushed her hair.

When she went out to the living room she found her father watching the preview channel, a scroll of all the programs that would air in the next couple hours. He looked overwhelmed. Shelby didn't see the remote. She went over to the TV and shut it off, stood before it and did a spin, her dress flaring at the bottom. Her father was trying and she was going to help him if she could.

Outside, her father opened her car door, ushering her. They drove down Route 19 in his plain sedan, then cut over to the expressway. They were both daunted by the silence in the car. Shelby had removed Kaley's car seat weeks ago, but it was still impossible not to notice the lack of Kaley in the back seat, singing and asking questions and thumping the passenger seat with her blunt little shoes. Shelby knew what point her father had reached. He had nothing left but hope and prayer and things like that. He'd reached the point where there were no more physical actions he could take, nothing to do but accept that he'd lost the fight for his youngest daughter and had to move on to other fights. He kept clicking the radio off and on, trolling the static-plagued stations.

"Let's not talk about her today," Shelby said.

Shelby's father patted her arm. He opened his window and turned the radio up. The station was an adult contemporary outfit from Tarpon Springs. They played a couple songs by Neil Diamond or whoever, then the DJ began plugging a bunch of charities.

Shelby loved the paintings of the desert. Though she'd never been to one, she loved deserts. She would save them until she was old; she would not visit a desert until she felt death nearing. The docent at the museum was infatuated with Shelby's father. She looked only at him when she spoke, and he kept ignoring her, gazing at the paintings.

Shelby decided that she was not utterly desperate. She decided she did not need hopes and dreams. She had a good dad to help and an interesting aunt to visit and a boy to chase. She was going to sit back and watch things get better. If she wanted an open destiny, she had to allow that destiny to take shape.

It had been a week. Nights and days. Too many hours to count. Toby couldn't stay away any longer. He had to see. Whatever it was, he had to see. Before school, he looped around toward the bunker, this long route to Citrus Middle that had once been a thrill and then a chore and then a ruinous routine and this day was a relief. Toby's feet knew where to step. His mind was losing darkness with the coming dawn. He felt old in his bones. He felt like the old man everyone had assumed he was.

He stepped over a fallen branch, heavy with young green acorns, and rounded the last pinch of a turn and when he came near he could plainly see that the bunker door was flipped open. He came to a stop, hoping the unfinished light was playing a trick on him. He knew it was no trick. Toby felt that he had a moment before he'd drown in panic. He breathed the morning air. He had a moment before his ears would shut down with heat. His legs started up again. He was approaching the open bunker. The woods were the color of pencil lead.

The broomstick was jammed in the latch. Kaley had forced the door open with a broomstick. The latch was probably broken now. Toby looked in and saw the cot against the wall and saw Kaley's fallen tower. She'd stacked blankets and pillows and cases of canned goods and the books Toby had brought her and she'd used the bucket the cleaning products were kept in and she'd pushed the latch open and pulled herself out. Toby had no idea when.

Time hadn't stopped. Minutes were still passing. Minutes could make the sun rise. Without minutes, there were no days, no years. Toby wondered if Kaley had been cooking this up for a long while or if she'd acted out of desperation. He wondered how many times she'd tried to reach the latch, constructed her tower and failed and waited it out for more building materials, or had Toby's absence prompted her to rely on herself? She was recast now. She had her own schemes. Her story was her own.

Toby dropped his book bag on the ground and pulled on his mask. He began jogging circles around the bunker, winding wider each time. He could've run forever. He didn't know if Kaley had been out for days or if she'd waited for the first light in the clogged vents this very morning. He knew she hadn't been discovered, rescued. Toby would've heard. He had to get to her before anyone else did. She couldn't be found anywhere close to the bunker, anywhere close to Uncle Neal's property. Toby's fingerprints were all over the bunker. What Toby could not think about was that she might be dead. He might find her dead or fail to find her, dead. All he had was what he felt, and he felt that she was alive.

The light was thickening. Toby knew Kaley hadn't found her way to the road. She hadn't gotten close enough to hear the cars whizzing past on 19. She was still in these woods. Toby was nowhere near stopping. He weaved around thickets and ducked low branches, his mask already sopping with sweat. Colors were showing now, the green leaves and white bay flowers and red azaleas. The kidnapping was, for the first time, just between Toby and Kaley. It had nothing to do with Toby's evil destiny, nothing to do with Shelby or her father, nothing to do with Uncle Neal, Toby's mother. It was just a crime, a violation of certain laws. The authorities couldn't punish Toby, but there were other punishments.

Toby was slowing. He'd thought he could run forever but he couldn't. His next lap would take him almost onto Uncle Neal's property, almost out to the swamp that extended back and blended into the springs. Toby thought he could hear the cars on 19, all rushing to get someplace important. He slowed to a walk. He had no bearing on the speed of the minutes. The minutes were not aware of his situation. He recognized every scent on the morning air, each of them full and slow. He pressed his palm against the rough bark of an oak tree as he stepped past it.

When he saw Kaley's stubbly orange hair reflecting the first honest morning rays, it took him a moment to believe it. He saw her skin and her scuffed white shoes. She was standing still. She was standing. She didn't see Toby yet. He watched her. She kept looking this way and that, deciding which way to go, her head full of her own thoughts. She couldn't move. She seemed not to want to. The cars could be heard, faintly, and their noise came from every direction.

Toby walked up and Kaley didn't run. Her face lost its alertness. She wasn't scared or defiant. Toby didn't know what to do. He felt he had no right to drag her, to pick her up or manhandle her. He felt unwilling. He felt like pointing Kaley in the direction of the road and nudging her into motion. He wanted someone to step in now, someone who knew what he was doing.

Toby made a noise and Kaley moved toward him. She wasn't serene or panicked. She may have felt just like Toby. He knew to begin walking and she walked next to him and he led her back to the bunker. They were far away from it, maybe half a mile. Toby felt like a tyrant. It wasn't merely a violation of laws.

"I'm sorry," he whispered. It was the first time he'd ever spoken to her.

She didn't look up. She kept dragging her feet through swaths of weeds, knocking the frail flowers onto the floor of the woods.

At school, Toby was feverish. He walked to class after class and then he walked to the lunchroom. The screeching of the other students, the reek of the county pizzas under the heat lamps, the fluorescent light glaring off the linoleum. He sidled back out against a current of bodies and found a quiet hallway. He walked as slowly as he could, perusing the tacked signs. Most of the classrooms were empty. Toby strolled down near the band room and back.

He went up the eighth-grade liberal arts wing, ducking under an ornate banner. He approached the teachers' lounge and could hear them inside—Mrs. Conner and the lady who taught Spanish. He hugged the opposite wall so he wouldn't be seen out the little window. Here was Mr. Hibma's door, open a crack. The lights were off but Toby heard a noise, a crunching sound. He nudged the door open and stepped inside, feeling like he was trespassing but also like he'd found an oasis. He couldn't remember being here just an hour before, sitting in this room for class. He recognized the noise now, a pencil being sharpened. He saw Mr. Hibma's desk. Mr. Hibma slouched in his chair, his back to Toby, turning the crank on the sharpener, which was bolted onto a big steel cabinet. The microwave beeped, startling Toby, and he looked over and saw a burrito in it. It smelled as bad as the county pizzas.

"Mr. Hibma," Toby said, not wanting to be loud but wanting to be heard.

Mr. Hibma's head moved slightly and his cranking let up. He didn't answer Toby, though. He began cranking faster, before stopping and sighing and holding the pencil in the air. The pencil was a nub, just the eraser and a point. Mr. Hibma dropped it in the trash.

"I'm supposed to be in lunch," Toby offered.

Mr. Hibma looked at the clock without curiosity. "What can I do for you, Toby?"

Toby had never seen Mr. Hibma humorless. He was like a dying plant.

"I need to talk to you," Toby said.

Toby had departed the lunchroom and had made his way to the liberal arts wing, had come into Mr. Hibma's classroom and was now standing here staring at his geography teacher. His stomach was a stone. Mr. Hibma was the only adult who could help or hurt him. Toby cleared his throat.

"I'm not really the problem guy," Mr. Hibma said.

"You are for me," said Toby.

"I wanted to be the problem guy, but I can't. At this point, I'm getting by hour by hour, class by class."

"That's how I get by," Toby told him.

Mr. Hibma splayed his fingers on the desk. "You've still got a chance, but it's too late for me."

"I came here to say something," Toby said. "Not to listen."

"Do you think you're my favorite or something? I gave you all those detentions because that's what teachers do and I was trying to be a teacher. I don't have a favorite. If you want to be somebody's favorite, start kissing ass. Definitely *don't* bother people during lunch."

Toby used the sound of Mr. Hibma's voice to brace himself. "You have to fix something for me," he said. "I don't want detention. I want to be in *real* trouble."

"You're not going to be young much longer." Mr. Hibma did something drastic with his mouth, some kind of smile. "Don't waste time trying to tell people about your problems. Do things that are youthful until you're not allowed to do them anymore."

The microwave beeped again. This time Mr. Hibma rose and pulled the burrito out with a paper towel and set it on a counter. He didn't return to his chair.

"That girlfriend of yours, I'd concentrate on her and quit going around seeking advice. It doesn't become you."

"I've never asked advice. You're thinking of someone else. Advice can't help me."

"You stole something or you broke something. That's all any of you kids can do."

"And what can *you* do?" said Toby. "I bet I can do worse things than you can."

Mr. Hibma glowered at Toby. Whatever he was feeling toward Toby, it was pure. Toby was catching up with the moment. Mr. Hibma was blowing him off, and he was allowing Mr. Hibma to do so. "You're not tough," Toby said. "Whatever other problems you have, another is that you're not a tough person."

Mr. Hibma pressed his thumb into his jaw. "That hasn't been decided yet," he said.

Toby had gone against his own closely held wisdom, had gone and tried to bring something important to an adult, and he was getting what he deserved. He felt he could breathe again. Mr. Hibma didn't seem to have anything else to say.

"I better go," Toby said. "Before the pizza's all gone."

"None of this is personal," Mr. Hibma told him. "Nothing, you'll find, is personal."

Mr. Hibma taxied past several pawnshops, a barber, a new chain restaurant that had decided to give Citrus County a whirl. He passed a sign warning drivers to watch for bears. WEST CITRUS U-STOR. There it was, the mini-storage complex owned by Mrs. Conner and her husband. Mr. Hibma parked and went into the office, where he was greeted by a woman about his age who wore a ball cap. The Conners weren't around, the woman told Mr. Hibma. "Just you and me," she said. She smiled and jutted her hip. It seemed to Mr. Hibma that this woman liked him, and he combated this by acting businesslike. He asked for a price list and chose a 13 x 9 unit that went for $51 a month. Mr. Hibma picked out a heavy lock. He wrote the woman in the ball cap a check, waited for the code to the gate, then went into the storage area and drove around until he located C-63. It was cool, and taller than it was wide. Mr. Hibma fetched a lawn chair from his trunk, a pad and pen, and a tall can of iced tea. He pulled the door of his storage unit down, sequestering himself inside.

Renting this place was the next phase in Mr. Hibma's campaign of friendliness toward Mrs. Conner. He'd begun bringing her coffee each morning, delivering it right to her classroom, and she was more or less eating out of his hand. When Mr. Hibma told Mrs. Conner about his acquisition of one of her storage units, he would gain her absolute trust. She would say nice things about him behind his back, stick up for him if other teachers gossiped about him.

Mr. Hibma had unfettered himself from the delusional project to mold himself into a standard-issue teacher, and he'd come to realize that all the energy he'd expended winning his victim over had not been in vain. It had been necessary. Everyone knew Mrs. Conner and Mr. Hibma were getting along now. When she turned up dead, Mr. Hibma could cry and express outrage like everyone else. He could say, "Why *now*, when I'd just realized what an inspirational, dynamic person she was?" He would mourn with the passion of the convert that everyone believed him to be. Everything was setting up for Mr. Hibma. He had to grit his teeth and weather the home stretch of the school year. It would take forever but it would also go by in a blink. If he couldn't bring himself to do what needed to be done, it would be because of his weakness and nothing else. Mr. Hibma didn't especially feel like a murderer, but maybe you didn't until you murdered. He had never felt, particularly, like a non-murderer. Someone had to commit all these murders that were always being committed. Why not him? Why couldn't his story be the story of a killer?

Mr. Hibma placed his lawn chair near the back wall and stayed quiet, the only noise the air conditioner, which was humping to keep the place at 78 degrees. He wondered what secrets were hidden in this place. What darkness had West Citrus U-Stor witnessed before Mr. Hibma happened along? What damning evidence was tucked away in these shadowy alcoves? None, maybe. Maybe it was all disassembled futons and china sets.

Mr. Hibma knew what the place smelled like. It smelled like his childhood attic—not a unique odor, just cardboard and mothballs. He wished he could remember more about his childhood, the period before adolescence, before his harrowing navigation of puberty. Those years when Mr. Hibma was a simple little fellow, wanting only to play and be fed and kept warm, looking up at the world without suspicion, were blurry. He recalled them in unsatisfying flashes.

He looked at the ceiling. He felt like he could hear his organs working, the muffled swishing of his heart. He felt the weight of his body pressing down on the chair. Mr. Hibma wondered what would have happened to him had he not been rescued from that nurse as an infant. She must've wanted a child badly, to give up her profession and commit a felony. Maybe she didn't want just *any* child; maybe she'd fallen head-over-heels for Mr. Hibma, she who'd seen thousands of newborns. It was plausible that the love the nurse had for Mr. Hibma was the strongest anyone would ever have for him. On the other hand, maybe Mr. Hibma would've died had his parents not reclaimed him. On the *other* other hand, maybe he was *supposed* to have died. Maybe he was only supposed to have been in the world for several days, not several decades.

Mr. Hibma put his pen down. He opened his can of iced tea and drank from it. He'd figured out what to do about his lost grade book. He would institute an unfathomable system of extra credit. The system would be applied retroactively, muddying the waters of quiz averages and presentation scores to the point where even the most fastidious kiss-ass could not question her grade. Mr. Hibma's new grade book would be a tornado of asterisks, checks, plus signs, plus signs within circles, smiley faces, and all in different colors, all blown about the columns at random. Under this system, the rich would get richer and the poor would also get some help.

Mr. Hibma heard a woman in clackety shoes enter the building. She walked past his unit and stopped a ways down the hall. There was the sound of a sliding door, what sounded like a huge deck of playing cards getting shuffled, and then the door sliding shut. The click of a lock. When the woman walked back by, her steps made a cushiony sound. She was wearing sneakers now. When the woman had exited and the door had closed behind her, Mr. Hibma took up his pad and pen. He had waited a few days so he wouldn't seem anxious. So he wouldn't say more than he wanted to say.

> D,
>
> My victim is tiny-minded and big-footed. There are several million like her but she is the one who matters to me. It is meant to be my plight to be tortured by her and women like her my entire life, and to never do anything about it except grow bitter, but I will shape the story of my life the way I want it shaped. I am no one's sad sack character.
>
> Mr. H

Toby walked onto the school grounds and went into the common area and sat on some carpeted steps until the warning bell sounded, then he rose and trudged toward the library to return his pole-vaulting manual and pay his fine. He sat through math and biology, skipped Mr. Hibma's class, then, during lunch, went outside near the portables. He'd avoided Shelby all day. He didn't want to be at school at all, but he didn't want to be at home either. The pole vault season was ending that evening and if he hadn't shown up at school then he wouldn't be allowed to participate. For some reason, he cared about finishing the season. He wanted to do something the way it was meant to be done. One thing. Toby had been the first alternate for this final county meet and the kid ahead of him had come down with bronchitis. Toby was going to face the Asian kid.

That afternoon, at the meet, Toby felt an odd lack of pressure. Shelby, sitting in the stands with her knees together and her lips pursed, did not make him nervous. Coach Scolle did not make him uneasy with his disdainful looks. Toby knew that it was all busywork. You were supposed to be cheerful about the busywork and worry about the busywork, but Toby could do neither at the moment. All he could do was succumb to it. This track meet was busywork. Dreaming was busywork. Coin flips were busywork. The Asian kid called tails. The coin broke the peak of its arch and began zipping toward the ground and Toby shot his hand out and caught it.

Another Sunday. Toby rose and put on shorts and shoes. He went to the kitchen for a handful of cereal, slugged it down with a sip of sports drink. Uncle Neal was in the living room, a room that went mostly unused, sitting on a folding chair. The last time Uncle Neal had been sitting in that spot was the day he'd hit Toby. Uncle Neal was crying or something. A book was open in his hands. When he saw Toby he pulled himself together with one great sob. His face was red, his eyebrows disarranged.

"What about the shed?" Toby asked him. "No hemlock today?"

"Done already," said Uncle Neal. He guided the book closed, looking up at Toby.

The book had small smudgy paintings on its cover.

"I found this," Uncle Neal said, trying to boast. "I rescued it from the trash."

"What trash?"

"At that big gas station by the county buildings."

The book was a collection of poetry. Uncle Neal combed his fingers over the front of it, like he was petting a cat. He snorted. "I'm getting bored with listening to the cops," he told Toby. "I haven't read a book since I was your age, and I want to read one more before it's too late. It was on the very top of the garbage, on top of a newspaper."

"Is it any good?"

"'Forgive, Satan, virtue's pedants.'" Uncle Neal raised an eyebrow. His throat was full. "'All such as have broken our habits, or had none, the keepers of promises, prizewinners, meek as leaves in the wind's circus.'"

Toby squinted. He was thinking about the poem or he was pretending to. He couldn't tell.

"Who needs a mother?" Uncle Neal said. "Mothers aren't everything. I had one, and look how I turned out."

Uncle Neal's smugness was still intact. His eyes were glassy, but he was smug as ever. Toby wanted to snatch his book from him and smack him with it.

"All mothers do is make sure you're presentable," Uncle Neal said. "You look presentable to me. I guess presentable for *what* is always the question."

"Do me a favor," Toby said. "Don't ever talk about my mother." Toby had caught Uncle Neal's bloodshot eyes and he didn't let go. He looked right through his uncle. "Do me a favor and don't mention mothers to me for any reason, ever again." He said this levelly, just the way he wanted to.

The old smirk came to life on Uncle Neal's lips. "Okay," he told Toby. "But now you're going to owe *me* a favor."

Shelby was getting to know the woods. She had a good idea where even the minor trails led. She knew where the turtle holes were, knew how to avoid the darkly shaded territories where snakes were likely to loiter. There were direct routes and routes that someone generous or ignorant might call scenic, half-a-dozen ways to reach the library. The substation looked dormant. There was an unfathomable current running through it, but it looked dead. The high school boys that hung out in the parking lot, crouching on their skateboards and sharing cigarettes, now recognized Shelby. As she passed, one of them doffed his cap and the rest of them laughed.

Inside, she signed up to use a computer. There was a line. She stepped over to a podium which upheld a monumental atlas. Bulgaria. The capital city was Sofia. Shelby had never heard of Sofia. It was the capital city of a major nation and she had never even heard of it. Mr. Hibma's geography class was fairly useless when it came to geography. There were thousands of countries, and Shelby had only been in one. In over thirteen years, she'd managed to experience one nation.

Shelby shut the atlas and found a chair off by herself, near the old card catalog. She breathed the library air, which smelled like all library air. She wanted it to be a cozy smell, like blankets from an old farmhouse or something, but really it smelled like book glue and old people. Shelby was worried about Toby. She wasn't intrigued by his darkness anymore, didn't burn to plumb the depths of it. She cared for Toby. She knew Uncle Neal was doing something to Toby, not just the marks on his head and neck that time, but more damaging things. Something had worn the Toby out of Toby. She wanted to know exactly what went on out at that remote property. She didn't want to go gallivanting off to a distant country without being sure Toby would be okay. She couldn't leave him to the wolves, and that's what Uncle Neal was. Toby was Shelby's affair and she had to get him in order before she left.

It was her turn on a computer. She scrubbed her eyes with her palms then logged on and went to her e-mail. Inbox—one new message.

> Niece of mine,
>
> Not much new over here. Interesting things occur less frequently than they used to—generally, in the world. I quit coffee. That's something, I guess. And I did this thing where you jump in freezing cold water for charity. It's like you have to do one or the other in the morning—drink coffee or jump in ice water. Well, sorry to cut this short but I'm late for a flight and I can't find anything.
>
> Aunt Dale

Still no allusion, as of yet, to Shelby visiting. Coffee or ice water. Shelby's aunt was a very busy individual with an ever-changing schedule. She was probably wary of inviting Shelby and then having to cancel, or having to work the whole time Shelby was visiting. Late for a flight. Shelby wished *she* were late for a flight. Aunt Dale was casual about these things, that was all. She wasn't a person who had to plot everything out way in advance. That's why she hadn't married that guy she'd been seeing forever; she didn't like to be hemmed in.

But Shelby didn't like that Aunt Dale seemed to struggle to find something to write. None of her previous e-mails had felt that way. Maybe Shelby ought to e-mail less often; maybe she was burning Aunt Dale out. It just wasn't Shelby's way to play hard to get. Her way was to hint, and if that didn't work, to come right out and take what she wanted.

She jostled the mouse and clicked on Reply.

> I've been wishing I could ride a train through the countryside, not one of our musty Amtraks, but a train where they serve soft cheese and pressed coffee and there's a lounge car full of fascinating people with red lips who all speak different languages and you sleep in a pitch dark bunk and in the morning there are snowy mountains out the window that make you feel small and safe.

One morning when Mr. Hibma had arrived at school early in order to map out his next few basketball practices, Mrs. Conner appeared in the doorway of his classroom. He had a notepad in his hands full of Xs and Os, new drills that would help his guards defend against backdoor cuts. He put the notepad down and looked up at Mrs. Conner and she invited him to come over and look at her books, to see if there were any he wanted. The lot of them were destined for a shelter her church supported, but she wanted to give Mr. Hibma a chance to pick them over first. She was making a gesture. Mr. Hibma had made his gestures and now she was making one.

He followed her into her classroom and it smelled like soap and coffee. It was a big corner room, windows on two sides. She pulled back the doors of a towering cabinet and a thousand spines spied out at Mr. Hibma. As he scanned the shelves, she told him she was honored that he'd chosen to entrust his possessions to her and her husband, that West Citrus U-Stor was the best facility in their region of Florida. She thanked Mr. Hibma for the calendar he'd bought her, one of those where you peel a sheet off for each day. The theme was little-known grammar rules. Mrs. Conner had it on her desk at home.

Most of the books in the cabinet weren't really books. They were books *about* books, manuals that instructed one how to teach certain books. There were collections of writing exercises, guides for building a curriculum. Mr. Hibma's eye was caught by a thick poetry anthology. He worked it out a couple inches and then pulled it off the shelf. Another anthology, essays about Florida cuisine. There was a *Complete Works of Shakespeare.* It was a fancy edition—probably a hundred bucks in a bookstore.

"I've never been able to understand Shakespeare," Mrs. Conner said. She whispered, but not like she was hiding anything. "I can follow the plots because it's right there in the teacher's edition, but I can't follow it line to line."

Mr. Hibma set the Shakespeare on top of the stack he had going near his feet. Mrs. Conner's face was deeply reflective.

"And those are the first ones you go for," she said. "The Shakespeare and the poetry. I kind of gloss over that unit every year. I show the movies."

Mr. Hibma looked at Mrs. Conner and he could imagine her dead without much effort. He didn't hate her. He didn't feel anything as strong as hate. That was good; he didn't want to murder someone because he hated them. He didn't want to commit a crime of passion. She would be quiet after Mr. Hibma killed her, and she would be a bluish color. Mr. Hibma had even less regard for her, seeing how easily he'd gained her confidence. She had no loyalty, not even to her own grudges. Mr. Hibma was a pet of hers, another of her successes.

"I'm not like you," Mrs. Conner said. She tapped Mr. Hibma on the forearm. "I'm not smart like you are." She tipped her face to his and then left the room, trusting Mr. Hibma, giving him time to look her books over in private.

A biography of the author of *The Yearling*. A biography of Dickens. Mr. Hibma couldn't concentrate on the titles. He didn't want any more of these books. He felt he had to take some, though. He felt like a child, alone in Mrs. Conner's classroom. He felt like a child who was being given too much slack.

Toby was not wandering the wilderness. He was taking a stroll like any reasonable person. He had made up his mind. At the end of the week, on Friday night, the same night of the week he'd taken her, he was going to bind Kaley's wrists and ankles, tape her mouth, stuff her in his rucksack, and return her to her home. Toby would be a failure, but he would be free. He'd be doing the right thing. Toby remembered when Shelby's father had spoken to the cameras. He remembered forgetting his thermos, the smell of the Register house. He hadn't been back inside it. He was afraid of that house. The last thing he wanted to do was bully Kaley again, be forced to physically move her. And this time he'd do it with open eyes, he'd do it without the strange trance he'd fallen into when he'd taken her. This had been the only answer all along, he saw. There was no more room for cowardice. He had to undo what he'd done. He had to cover the same tracks in the opposite direction, lugging Kaley, lighter on his back though older. Whatever he'd done to Kaley would be over. He could end this and she could begin recovering. And then Toby could be with Shelby. He'd been Shelby's greatest enemy and now he'd be her greatest ally, and she'd never know about any of it. They could start over. They could be themselves. They could find out what their selves were.

Toby wouldn't have to go in the house; he could leave Kaley on the porch or even the edge of the yard. He would leave her at the edge of the Register yard, and in case she didn't work her way free of the bag, he would leave an alarm clock resting nearby on the grass. He would get one of those extra-loud alarm clocks meant for old people—steal it from the drugstore, he supposed. He would never have to wear the mask again. He would burn the mask, burn it to get rid of it but also burn it because he hated it. He'd worn it to hide his identity and now he wore it out of shame. Toby kept strolling. Things were coming clear. He felt a little like his old self, resourceful and lean, nothing to worry about but getting caught. He felt simple again; he had an operation to execute and he would either be caught red-handed and take what was coming to him or he would get away with it. But Toby knew no one would catch him. He knew the woods. He knew the night.

Earlier that day, after school, he had carried his mother's mirror out to the delivery bay. He'd knocked it against a steel corner of one of the dumpsters hard enough to run cracks through the glass, reached his arm into the dumpster, held the mirror as far down as he could, and released it. The mirror couldn't help him and he didn't want help. His mother couldn't help him. Mr. Hibma couldn't help him. Nothing could. Toby was a shade of gray, like the rest. And maybe now he could be happy like the rest. He could be an idiot punk with just enough poison in his heart to make a fool of himself. He could be another punk with a girlfriend who was too good for him. Toby wasn't evil and he wasn't meant to get Bs and pole vault. His real self was the petty vandal who broke bird eggs and made prank phone calls. His real self wanted to flirt with the world like everyone else, flirt with trouble and flirt with Shelby and flirt with whatever else came along. He wasn't meant for damage, only damage control. Someone else should've found the bunker.

Toby halted. It was the spider web with the big beetle in it. The beetle was dried up and dead, its armor still shiny. It wasn't wrapped. The spider was nowhere to be found, the web in disrepair. The spider had given up and abandoned its web. A breeze that Toby couldn't feel was swaying the loose filaments about. Toby reached with a stick and destroyed what was left, the beetle carcass dropping to the floor of the woods and getting lost.

Shelby was lying out in the sun. She was on her back patio where she'd spread a few towels and brought out a throw pillow for her head, the telephone, an apple. Very soon, tomorrow maybe, she was going to start eating correctly—healthy foods in decent quantities. Very soon she was going to start reading again, real reading. Not today, but soon. She was going to go on an overseas trip to a strange, cold country. She was going to get a tan first. She would be exotic with her tropical glow. She'd be cupping hot beverages and eating eel and meeting musicians and buying boots that were at once rugged and soft. She'd mingle with faceted Icelandic teenagers, rather than with skateboarders and Baptists. When she returned, she'd gaze upon the burnt yards of Citrus County with forbearance, with neutrality. She'd tell Toby every single thing about her trip, every solitary detail.

It was one in the afternoon. Shelby had left school during her lunch period, cutting psychology and algebra out of her day, and it felt like a sound decision. She felt better off. This was one thing she would make no promises about; she would continue to skip school whenever she felt it would benefit her, whenever she felt school would do her no good. She had her science book on the patio with her, and also an erotic novel, and she planned to switch back and forth chapter for chapter.

Shelby perused the periodic table of elements for fifteen minutes, cooling her mind with rows of letters and numbers, then slid the science book aside and flipped onto her back. She opened *The Wild, Warm Winter of Shauna Black*. A girl in her twenties, a virgin, went to a bar and picked out a guy and they went to a hotel. The girl was scared, wouldn't come out of the bathroom. Description of the bathroom. Guy talking his way into the bathroom. Kissing and whispering. Fingers slipping beneath panties. In the space of the next paragraph, the author referred to Shauna's nether regions a dozen different ways, in painstaking detail, dragging each moment out and piling on the adjectives. And surprisingly, it was effective. It was working on Shelby. At the same time as she felt the tightness and tingle of the sun doing its work on her tummy and thighs, she felt the perk of sex inside her. Shauna was holding herself back, reluctant to give up what she had held dear for so long. Shelby rolled on her side, collecting herself before going further. She was sweating. The man clutched Shauna high on the leg and put her where he wanted her. He unbuttoned her blouse, put his thumb in her mouth. Shelby put her own thumb to her lips. She could hear the sound of bees.

The phone rang and Shelby flinched. She shut the book and flopped her arm behind her, finding first the apple and then wrapping her pinkie around the hot metal antenna. She squeezed the phone in her hands, stifling everything she was feeling in her body, blocking out the sun and blocking out what was happening to Shauna in the hotel room.

She pushed the Talk button and said hello.

The voice on the other end was composed, with the slightest grain to it—a man's voice. "I'm looking for Mr. Ben Register."

"You've got his secretary."

"My name is Finch Warren."

"I've never heard of you."

"Most people haven't," Finch said.

"It's 1:45 in the afternoon. Don't you think my father might be at work?"

"You're the older sister," Finch said.

"Now I'm just a secretary."

Finch cleared his throat. "I'm a writer. I teach at USF. I wrote a memoir that was short-listed for the Blackburn-Hickey award. I want to write a book about you and your father." He cleared his throat again.

"I'm still here," said Shelby. "I haven't hung up as of yet."

"I thought we could take a cut of the proceeds and do something for Kaley, like dedicate a scholarship in her name."

"*I'm* going to need a scholarship before long," Shelby said.

"You won't need a scholarship if this book does what I think it will."

Shelby opened her science book and looked down at a diagram that explained nuclear energy. She didn't hear bees anymore. There were drowsy clouds spread evenly across the sky.

"I can get my own scholarship," Shelby said. "I'm going to start getting back on top of my grades, Finch. Me and my dad are going to start getting on top of things, and I appreciate your interest but I'm afraid we're not going to have anything to do with your book. I've heard you out and given you an answer."

"I wouldn't prefer to do the book without you."

"Of course you wouldn't," Shelby said.

"Maybe you should take a little time to think about it. Talk it over with your dad."

"It doesn't take me long to think. I'm fast and accurate when it comes to thinking."

Shelby picked up the apple. Her limbs were heavy. The phone felt like a brick. She thanked Finch for his time and got off the phone. She knew she ought to feel insulted by someone suggesting that money be made off Kaley's disappearance, but she didn't. Finch Warren was doing his job. Everyone in the world, they were just doing whatever they got paid for.

Shelby carried the phone inside and put it on its cradle in the kitchen. She could feel all the shame in her. Not for any specific deed—shame for being able to carry on. She could eat, put on clothes, read trashy books, clean house, make summer plans, worry about things going sour with a boy. Shelby was not a good person. Her mother had hardened a portion of her and her sister another portion and now she wasn't a good person.

She was still holding the apple. She dropped it in the trash, then stood at the kitchen sink and drank a glass of water. She went to the patio, gathered everything into the blanket and hauled it inside. Shelby picked up the Shauna Black novel and her stomach felt sick, like the water she'd drank had been sour milk. She took the book to the kitchen and rested it in the trash can. After a moment, she pushed it down under the other trash.

On Sunday Mr. Hibma's girls had dispatched Pasco Middle, the black school, by thirteen points. Though Pasco was in a rebuilding year and three of their starters had been suffering from the flu, this was still something to be proud of for Citrus. All that build-up for Pasco, and then it hadn't even been a close game. Pasco seemed to concede early in the second half, shorthanded as they were. They didn't put on a pressure defense. They didn't take quick shots. When the clock ticked down to all zeroes, the Pasco players absorbed the loss with a dignity that diffused any desire on the part of the Citrus players for a raucous celebration. Even Rosa and Sherrie lined up and shook hands. The win had vaulted Mr. Hibma's squad into the district semifinals, and he'd given them two days off from practicing, telling them to recharge and get ready to play by Wednesday night. Mr. Hibma tried to enjoy the win, but he found that winning was not what he relished; it was seeing the other guy lose. He loved to see his opponent frustrated, and Pasco hadn't given him that.

Now it was Wednesday evening, back at the gym, and Mr. Hibma was thrown a nasty curve. An hour prior to the game, with his players straggling in and starting to stretch, a girl wearing a choker walked up to Mr. Hibma and handed him a folded sheet of paper. The girl stared at Mr. Hibma and he stared at her. This girl knew how to deliver bad news. She was a pro. The moment Mr. Hibma looked down at the note and began to unfold it, the girl spun and sashayed out, her heels slapping in her sandals.

> Mr. Hibma,
>
> Rosa and I can't play anymore. We wanted to beat Pasco and we did that. We're going to states in shot and discus and that's priority. Thanks for being our coach. Thank the girls for being our teammates.
>
> Sherrie

Mr. Hibma let the girls mill about, let them run their layup lines. He could tell they were wondering about Rosa and Sherrie, hoping they'd had a flat tire or woken up late from a nap, hoping they'd bustle through the double doors any minute, polishing off some tacos, yanking off their warm-ups. The Citrus fans—an ever-growing contingent of boyfriends, a few parents, a smattering of bored elderly—were also worrying about Rosa and Sherrie. The other team was looking down toward Mr. Hibma; they'd noticed, too. The Dade Chargers: solid and unspectacular. They'd advanced to the semis by making free throws and not turning the ball over. This was how they won; they showed up with their sound fundamentals and waited for something to go wrong with the opponent.

When there were twenty minutes to tip, Mr. Hibma pulled his team into the locker room.

"They're not coming," Mr. Hibma said. "So there it is. This is no time for looking around and blinking. Rosa and Sherrie are off the team. And that, just then, was the last time we're ever going to mention them." Mr. Hibma allowed a moment of silence, a period of grief. When he spoke again, his girls would know they were expected to be recovered from the loss of their largest, meanest comrades.

Mr. Hibma knelt in front of his point guard, his hands on her bony knees. "I want you to push the ball every single time you get it. Even if you're one on five, you push all the way into the lane and figure out what to do when you get there."

The point guard nodded. She liked having a lot asked of her.

"Under what circumstances will you walk the ball up?"

"None," she answered.

Mr. Hibma moved on to the fast girl, told her she was going to be the star of the game, that she was going to make a dozen layups. He told the three-point-shooting twins to stay right next to each other the whole game, to set screens for one another like a revolving door. Mr. Hibma had instructions for everyone. His troops were captivated. He stood back and addressed the whole team.

"You all know what's going to happen on Thursday," he said. "We're going to run into Ocala. We're going to be outclassed. We're going to be outcoached. Ocala is in better shape than we are and they possess a killer instinct." Mr. Hibma jabbed his finger in the air. "But," he said. "But tonight, we will pummel these spineless Dade Chargers. We will be a dizzying storm of audacity."

The girls didn't know what audacity was, but they knew they were about to embody it. Mr. Hibma wanted the Dade Chargers to lose in the worst way. He wanted their parents to scream at the refs. He wanted their coach to feel powerless. Mr. Hibma, for the first time since he'd been a coach, was not faking. He wasn't acting like what he thought a coach would act like, but was speaking from his guts.

"There will be no chatter once we leave this locker room. Not one word. No smiling. No looking at boyfriends. I'm going to sit on the bench silently with one leg crossed over the other. You are a silent avalanche."

Mr. Hibma paced, letting his words get heavy and sink to the floor and settle. His players had frenzy in their hearts. They were trembling.

And they triumphed. Mr. Hibma had never seen a team so thoroughly psyched out as Dade. After the final seconds ticked off the clock, all the voice Mr. Hibma's players had held inside exploded into the gym. The fans wailed. Even the other coach, it seemed to Mr. Hibma, understood that the good guys had won.

Mr. Hibma guided his car along the roads that led to his villa. He stopped at the grocery store and picked up wine, hummus, pickles, salami. He ran his car through a car wash then pulled around to get gas. Mr. Hibma was leaning on his car, the trigger of the nozzle locked in place and pumping steadily, when an SUV pulled up across from him and the most curvaceous woman Mr. Hibma had ever seen stepped down from it. She was wearing a purposely tattered T-shirt, overmatched shorts, and canvas shoes. She was not from the area. Her ankles and knees and waist were delicate and in between those points was bursting, fecund flesh. Her face was an arranged jumble of plump cheeks and full lips and dark eyebrows.

When Mr. Hibma's tank was full, he replaced the nozzle on the pump and screwed on his gas cap. He fondled his keys in his pocket. He stepped around the pump and emerged next to the woman's SUV. She was facing away from Mr. Hibma, kicking some hosing out of her way, fixing up a place to stand. Her calves were flexing preposterously.

"Miss," Mr. Hibma said.

The woman turned, caught off-guard. It was night and she was at a service station in a redneck county.

"When a man sees the sexiest woman he'll ever see, he knows he has received a gift that will enrich him and curse him. You have broadened my notion of feminine allure. Because of you, this gas station will be one of the places in the world most dear to my heart."

The woman giggled breathily. She gave Mr. Hibma a look that meant he ought to know better.

The woman's nozzle clicked, her tank full, and Mr. Hibma did not miss his chance for a well-timed exit. He backed out of the woman's sight, slid into his car, and pulled away from the gas station. The whole way home, he kept looking at himself in the rearview, wondering about himself, doubting very little that the person he saw in the mirror was a cold-blooded killer, doubting very little that he could pull off a grand act that would transform him. It wasn't that complicated. Your mind told your body to do things and your body obeyed. If he needed to coach, he could coach. If he needed to charm a sexy woman, he could charm a sexy woman. If he needed to kill Mrs. Conner, he could kill Mrs. Conner. He could sit long hours in his storage unit and let his soul curdle. Mr. Hibma wasn't stuck in his life. He was cocked and loaded, ready to blow his life apart.

On the way into his villa he checked the mail and, he should've known, there was a letter from Dale waiting for him. The address of his PO Box in Clermont was written in Dale's hand, and beneath that a yellow sticker had been affixed which directed the envelope to Citrus County.

> Mr. H,
>
> Write me once more, to let me know where to be and when to be there. I'm game, as you've gathered. At the very least, as game as you are.

After school, Toby and Shelby walked past a trailer park where only old people were allowed to live. They went into the woods and passed a hill of tires and kept going until they reached the old warehouse, the one with all the statues leaning against it. Toby had walked past it a bunch of times but had never tried to venture inside. The door didn't have a knob. Shelby lifted the thin rod out of its setting and Toby gave a shove and they were looking at the dim immensity of the place. Boxes were everywhere, none of them closed. Bibles and shoes. Heavy, glossy leather bibles and plain black shoes. And that's what the place smelled like, brand-new rubber and old, old words. Shelby started kissing Toby and he was ready. He could enjoy kissing her now. He wanted to do nothing *but* kiss her. In two days he was going to put everything right and his mind would be empty and ready for brand-new inventory. He wasn't using his faulty instincts anymore. He was thinking. He was thinking of the new day that would dawn, when everyone would wake up where they were supposed to. Shelby wouldn't come to Toby's house and he wouldn't come to hers but the rest of the county would be their stomping grounds, their kissing grounds.

Shelby backed into the shadows and reclined herself on some boxes. Toby wondered if she was on shoes or bibles. She undid the buttons of her shirt and calmly drew one arm out of its sleeve and then the other. She was wearing nothing underneath. Toby's mouth was dry from nerves and it was dry from the lack of Shelby's mouth. He'd been watching her body for months and now here it was. Shelby was so pale and somehow her breasts were an even lighter shade. They were of a shape and character that Toby could not have imagined. He reached and placed his hand on one of them and a husky squeak escaped Shelby. Toby didn't want to be scared again. He didn't want to feel like a sucker. He wanted to feel what you were supposed to feel.

Shelby wanted this to go further, but she wasn't going to lead Toby anymore. She wanted *him* to do something. He reached with his free hand for her shorts, no idea what was going to happen. She was right in front of him, but it seemed like he had to reach a long way. He fumbled with the button for a moment, his fingers stupid, and then Shelby was reaching for him, clutching at him.

Toby stepped back into a stack of boxes and they teetered and almost fell.

"I don't want you to touch me this time," he said.

"Why not?"

Toby didn't know what to say. He wanted to be able to keep his nerve, to touch Shelby because that's what she wanted. He reclaimed the space between them, and then both of them were holding still and listening. They heard a car. The noise got steadily louder until it was right outside the warehouse. The car didn't have a muffler or something. The doors opened and then slammed. Toby handed Shelby her shirt and she accepted it and began buttoning it up. The two of them crept over to the wall and found a warped spot where they could see out. There were two men, both with flattop haircuts and one with an enormous class ring. They were talking about which statues to take, which would sell for the most, their voices raised because of the grumbling engine. Toby and Shelby could see the men but not their vehicle. They kept carrying statue after statue. It must've been a big pickup truck. They must've been piling the saints and knights one on top of the other in the bed like a bunch of dead bodies. The men may have owned the statues or they may have been stealing them.

That evening, Shelby asked her father to drive her to the library. She'd done enough walking in the woods for one day. They cruised along the edges of some cow pastures, slowed at a recent sinkhole that had collapsed half of a diabetes clinic. They pulled onto the dusty road, passed the power substation.

Lately, Shelby's father's breakfasts had gotten more elaborate—honey-pecan sausage, omelets, pineapple juice. He made himself read the paper each morning, grinding through the major stories of each section no matter how little they interested him. He gave Shelby gifts, the latest a book in which a bunch of poets wrote about their favorite pop songs. Shelby's father had learned how to force his mood, to keep himself in the middle ground, neither manic nor hopeless. He seemed a bit lighter in spirit, perhaps because he had less of it. He would find peace, even if it were some compromised brand. Shelby could feel it; he would survive.

Shelby's father parked the car and the two of them sat staring at a poster for a fundraising picnic to benefit the manatees. Shelby looked out her side window and saw the high school boys, with their falling-off black jeans and frayed shoes. They were cowardly and dangerous, a pack of hyenas.

"I don't get manatees," Shelby's father said. "I don't get the big fascination. If I'm still around when they kick, let's have a party. We'll make margaritas."

"I understand manatees," Shelby said. "They're like friendly dinosaurs." She got out of the car and leaned in the window. "Back in ten."

Shelby walked along the front planters. As she passed the high school boys, one of them mumbled something, too low for Shelby to make out. Shelby went up the stairs without looking at them and went inside and got into her e-mail. If Aunt Dale still hadn't invited her to Iceland, she was going to have to come out and ask. It was a rude thing to do, but less rude, Shelby thought, than leaving someone hanging for weeks. And maybe, as strongly as Shelby had been hinting, Aunt Dale hadn't really comprehended that Shelby wanted to visit right now, as soon as possible, that Shelby wasn't being hypothetical.

There it was, the message in the inbox.

> Shelby,
>
> I want you to know that I would really enjoy a visit from you, but unfortunately I'm not going to be able to make it work as soon as this summer. I've been hoping my schedule would clear a little, but it's only grown more impossible. I'm hoping to take real vacation time (what's that?) this spring, a sabbatical I'm going to call it, so maybe we can work something out, maybe on your spring break. It'll be good and snowy for you. That may be better anyway, because I'm sure your dad still needs you around down there. I'm really glad we've gotten back

> in touch like we have. I'm sure there are a lot of interesting things you can get into down in Florida, and I'd like to hear about all of them—not too interesting, I hope. Wink, wink.

Shelby signed out, but she didn't get up from her chair. The people in line could wait. Aunt Dale was ditching her. Shelby didn't need to read it again. She got it the first time, she was being ditched. Aunt Dale was bowing out. The only reason it had taken her so long to say anything was that she knew she was going to hurt Shelby's feelings. And she had. Wink, wink? What was that about, Toby? Of course Shelby's dad needed her around, but what about what Shelby needed? Next spring. Next spring felt like another eon. The world could end before next spring.

Aunt Dale, Shelby saw, was a coward. Maybe next spring, like everything was fine. She was full of shit, this lady. Nobody was *that* busy. And using Shelby's dad as an excuse. Aunt Dale was afraid of helping her flesh and blood. She was scared of Shelby, like everyone else.

Shelby picked up some pieces of scrap paper and tore them into little pieces and brushed them off the counter and into a wastebasket. She was annoyed that she was still susceptible to disappointment. She still lost her balance when a rug was pulled. She didn't want to e-mail anyone ever again. She looked around at the other people, all staring at their screens. They were researching God-knows-what. They were trying to figure out what to feed a sick sheep, trying to buy a used engagement ring, looking for a cheap fishing boat. They were all better people than Shelby's aunt. They would do anything for their families. They knew what was important. Aunt Dale was conducting a busy, glamorous life, and Shelby was a burdensome interruption.

Shelby stalked through the library and shoved the front doors open, then sauntered down the front steps. She rounded a planter and jumped across the walkway, landing a couple short feet from the high school boys, causing the closest of them to give ground.

"The only way you guys will ever get to second base is with each other," she said. "None of you, in your lives, will lay your hands on a girl like me."

The boys glanced nervously toward Shelby's father in the car. They laughed a little, believing they could turn Shelby's words from an insult into a joke.

"That's why you stand out here and make remarks," she said. "You're not even rednecks or thieves or perverts or drug dealers. You're worthless."

"I am too a redneck," one of them said, the one with the closest-set eyes and tightest ball cap. "And I'm the type of redneck doesn't allow people to insult me."

"Nobody thinks you guys are funny and nobody's afraid of you."

"We're just some boys who like fresh air and company," one of them said, the one with the wispy, pitiful mustache. "You like to read, we like fresh air and company."

Shelby looked at the one who said he was a redneck and he was champing at the bit. She wished he would jump at her or raise his voice. She wanted to see her father beat the hell out of one of these kids. This was what she was stuck with. Citrus County. These were her people now. No one in Iceland was hers. Her mother and her sister were not hers. Toby—who knew? The whole county was full of these kids, these punks, full of their parents.

Shelby looked toward the car and her father was indeed peering rigidly in her direction, the look on his face all business. He was trying to figure out if these boys were her friends or what. Shelby looked individually at as many of them as she could, into their hollow eyes. The boys didn't move. There wasn't a peep to be heard. They were of one mind, done in. They were survivors, these boys. They couldn't afford to have fight in them like Shelby did. They knew when they were beat.

After the final bell sounded and Mr. Hibma's last class of the day spilled out into the hall and blended with the rest of the freed students, Mr. Hibma shut off the lights in his room and sat at his desk. All the clubs had wrapped up. Most of the sports were over. This was the time of year when even the teachers bolted right after the final bell. It was the beginning of summer, a time to be happy. Mr. Hibma clacked the heel of his shoe down on the linoleum and listened to the echo, and for once it wasn't a dispiriting sound. The clack of Mr. Hibma's heel was not in a minor key; it was the first note of a crescendo.

He spun his chair around so that he was facing his computer, blew on the keyboard, then backed his head away as a plume of dust rose. He turned the computer on and listened to it come to life, waving dust away with his hand. He watched the green light flicker and then steady, made sure there was paper in the printer. Mr. Hibma got into the word processing program and typed the following:

> The moon is more serious each night and the sun sillier each day. I could do without anything. I could do with nothing. The Publix. 1315 Cooper Road. Clermont, Florida. 5 in the afternoon. June 1.

Mr. Hibma walked to the end of the hall and looked out over the parking lot. He saw the buses pulling away, saw the grassy plot where the flag corps practiced. He saw Pete and the Spanish expert walk out together and slip into the same car. He saw Vince drifting from crowd to crowd, offering his gum. Mr. Hibma had no idea if Dale was going to show up. He knew he'd corresponded himself into a corner, and he was glad for that, but whether Dale would physically appear was of little consequence now. Mr. Hibma didn't need Dale anymore, didn't care to impress her. He understood that she didn't take him seriously. She *wanted* to be disappointed. That was how she lived—in search of disappointment. Had she taken Mr. Hibma seriously, even a little bit, she never would've responded. Mr. Hibma was trying to change his life and she thought he couldn't. Mr. Hibma was going to shock her; he was going to stick her with a heavy secret, a problem, and she was going to have to carry it.

He would go to the FedEx in Clermont this afternoon—no messing around with the post office—and tell them to deliver the letter on the morning of the 29th. He didn't want Dale to have time to think anything over. If she *did* come, he wanted her rushing to get to him, wanted her to arrive bedraggled, beginning to lose her doubt in Mr. Hibma—her doubt, all she had. He wanted to see her screech into the Publix parking lot in her rental car, panicked, hoping she wasn't late, hoping Mr. Hibma was bluffing, hoping not to have to talk him out of anything. And what would Mr. Hibma do? He couldn't meet her there. He'd wander the parking lot and watch for her, and he'd know her when he saw her, and he'd pass close enough to smell the airplane and the foreign air on her, and he wouldn't say a word. Afterward, if she wanted to reveal what had passed between them, wanted to turn Mr. Hibma in, so be it. That would be *her* business.

Mr. Hibma was bursting with a foreign feeling. Or perhaps the absence of a familiar feeling. He didn't feel defensive. He did not feel put-upon, attacked. He was on the move. No other way to move forward had presented itself, and he wasn't running from the way he had.

Shelby decided to follow Toby on Friday afternoon. A week left in the school year. She couldn't think of a thing to hope for, and that was good. What she was going to do was hunker down in Citrus County. If she had to be here, she was going to *be* here. Her passport had arrived in the mail and she had promptly carried it out to the backyard and burned it in a coffee can, the white smoke trailing with the breeze into the treetops. Shelby hadn't had to coax the fire. The passport went up like kindling, like it knew it was meant to be burned. Shelby had also removed the photograph of Aunt Dale from the hallway. It wasn't hers to burn, but she'd stashed it out in the utility room. She wasn't about to pass by the lady every time she went to the bathroom. Her father would ask where the picture went, and Shelby would have to come up with something.

Shelby knew the general direction through the woods Toby started in on the way to his house, but she didn't want to miss him somehow, didn't want him to evade her by taking an alternate route, so she blended into a crowd at the end of the science wing and tracked Toby straight from his marine biology class. He nudged past a gaggle of short blondes, crammed his whole bag in his locker, then proceeded at a mourner's pace out the lunchroom exit. He didn't stop to talk to anybody. He broke from the parking lot into the woods at a spot that didn't seem to have a trail. Shelby followed. There was a trail all right, winding and shadowy. Shelby felt exposed in the woods. She wasn't sure how far behind to stay. Toby kept his eyes on the forest ground, never turning around to check what was behind him. He'd worn a bright red T-shirt that day, so whenever Shelby let him get a few steps too far ahead, she had only to rush forward until the shirt called out through the underbrush. Shelby fell into a rhythm. She kept at least one tree directly between her and Toby. The multitude of bugs in the woods were providing their standard crackling hum, drowning out any noise Shelby made by snapping twigs. She felt dishonest but full of purpose.

They came to an open area, what would have been a meadow if there were such a thing as a meadow in Citrus County, and Shelby let Toby get ahead. She watched him drag through the sandy clearing and into the woods on the other side. Shelby wasn't a spy, she was a girl in love. There was something delicious about watching Toby with him not knowing she was there. She could see a lot of the tired sky, could see the spot where the sun, in a few hours, intended to set.

She came out into the brightness and hurried across, peering ahead for the red T-shirt, and in a moment there it was, bobbing in the foliage. Toby had sped up. They pushed past bunches of cross-trails, tracks in them from dirt bikes and dogs and raccoons, and they shuffled past countless rabbit holes, countless isolated bogs that hid countless snakes. They passed a shopping cart full of beer cans. They'd been walking for close to an hour. Sweat was dripping off Shelby's nose. She could taste it. The sun was a bald eye. It was clearing away the clouds, making preparations.

The best odds were on Uncle Neal being exactly how Toby had described him, bewildered but volatile. Probably the house would look normal, and Toby would take a shower and play solitaire or something, and Uncle Neal would be down for his pre-dinner nap. Probably Shelby would find nothing damning about the household, but she had to check. She had to see where Toby lived. She was doing this partly for herself, she knew, following Toby for her own reasons. At night, when he was at his house and she at hers, she would be able to picture Toby safe in his bed. She would be able to see him drift off to sleep as she drifted off to sleep. He was her only friend, and at night she knew that more than ever.

Shelby sensed something above her and took a bad step. It was an owl. The thing was ten feet over her head. The owl didn't like having people in its woods; that was clear from the look on its face. Shelby whispered hello to the owl and it did not blink. It was a haughty little statue. Shelby wanted to throw something at it, but she was afraid. It was like the snake on her patio. It wasn't going to move until Shelby went away. She had to keep going. She got back on Toby's trail, and soon saw power lines. The woods grew less wild. Toby's red shirt bumped up onto a porch. Shelby had made it. The house was in view. Toby dug out his key, wiggled it into the lock, and went inside.

Shelby pulled her shoulders back. She took stock, drifting around the side of the property. No flowerbeds, not even grass to speak of. No sports equipment or bikes lying around. No dog, no cat. The house was the color of an old gym bag. It had a wide front porch with a rocking chair. The place appeared tidy in its spareness, except for the gnarly live oak branches hanging near the roof, some of them scraping when the breeze picked up. There were no squirrels, no vultures soaring high above. The blinds in most of the windows were open but Shelby could not see in. She was too far away and the house was dim inside.

She made her approach near a shed that looked at once dilapidated and sturdy, some kind of greenhouse. It smelled cramped, like things overgrown. In the woods, Shelby's footfalls had been drowned out, but now she could hear the soggy ground compressing under her boots. She could hear the wind brushing the back of her neck. There was one window on this side of the house, all the way at the back, looking like a mistake. It looked like the windows they put in the walls of fortresses, to see the enemy coming. Shelby slipped across the yard and rested against the worn stucco. Her heart was beating so quickly it seemed to have stopped.

She shuffled down the wall. The blinds of the little window were open. She inched her face, seeing more and more of the room inside. She placed her forehead against the cool glass. She was looking at Toby's bedroom. This was it. There was his dirty laundry in a basket, the shirt he'd worn to school yesterday, his track shorts. The bedroom door was closed and Shelby knew that at any moment it might fly open. There was a big closet in Toby's bedroom, the doors not fully closed. Dog-eared cardboard boxes. A stack of folded sweatshirts he'd retired for the summer. There was no TV in the room, no radio. Toby had hung no posters, had no bookshelf. He didn't read comics or play video games. There was a case of soda on the floor near the bed. The cords for the fan and the light hung low, so he could reach them while lying down. The carpet was a couple shades of marbled brown. Shelby locked the image of his room into her mind, the garish hue of his bedsheet, the water stain on the ceiling, the riveting stillness. She felt satisfied, like now she would be playing with house money. There were shreds of peace within her, blowing around like confetti. Shelby didn't need Aunt Dale. She didn't need to go to Iceland. It didn't matter where you went. *Where* meant nothing. Maybe, Shelby thought, she'd always been playing with house money. Maybe everyone was, every day they were alive.

The house was a perfect rectangle. Shelby stuck to the wall. She moved down from Toby's room, stepping over dry, stubborn bushes. If she saw Uncle Neal, then great; if not, that was okay, too. She didn't need to see him. What would it help? She'd seen where Toby ended up every night, and that was the important thing. She came to a larger window. The blinds were dropped all the way, but a few of them were bent, as if something had been thrown against them. Shelby positioned her eye and saw a big, empty table and some metal folding chairs. The edge of a counter was visible, a big bowl of matchbooks. Everything was so still inside, same as Toby's bedroom, like a museum exhibit. Maybe Uncle Neal wasn't even home. Maybe he was out of town on a job. Shelby hadn't seen any cars out front, but she hadn't seen a proper driveway, either.

A blackbird began ranting from behind her and she got moving again, passing a lonely wooden door. There was no back patio, no steps or anything, just a door painted a shade darker than the house. The next window was small, at eye level. Shelby had a full, obscene view into the kitchen. There were puny oranges on the sill. A large portion of the counter space was given over to two-liter bottles of soda, all lined up stiffly like an army unit. There was a tray of what appeared to be surgical tools, soaking in a tinted liquid. Shelby was gazing at the tray when there was movement off to her right. She froze, couldn't do a thing, couldn't even unlock her knees and drop. But freezing was the correct thing to do. It was Toby, and he hadn't noticed her. He was looking at nothing, talking to himself. Shelby watched him shuffle into the woods on one side of the house and once again she was following him.

She tracked Toby and tracked Toby, and the whole afternoon seemed like one moment now, one sprawling moment. The shadows congealed, preparing to be phased out. There was a line of weather-beaten stakes hammered into the ground at even intervals, a lot of trees with pink ribbons on them. Shelby noticed there were no more tracks of any kind in the marled ground. She realized she was behaving like a crazy person. She was stalking someone through wild unfamiliar acreage, afternoon giving way to evening. She wondered whether, if Toby got away from her, she would be able to find her way home. The trees looked forgotten. They were real trees, like up north—maples or sycamores. They'd never lost their leaves. The back of Shelby's shirt was damp and sticking to her. She knew she should stop now, knew she should go back. And then Toby dropped to one knee. Shelby eased closer, to see what he was doing. He tossed moss clumps and branches this way and that. He dragged a raft of brush. All his movements were void of emphasis, nothing but utility. Shelby got low, observing Toby through the fronds of a palmetto stand. Her thighs were numb, exhausted from traipsing through the sandy woods, and now from crouching. Was Toby making camp? Maybe things at his house *were* that bad. Did he sleep out here, in the woods?

Toby rose and leaned and pulled up some kind of door, and when he did, the acoustics of the world warped. All the sounds slowed. Shelby grasped a palmetto frond, down near the base where they were sturdy, and pulled herself farther into the stand, the blades of the frond digging into her soft palm. Shelby's body knew something was happening; the animal part of her knew. Toby descended into the ground, pulling something onto his head. He had been standing there and now he wasn't. Toby had some kind of underground lair. Shelby was close to the real, secret Toby. She had to stay hidden. If Toby discovered she'd followed him out to this place, this place he considered all his own, he wouldn't ever trust her again. Shelby had to wait him out.

After just a minute or two, he was back. He emerged and peeled off what appeared to be a ski mask and flipped the roof of his lair back over. He let it close with its own weight, like the hood of a car, and then, without bothering to drag the branches back on top of it, went back through the woods the way he'd come. Shelby watched his red shirt get smaller and smaller. She didn't follow. She remained hidden, waiting. It seemed foolhardy, leaving her hiding space, abandoning the palmetto. She was about to betray Toby. She stood up and approached. The door was octagonal and had one little handle that latched and unlatched it.

Moss and mushrooms were all over it. It was out of place, how moist and muddy the hatch was, in an otherwise dry section of the woods. Shelby began to reach for the handle and she heard a sound from inside. Her guts performed one ponderous flip. A small voice, muffled. It was singing. A child's voice. Shelby knew there were physical actions she had to undertake, and the first one was lifting this hatch open. She was going to concentrate on the actions. She was going to keep doing the next thing.

Toby awakened with a craving for an icy soda. His throat felt like it needed to be scoured. The lights in the room were off, but the door was open and even the scant light from the hall was harsh in Toby's eyes. It was exactly as dim outside the window as it was in Toby's room. It was dawn or dusk. In the coming hours, Toby would be expected to fall back asleep or he would be expected to face a day.

Toby had never been in one before, but the sour, sprucy smell and the gamut of beeps he heard—monitoring machines, the bing of the elevator, the buzzing of the nurses' call buttons—all came together in a way that could only be a hospital. Toby remembered being brought here. He'd been loaded into the back of a van. Stale rock music had been playing on the radio. He remembered a wheelchair, an elevator, but before that a police station, another place he'd never been. The station had seemed tiny from the outside, but inside it went back and back. Phones had been ringing and no one would answer them. A lady had administered a bunch of tests on Toby, then he'd been given a hot dog with no bun and a very small apple. This memory was sharp, the smallness of the apple. Toby had eaten it in three or four bites and hadn't touched the hot dog. What Toby did not recall was the police arriving at his uncle's house. He remembered walking back from the bunker after making one final check on Kaley. He'd had her dressed the way he wanted her and had let her hair grow out in the past weeks until it looked like that FBI agent's hair. He'd gone back to the house to wait for night to fall, not meaning to go to sleep. He'd stretched himself out on the floor of his bedroom, wanting to get down onto something firm and permanent rather than his mushy mattress, and the next thing he knew he'd been awakened by a shot. He'd wanted to be shocked by the sound, that flat, resolute clap that could've come from Toby's closet or from miles away, from some distant, cool place. He'd gone to the living room, and from there he could hear the radio from his uncle's room, excited cops barking away. They'd found the Register girl. There were a bunch of them talking, all failing at keeping a calm, determined tone. Code numbers and directions. They'd kept saying Toby's uncle's name, Neal Showers. The singed smell of the shot was lingering in the house. Toby had known, had come to understand, that his uncle was in the next room, dead. His uncle wouldn't make any more decisions, wouldn't clean another thing or smoke another thing. Toby couldn't bring himself to go in there. He remembered how it sounded, strangers on a radio talking about Uncle Neal, calling him all kinds of names that regular, tame people called people they didn't understand.

It was morning. Outside the window of Toby's hospital room, the sun was rising. He propped himself on his pillows. He saw the TV up in the corner of the room, saw the remote control on the dresser beneath it. He wasn't squinting anymore. Another type of beeping was coming from outside, a big truck backing up.

Toby remembered riding in the back of the police car. There was a metal screen separating the front seat from the back. Two cops sat up front and one sat next to Toby, a guy with a thin, sly mustache. The guy kept asking Toby questions, mostly easy ones like his age and what sports he liked, but then he'd slip in questions about Uncle Neal. Toby had known enough to say nothing.

Uncle Neal was gone. Toby's uncle was dead. Toby would never know if he'd killed himself because he thought he'd be blamed for the kidnapping, or because he'd been looking for an excuse for a long time and this seemed like a good one, or if his uncle had meant to take the rap for Toby. Maybe, for the first time, Toby's uncle had looked out for him. Toby had hastened his uncle's suicide and his uncle had kept Toby out of trouble. They'd helped each other. Toby was very glad he hadn't gone in and seen his uncle dead. He didn't want that in his mind. That wasn't the kind of thing, he imagined, you could clear out with a long walk.

Toby heard steps approaching his room and then a nurse with black shoes was in the doorway.

"Want the light on?" she asked.

"No," Toby said. "If that's okay."

The nurse came over and pulled Toby straighter and plumped his pillows. She didn't seem fond of Toby, but was nonetheless going to be a proficient nurse.

"Did they get me from my uncle's house *last* night?" Toby asked. "Or was it the night before?"

"It was last night," the nurse said. "They gave you something for sleeping. That's why it feels like you got hit in the head."

The nurse had a mint in her mouth. The mint was gleaming white, and made it easy to see that her teeth were not. She opened a couple drawers and was not displeased at what she saw in them. She glanced at Toby's chart, then went and pulled the blinds all the way up. She told Toby she'd be back in a few minutes to help him to the shower. The doctor would be coming by in an hour or two, and she wanted Toby alert.

She picked up the remote control and walked it over to him.

"Could I get a soda?" Toby asked. "A soda on ice?"

"I suppose you can have a soda."

"Are there cops here?"

The nurse nodded. "They're down by the nurses' station. They're wearing regular clothes. I think it's supposed to be a secret you're here, but we'll see how long that lasts. Those guys won't bother you. They're down there flirting with Stacy."

"I don't want to see any cops right now."

"I wouldn't worry. Stacy's got her low-cut scrubs on."

The nurse tapped the door frame, meaning she was leaving.

"Maybe two sodas," said Toby.

"A double." The nurse might've smiled.

"Is the little girl here?" Toby asked. "Is Kaley and her family here?"

The nurse made a noise. If she'd smiled, that was over now. "No, sir. They took that child down to a fancier place than we got."

The nurse left and Toby turned his attention to the remote control in his hands. Menu. Mode. Function. He hit the power button and the screen snapped to life. He heard the announcers before he could make out what was on the screen. It was a soccer game, from Mexico or somewhere. People holding banners hopped in the stands. Toby pressed the arrow. A show from the eighties about teenagers. A show about barbecue. Toby needed a news network. He found one, and turned the volume up a notch.

There was a shot of Uncle Neal's property from above, from a helicopter. Toby could hear the blades whirring. The sight of Uncle Neal's place gave him a pang—for what, he couldn't say. A woman with a flinty voice began speaking, referring to Uncle Neal's property as a compound. All of it could have looked placid and everyday—the house, the shed, the winding dirt driveway that stopped a ways short of the house—but with the wobbly camera and the eerie music swelling up, everything was sinister. The woman mentioned Kaley and a picture of her appeared in the upper corner of the screen. The woman was in disbelief that Kaley had survived her ordeal. They had a different picture of Kaley now. In this one, she was held aloft by someone and was clutching a popsicle. Next to the bright orange of the popsicle you could see just how gaunt and colorless she'd grown, like the mint and the nurse's teeth. Kaley looked terrible, really. She would've died. Toby could say that now. Anyone that laid eyes on her could tell she wouldn't have lasted much longer. The station left the picture of Kaley in the corner of the screen while the anchorwoman returned her attention to the Showers compound. The shed, she said, was packed with hemlock plants. There were drugs all over the house, few of them strictly illegal. No food in the fridge. Old carpets that had never been cleaned. The anchorwoman said a lot of folks believed Neal Showers had gotten off easy, killing himself, that he should have had to face Kaley's father and have his day in court and try his luck in prison. Toby looked down at his hands. They were pale, weakly veined. They didn't seem capable of the things they'd done. Toby wanted to know how they'd even found Kaley. How had it all broken loose in the first place? No one was saying.

In time, the station cut away from Uncle Neal's place. They showed the anchorwoman. She guided her bangs into place and then started talking about Shelby, speaking reverently, speaking of Shelby as a hero. She had followed the nephew out to the bunker. Neal Showers had been sick enough not only to kidnap a little girl, but to force his nephew to help with the keeping. The anchorwoman was flabbergasted at the things that happened in the world. She promised that in the coming hours she would have full reports on Shelby, on the nephew, and on the bunker itself. She promised to describe in detail the conditions the little girl had endured.

Toby removed his blankets and sat himself on the edge of the bed. Shelby. Shelby had figured it out. Somehow Toby was glad it had been her and no one else. She had never underestimated Toby, had she? Toby was relieved that Shelby knew the truth about him. He made his way to the window, one hand on the wall, and pulled the cord, dropping the blinds. He twisted the plastic staff and the room grew dim again.

The commercials came and went and the anchorwoman began talking about Toby. Earlier she hadn't said his name, but now she did. The woman spoke of him in pitiful tones. She said the name Milton Hibma. Mr. Hibma? Here he was, wearing a tie. Mr. Hibma was trying to get temporary custody of Toby. He was the boy's geography teacher, the woman explained, a single man with no children. Toby had no family, no godparents.

Toby remembered. Mr. Hibma had been waiting at the hospital when Toby'd been transferred from the police station. Mr. Hibma had left him food from the taco place. Nachos. Toby rolled to the edge of the bed and lifted up the trash can. The carton was inside, the cheese containers. Toby didn't remember eating anything, didn't feel like he could've.

Toby shut off the TV. He was so thirsty. Mr. Hibma wanted him. Could that be true? Mr. Hibma didn't bother with troubled kids. Since Toby had gone and tried to confess to him during lunch that day, Mr. Hibma had barely looked at him. Toby had woken up in an altered world. It only *looked* like the old world. Toby would have to change. He'd have to take the new world in stride. He had to shake the feeling that he was going to be punished, that he deserved justice. He was being treated as a victim. He was a type of victim; that's what they all thought.

Mr. Hibma had been up late, switching between a show about temp workers and a long commercial for a video of girls revealing their breasts. He had been preparing to turn the TV off and face the noiseless night, flipping through the cycle of channels one last time, when there was a newsbreak. The pictures in the corner of the screen weren't matching up with the hastily written script. Shelby Register's little sister had been found. She'd been rescued, alive. Mr. Hibma had listened to a description of Neal Showers, who'd killed himself, and whose nephew was now in the custody of the Citrus County Sheriff's Department. Mr. Hibma sat up and took a swallow of stale tea. Neal Showers. That was the name Toby had always forged on his detention forms. Mr. Hibma could see the careful cursive. It was Toby who was at the police station. Toby.

Mr. Hibma threw back a shot of bourbon, brushed his teeth, and tore down the empty roads that led to the county offices and the jail. This was the change. Mr. Hibma saw it. He didn't have to love the kiss-asses. He had to love who he loved. He could be his own kind of teacher, one who took an interest in the Tobys of the world. Mr. Hibma didn't *have* to give Toby all those detentions. He respected the boy. Mr. Hibma had been misguided in trying to take the drastic alteration of his life into his own hands. As usual, the world was supplying the change. As usual, Mr. Hibma was a character, not the author. And thank God. Mr. Hibma wasn't up to being the author. He didn't know how to save himself. Never was he less skilled, more doltish, than when he tried to figure and plot his own life.

When he arrived at the station, he drove around the building, deciding where to enter. There were media vans and he didn't want to be near them. He found a side entrance that seemed meant for deliveries, then collected every bit of identification he could out of his glove box and wallet—documentation proving his residence and place of employment and the status of his automobile insurance, credit cards and a valid driver's license. He had a social security card, a punch card for a smoothie shop.

Mr. Hibma went and knocked on the door until someone answered. He asked for the guy's supervisor, saying he had information regarding Toby McNurse, and was taken to a small room with speckled tile on the floor where he waited for almost an hour. He decided, after much consideration, to leave the room, and he soon found the infirmary, where a nurse informed him that Toby had undergone his tests and was now resting. The nurse seemed a sympathetic person, so Mr. Hibma told her why he was there, that he wanted to claim Toby, that he was one of Toby's teachers at school and that the boy was fond of him and that he was meant to help this kid and probably not meant for a damn thing else.

The nurse sat Mr. Hibma down and gave him some coffee and again Mr. Hibma waited for an hour. He felt like *he* was in trouble. His hair felt greasy. He was on the verge of tears. He realized that he was very tired and agitated and that when he finally got to talk to someone with pull he was going to come across as raving. He drank more coffee. He could sit for ten more minutes, he told himself, and then he would have to go explore another part of the building. Mr. Hibma wondered if he was on camera. He imagined that by now the police social workers had confirmed that Toby had no family. They were doing a background check on Mr. Hibma. There were lawyers back there. The chief. Mr. Hibma needed a bathroom. He needed to piss and splash water on his face. Mr. Hibma thought back to the only other time he'd been in a jail. In college he'd missed a court date for underage drinking and cops had come to his apartment at six in the morning and pounded on his door. They had sat the eighteen-year-old Mr. Hibma in the back of a long van and then proceeded to pick up every deadbeat dad in town. It was something they did once a month. For hours upon hours Mr. Hibma had watched lawyers dragged from offices, mechanics led out of garages, old leather-skinned black guys called up from fishing holes.

The door to Mr. Hibma's little room swung open, causing him to spill coffee on his leg. A large, relaxed cop entered, not wearing a uniform but just a polo shirt with a badge embroidered on it, followed by Mrs. Conner. Mr. Hibma was dumbstruck. He did all he could, which was to sit up with a formal bearing and wait to be spoken to. Mrs. Conner smiled solemnly at Mr. Hibma, as if proud of him. The cop started talking. He was Mrs. Conner's husband, Sergeant Conner. He'd been retired for years, but still had influence around the station. Mr. Hibma had pictured Mrs. Conner's husband wearing a polo shirt and here he was, wearing a polo shirt. Toby was going to be released to Mr. Hibma on a trial basis, for thirty days. Thirty days was the minimum. If Mr. Hibma couldn't make a thirty-day commitment, he should speak up now. Sergeant Conner went on, Mrs. Conner beaming at his side. Mrs. Conner considered Toby a problem child, Mr. Hibma gathered, and believed Mr. Hibma was doing a saintly deed taking him in. Mrs. Conner had put in a good word for Mr. Hibma. She and her husband were pushing this through. It was just a matter of time and signatures. Her husband explained that Toby would be moved to the hospital for a short while, then would return to county custody for a week or so, until the hullabaloo died down. After all that was over, he would be Mr. Hibma's temporary charge. Mr. Hibma had never seen Mrs. Conner out of school. Everything about her seemed exaggerated. Her hair was a vibrant red. Her teeth were big and straight. Her blouse was of some rough, stiff material and her perfume shrunk the room.

The next day, Mr. Hibma rose late. He got up from his couch starving and foraged in the kitchen. Crackers. They were stale but they'd work. Mr. Hibma chewed up half a tin of ginger candies. He made tea and drizzled honey in it and took it to the couch.

Mrs. Conner had come to his aid. Mr. Hibma's campaign to befriend her had paid off. He was a friend of hers. Mrs. Conner was his buddy. His friendship with Mrs. Conner was cemented, while whatever he'd had going with Dale had ceased. The moment he'd gotten home from the police station he'd sent an e-mail off to Dale, to her website anyway, the first e-mail he'd sent in a very long time, telling her he wasn't going through with his proposal, that he was shutting down the project. Mr. Hibma had not offered an explanation for his bailing out, had not told her that unlike her he now had something worthwhile to do with his life, had not revealed the fact that he was Shelby's teacher and wasn't really from Clermont. Dale had shot back a reply within five minutes saying she had never intended to come to Florida, that she'd been stringing Mr. Hibma along for fun, not that it had turned out to be much fun. He wasn't capable of art, she'd told him. He didn't have it in him. Did he honestly think, she asked, that she didn't get crackpot proposals like his every other day? She knew Mr. Hibma's type. He was a loser and his plans were the typically grandiose plans of a loser.

When the Registers returned home from the hospital, Shelby's father began building a fence around their yard. He had a post-hole digger and a bunch of lumber delivered, and he pulled his table saw and some other tools out of the garage. The fence was eight feet high. Shelby's father started right in front where the media hung out. The churchies offered to help with the fence. When Shelby's father turned them down, he did so with a gruff dignity that Shelby admired.

He spoke to Shelby a lot in the afternoons, both of them drinking coffee, while Kaley napped. Shelby mostly listened. She liked coffee. She liked measuring the grounds and pouring in the water and dropping in the sugar lumps. She liked the saucers and the spoons and the tiny pitcher that held the cream. The aroma of the coffee and the sound of her father's voice were things she looked forward to. Kaley gave Shelby and her father feelings they didn't want. Her father longed to dive back into Kaley, but something kept him from doing so. It was hard for him to touch her, and he spent most of his time watching her from across the room. He needed to finish grieving the loss of her, even though she was back. It felt like Shelby and her father were expected to be celebrating, but that wasn't the mood in the house. The mood was bewildered relief. They felt behind, out of the loop. Just as she had right after Kaley had gone missing, Shelby had the overpowering feeling that her life's course was being charted by outside forces. She felt that her heart's work would never be her own.

Every second Shelby had spent with Toby, every moment she'd spent thinking of him, counted against her. She felt pity for him, like she ought to be helping him right now. It was absurd, but she wanted to smell him. He was another person lost to Shelby. The past was against her and the future could see her coming, easy prey.

As for Kaley, she was frighteningly skinny, listless. She wasn't cuddly anymore. Her memory was porous. She was picky. She didn't jump into hugs, but braced for them. At bedtime, she put up no fight. After all that time with nothing but a cot, now she wanted nothing but her bed. The same bed she'd been snatched from. Shelby and her dad had never gotten rid of it. Shelby knew it would be a long time before Kaley was back to something like normal. It was hard enough to feel you had a place in the world without that place being jerked out from under you. They'd kept Kaley in the hospital for forty-eight hours. Incredibly, she didn't appear to have been abused, not physically or sexually, a fact that confused everyone from cops to reporters to TV psychologists. It was news no one knew what to do with, but it was the best news Shelby had ever received, the only good news in the world. After Shelby heard this, she didn't want to hear anything else.

A minor parade was held for Kaley in Crystal River, put on by the banks. Shelby did not attend, nor did her father or sister. The media had broken into two camps, one at the Register house and one outside the gates of Mr. Hibma's villa complex. Their attention was steady, but not passionate. Shelby grew accustomed to the idea of the media's presence, and once her father's fence was completed, she often forgot they were out there at all. The police, because, Shelby figured, they'd had nothing to do with cracking the case, showed waning interest. Kaley had been in Citrus County the whole time, right under their noses. And there was no sign of the pixie-cut FBI agent. A pair of new agents, men, had shown up at the hospital and halfheartedly took some notes, but everyone seemed to realize that the whole affair was now in the hands of lawyers and doctors and social workers, not people with badges and guns.

Shelby's father took Kaley for a walk toward the school, reclaiming the sunny outside world. Shelby was alone at the house. The media wasn't even out front today. The fence had done the trick. Shelby was determined to have a reasonable little meal, but it wasn't going to happen. She was cold. The phone kept ringing. That writer guy had called again, now that the book could have a happy ending, and again Shelby had put him off. She thought maybe *she* should write the book. Maybe she could get signed up for home-schooling and next year she could stay in her nightgown and write all day.

She decided she could eat some croutons, but then she just stared at the box. She felt trapped in the kitchen, trapped in the chilled, over-air-conditioned house, so she went out into the front yard. She opened the gate of the fence her father had built and stood in the middle of the road. The clouds were too close, the trees too green and intent, the dust from the road insidious, the air full of mildew, the calls from the crickets and frogs exuberant. Shelby stood amid all that, the sun baking the top of her head with what Shelby was expected to believe was disinterest, not intending harm or help, the sun, like it would do to anyone who happened to be standing where Shelby was standing.

Mr. Hibma sat through the middle school graduation ceremonies, up in the front corner of the gym where he could be the last one in and the first one out. There was no good reason to attend, but he found he wanted to punctuate the year and be done with it, to feel he had nothing to think of but the future. He sat through the speeches and then the interminable calling of names, catching a couple curious stares from people in the crowd. People knew he was taking in that boy who was caught up in all the nastiness at his uncle's compound, but none of them knew Toby personally and few of them knew Mr. Hibma. In the gym, Mr. Hibma felt a bracing normalcy. The gym was saturated with parental pride and volleyball banners, and there wasn't room for anything else.

Afterward, he sat in his car in the parking lot. This might be the last time he ever saw this school. He watched the families all find their cars, the lot overrun with little brothers and little sisters, like rats on a ship, dodging and darting and impossible to corral. In the end they *would* be corralled, though, every single one, and forced into a car, and the cars would all pull away. During each basketball practice and each game, Mr. Hibma understood, a small girl Mr. Hibma had never met and who meant nothing to him had been held captive in a bunker. There were millions of little girls in the world, and one of them, while each and every basket of the season was scored, had been held captive in a bunker. During Mr.

Hibma's lectures and all the trivia games and presentations. When Glen Staulb died. Through all that nonsense with Dale. While Mr. Hibma had sat quietly in his storage unit, the girl had sat in the bunker. There'd been earthquakes on many continents. Songs had been written, many of them designed to be sorrowful. Elections had been rigged. Inventions had been thought up, patents sought. Countless people had been born, countless had died. Mr. Hibma couldn't tell if all the events of the past months seemed momentous or meaningless. He thought about Toby coming and trying to talk to him during lunch period, and Mr. Hibma did not feel bad. A couple short days and he would begin redeeming himself. There would always be a multitude of awful people, but Mr. Hibma would not be one of them. Now that it was all happening as it was happening, now that he had a part in this new beginning, he felt that the worse he'd been, the better he'd be.

Toby slipped his shoes on and left the county house one morning while everyone was in a meeting. It was only a couple days before he went with Mr. Hibma, but he needed a field trip, a break. He sneaked out the back door, hoping not to be seen out any of the windows. The staff at the county house had made a point of making Toby feel like a guest rather than a prisoner, of impressing upon him that this wasn't a jail and he wasn't in trouble. He walked out past the last of the identical buildings, past a stagnant pond, through a field of sandspurs that had once been used for soccer, and into woods he'd never been in before. There was no telling where these woods stopped. Maybe they spread all the way to the other coast, to the space center. Somewhere in these woods, far away, a larky picnic was transpiring. Somewhere in them, a dog was being put down. Somewhere, people met to worship their gods. Toby would get in trouble for this, for escaping. He'd be put under watch, some casual form of lockdown, but it was worth it to get out in the fresh air on his own. He'd been breathing county air for more days than he cared to count.

Toby poked around until he picked up a trail that unfurled along the edge of a pasture. He would walk this trail to the end and then turn around and walk back. That was all. He would happen upon no hindrance or encouragement. There were things he was free of—not just the county house, but things he was permanently free of—and he felt the freedom in a tangible way, in his guts. He was free of the bunker. He never again had to approach it through dwindling or gathering shadows, never had to smell it, never had to wonder what it meant that he had found it and no one else. It was everyone's now. The bunker wasn't Toby's to lose. It belonged to the news shows. It was powerless.

He tugged a baggie of nuts out of his pocket. These woods were quieter than his old woods. Spindly steers looked at him dryly. Toby tightened his sneakers. He guessed that what he was feeling was hope. He had a different plight now. He had no plight at all. He wasn't a bad luck case. He'd made a hell of a mess, but it looked more and more like the clean-up would be someone else's business. He'd performed well at the meeting or hearing or whatever they called it. There'd been a social worker and a cop and a psychiatrist and a couple other people, and none of them liked each other. They all had different agendas, and this kept Toby from ever feeling pinned down. And Toby hadn't even felt like he'd been lying. He'd felt like he was doing right by himself. He worried a little about what the cops might get out of Kaley, but Toby knew he could always muddy the waters. He could muddy the waters to the point where nobody wanted to dive in.

The pastures gave out and the air changed. Toby smelled cars on the breeze, and in another five minutes he broke from the woods onto a vast construction site, apparently shut down, that was bordered on the far end by an expressway. Toby had heard about this road. It went to Tampa. It was Citrus County's last chance to become part of the rest of Florida. Toby was in the middle of nowhere. The only other human beings around were the truckers, rushing past one at a time in their semis, each truck dragging with it the same windblown wail.

Toby could not stop thinking about Shelby. They would never have another way to think of each other but this way. Toby's guilt was towering in another plane. He didn't feel it. It was so big, it was elsewhere. Toby hoped, because that was all he could do, that he was capable of thinking of all that had happened with Shelby as a sad, unlucky, disheartening jumble that had been thrown at him and that he'd handled the best he could. That's what life would be for Toby, figuring out the best ways to think about the things he'd done.

Toby wasn't ready to turn back. He went into the almost-finished building. It was going to be a do-it-yourself warehouse store. The shelves were all up, not yet stocked. There were signs to help shoppers find large appliances, paint, lumber. Toby wandered and found himself in the garden section. The plants had been delivered and left to fend for themselves, plants from unimaginable states and provinces and hemispheres. Some were bursting their pots and growing down to the floor, some were dying. Leaves covered everything. Toby found a hose and followed it to its spigot, reeling himself toward the wall. He turned the valve and heard the sound of water finding its way and felt the hose stiffen in his hand. Every plant in every row, the rotting and the unruly, was due a share.

ABOUT THE AUTHOR

John Brandon was raised on the Gulf Coast of Florida. During the writing of this book he worked at a Frito-Lay warehouse and a Sysco warehouse. During another part of the writing of this book he was unemployed. During the revising he was the John & Renee Grisham Fellow in Creative Writing at University of Mississippi. His favorite recreational activity is watching college football. This is his second book; the first was *Arkansas*, also a novel.

The author thanks Paul Winner, Anna Keesey, Tim Hickey, and Heather Brandon. Their help was invaluable.